Timeslip Troopers

Timeslip Troopers

by
Théo Varlet & André Blandin

translated, annotated and introduced by
Brian Stableford

A Black Coat Press Book

Visit our website at www.blackcoatpress.com

ISBN 978-1-61227-078-4. First Printing. March 2012. Published by Black Coat Press, an imprint of Hollywood Comics.com, LLC, P.O. Box 17270, Encino, CA 91416.
Printed in the United States of America.

Introduction

La Belle Valence by Théo Varlet and André Blandin, here translated as *Timeslip Troopers* (the full significance of the original title, as explained below, cannot be transferred into English), was published in Amiens by Edgar Malfère in 1923. It was, apparently, the third supposedly unpublishable manuscript handed over by Malfère to Varlet for rewriting, following the two volumes of *L'Épopée martienne* (1921-22),[1] whose first drafts had been provided by Octave Joncquel. How extensive Varlet's rewrite of *La Belle Valence* was, or why it was thought to be required, I have no idea, but it is not surprising that the novel had had difficulty finding a publisher in Paris, on account of its subject matter alone, thus ending up in the hands of Malfère, who had a reputation for dealing in bizarre and edgy material.

Whether it was actually written in the trenches or shortly after the author's return therefrom, *La Belle Valence* present an image of life and attitudes therein that was somewhat at odds with the notions promoted by wartime propaganda. It suggests, with a laconically cynical black humor, that the soldiers of France did not spend their free time dreaming about a future era of peace and harmony or about distinguishing themselves heroically in defense of the fatherland, but of massacring enemies who were too ill-equipped to fight back and then surrendering themselves to the orgiastic delights of

---

[1] Translated in a Black Coat Press edition as *The Martian Epic*, ISBN 978-1-934543-41-2.

alcohol-fueled pillage and rape. If that were not enough, it blithely takes for granted the fact that a group of French officers accidentally timeslipped into the middle of a 14th century war between Muslims and Catholics would unhesitatingly side with the Muslims, as the contemporary custodians of civilized values, against the adherents of the religion to which they no longer even pay lip service. Both of these notions were liable to upset a portion of the potential audience, and make some of its members apoplectic. Given that Varlet was probably given instructions to tone down the controversial content, we can but wonder what the original was like—although, as a committed pacifist and non-believer, Varlet was presumably fully sympathetic to Blandin's aims in highlighting the hellish hypocrisies of war and faith.

As to who "André Blandin" was, no information seems to be available save for what can be inferred from the text—that he was almost certainly a French officer who served on the Western Front during the latter part of the Great War and was extremely disenchanted by the experience. The name is a common one, and internet searches readily turn up a plethora of André Blandins, none of whom seems likely to be the author of the present text. We can be fairly sure that the original author of *La Belle Valence* was not the roughly-contemporary Belgian painter André Blandin (1878-1945), who corresponded with Guillaume Apollinaire and exhibited in Paris, not so much on grounds of discrepancies in apparent nationality and military experience, but by virtue of the fact that the Belgian Blandin was an accomplished writer who collaborated on a book of parodies of contemporary Belgian writers published in 1914, and would surely not have produced an unpublishable manuscript in need of doctoring by Théo Varlet.[2] If the original author of *La Belle Valence* went on to write other novels, he presumably did so under another name, but the probability is that he disappeared in the same way as Varlet's other Malfère-supplied collaborator, Octave Joncquel. Indeed, given that more than one André Blandin was killed in action during the war, it is possible that the manuscript was given to Varlet posthumously.

La Belle Valence is one of several French texts directly inspired by the example of H. G. Wells's *The Time Machine* (1895; French tr. 1898), following in the footsteps of Octave Béliard's *Les Aventures d'un voyageur qui explora le temps* [The Adventures of a Time-Traveling Explorer] (1909), which also sent its protagonist in the opposite direction to the one taken by Wells's hero. It has more in common thematically, however, with Mark Twain's *A Connecticut Yankee in the Court of King Arthur* (1889), whose timeslipped protagonist sets out to import the advantages of 20th century civilization to the legendary King of England, but eventually cannot prevail against Dark Age obduracy. (Blandin would not have known about Enrique Gaspar's *El anacronópete* (1887), the first novel featuring a time machine that takes trips into the past.) Unless the other literary references in the text were imported by Varlet, Blandin was obvious well-read, and if the title was Blandin's, it gives evidence of a certain literary sophistication in itself.

---

[2] Biographical and bibliographical details of Théo Varlet's career can be found in the introduction to the Black Coat Press edition of *The Martian Epic*. Black Coat Press has also published a translation of his solo novel *La Grande panne* (1930) as *The Xenobiotic Invasion*, ISBN 978-1-61227-054-8.

La Belle Valence translates literally as "Beautiful Valencia" or "Valencia the Beautiful," and refers in a straightforward sense to the destination of the time-slipped soldiers, but the phrase is used by them even before they know where they are, the first time they find oranges growing on the local trees. "Valence! La Belle Valence!" was once the standard cry of Parisian orange-sellers in the 19th century, and although it had fallen out of use long before the Great War, it had retained a nostalgic familiarity by virtue of numerous literary references; it is one of the Things Past fondly remembered by Marcel Proust in *À la recherche du temps perdu* [In Search of Lost Time] and is also cited in Joris-Karl Huysmans' *Les Soeurs Vatard* [The Vatard Sisters]. More pertinently, it was used as the opening line of a song written by the librettist Maurice Franc-Nohain for Maurice Ravel's comic operetta *L'Heure Espagnole* [Spanish Time] (1911), which features a clockmaker named Torquemada and has a farcical plot in which two of the characters spend much of the time hiding inside the cases of grandfather clocks—a combination of images that surely played some part in the inspiration of the plot of *La Belle Valence*.

More detailed discussion of the plot of the novel is certainly warranted, but is best postponed to an afterword in order not to spoil the suspense of the reading experience. It is, however, worth noting that the work of translation was made difficult by the fact that the soldiers—especially the enlisted men and the major—speak in an elaborate *argot* that is sometimes further complicated by a tortuous eye-dialect applied to the speech of characters supposedly hailing from the south of France. How closely this colorful vocabulary resembles the actual *argot* of the trenches I cannot tell, but it must have posed a stern challenge even to its contemporary readers, let alone 21st century readers.

There seemed to be no point in offering literal translations of numerous colorful slang expressions, and even those that I have translated straightforwardly because the translation is able to carry a similar implication in English (*poule* into "chick," for example) are bound to ring slightly false. I have made no attempt at substituting the eye-dialect, because it would be simply absurd to try to make a Provençal sound as if he were a Cockney or a native of Brooklyn, but I have tried to find English or American slang expressions that reproduce intended meanings similar to the words and phrases in the text's dialogue, while leaving a few terms in the original, in order to preserve a French flavor while retaining a reasonable measure of reader-friendliness. The result is admittedly artificial and sometimes awkward, but it seemed to be the best solution.

French is, for various reasons, better supplied with mild *doubles entendres* than English, so the passages in which the *poilus* are telling obscene stories presented particularly difficulties. I have attempted to solve them by means of similarly-pitched implication, only descending to frank obscenity when the original text does (rather sparingly, although it does not entirely shirk "the word of Cambronne"), but was occasionally forced to improvise. Although this might have been one of the aspects of the original toned down by Varlet, the text is conspicuously liberal in this regard, for its time—although one of the three appendices attached to it in the 1996 Encrage reprint (from which my translation has been made) points out that there are other *romans scientifiques* from the same period that are similarly free in their handling of explicit sexual materials, notably Maurice Renard's

Le Docteur Lerne sous-dieu (1907)[3] and Victor Margueritte's *Le Couple* (1924).

Although early time-travel stories tend to suffer somewhat by comparison as a result of the rapid sophistication of such stories in the latter half of the 20th century, which drew considerable narrative energy from elaborating the intricacies of "time paradoxes," *La Belle Valence* still holds up remarkably well as an exploratory endeavor, and the quality of its cynical black humor has not diminished at all, perhaps even gaining something by virtue of contemporary trends in humor and *weltanschauung*. At any rate, it deserves to be recognized as one of the finest *romans scientifiques* of the period between the end of the Great War and the birth of American science fiction, when the European crop of post-war speculative fiction was thinned out by postbellum prejudices, but nevertheless included some exceptionally juicy fruits.

Brian Stableford

---

[3] Translated in a Black Coat Press edition as *Doctor Lerne,* ISBN 978-1-935558-15-6.

Part One
THE DISPLACEMENT

I. The Englishman's Cellar

"Pernod, you say?"

"Yes, old chap, Pernod. And Benedictine, kummel, Cointreau, whisky, gin—how do I know? Not to mention champagne and wine, naturally. Hold on—here's your bolt-hole."

And by means of a short communication tunnel dug under the walls of a pretty white house in the style of a villa, the two officers quit the trench to go into a cellar. It was scarcely possible to see in there, by means of the light coming through a narrow air-vent, but Captain Loubet, taking out his lighter, lit a stout oil-lamp suspended from the vault and the subterranean space brightened. One table, three chairs, two iron-framed beds, one Henri II bookcase with a glass front fitted with green curtains, sketched out an accommodation, in a corner where the floor-tiles had been swept clean. Further away, the clutter commenced: a mass of furniture and other objects, piled up at random, obstructed the greater part of the cellar, and only a narrow path cleared around the periphery gave access to the carefully-labeled racks where multiple rows of bottles were superimposed in good order.

Such was the sumptuous domain in which Lieutenant Marcel Renard was about to succeed Captain Henri Loubet for the next fortnight.

The captain enjoyed the lieutenant's bewilderment.

"Takes you aback, doesn't it, old chap, to find this at the front line, after 30 months of war? I had no suspicion of the riches myself, to begin with. My predecessor had no idea this cellar existed. The door was walled up, you see, along with the air-vent. As the sector was quiet, I lived on the ground floor for the first few days, but when a few big shells from Metz fell on us—in error, I think, having been aimed at the battery on the flank—I thought it more prudent to take shelter. My orderly, a cunning fellow, ferreted around, sniffed out the camouflage, found the door…and here we are!"

While talking, the captain opened the bookcase with the masked glass panes, the shelves of which were garnished by a collection of bottles. "This is just to have a small selection close at hand, without searching the racks. I had the books thrown into the river. Pernod for me—what about you?"

"OK, Pernod," the lieutenant accepted. "But tell me, Captain, is this the stock of a wine-merchant, then?"

"Not at all. It appears that it was the villa of a so-called Englishman before the war, who passed himself off as an engineer—but he was really a Boche, and he was sentenced to be shot as a spy in '14…at any rate, may the old bibber rest in peace. Thanks to him, I've not been too bored here, and you'll owe him the same gratitude, and others after you... To the health of the English engineer!"

They were putting down their glasses when two *poilus* came in. One, with the look of a street-porter about him, was bent down under the weight of a trunk;

the other was marching beside him discreetly, guiding his companion by means of unctuous little gestures that were almost sacerdotal. He had him deposit the trunk on one of the beds, then sent him away with a amiable smile.

"Thanks, Saucisson. Go fetch the other one now." Then he turned the clean-shaven face of a perfect flunkey to Renard, and with his eyes respectfully lowered, said: "Would the lieutenant care to indicate a cupboard where I can arrange his linen and effects?"

His accent was less distinguished than his outfit, and the latter, which was probably unparalleled throughout the sector—a jacket elegantly pinched at the waist, yellow shoes, an embroidered silk skull-cap—revealed numerous whims that the captain seemed to be studying with a disgusted expression.

The lieutenant pointed to the Henri II bookcase. "There, Jasmin. You have only to take out the bottom shelves and put the bottles on the ground to one side. And if you'd like to pour yourself a glass of Pernod, go ahead."

"The lieutenant knows that I don't indulge," the man murmured, as he set to work.

"That's my orderly," Renard explained, in a whisper, seeing that Loubet was about to make unkind comments about his costume and declaration of sobriety. What can you do?—he's the former *valet de chambre* of the Duc de Pinchefalise. I sometimes joke about his exaggerated distinction and his family name, which drives him to despair—he's called Wambrechies; Jasmin Wambrechies—but apart from that, I've nothing for which to reproach him; he serves me to perfection. He has no peer for finding chocolate."

"You even permit him to hire domestics?" muttered the captain, recalling the arrival of the trunk.

"Oh, the other one's my new colleague's orderly. They share the work—and, my word, it goes very well like that."

The said colleague, the sublieutenant of the eighth, made his appearance in the cellar at that moment. He was a tall blond young man with a serious and thoughtful expression, whom Renard introduced to the captain by the name of Henri de Lanselles, although his monocle had earned him the more familiar nickname of Monocard. He came to announce that the relief was complete.

Loubet gave the new arrival the honors of *his* cellar one last time, then darted a farewell glance at the precious bottles and, after a brief hesitation, took hold of a bottle of Pernod, which he wrapped up in a newspaper and hid in the vast pocket of his trench-coat.

"In memory of the Englishman," he sniggered. Then, shaking the hands of the two officers, he wished them god luck and went out to rejoin the company that was standing down.

Assembled on the edge of the village, behind a large brick building, the men of the tenth, kitbags on their backs, were only waiting for their captain. The trench stretched away in front of them, and further away—in the forest with bare branches that sheltered the artillery battery, which had been crossed many times in the last fortnight for fetch provisions from Landremont—the road. And today, the road led to the rear, to rest, and, for some, to paradisal leave.

While Loubet headed in that direction, through the subterranean tunnel that cut diagonally through the entire village, the two lieutenants proceeded with the ritual assembly of the eighth, who were about to occupy Port-sur-Seille.

Port-sur-Seille, grouped on the left bank of the river, still had numerous houses standing, which permitted the communication trenches to be forsaken and prudent circulation, even in broad daylight, through the streets and terraced gardens. Only on the eastern side, toward the river—beyond which was no-man's-land, then desolate brushwood, Boches and 20 kilometers further away, the silhouette of Metz and the hummocks of the fortifications—did they burrow underground in the listening-posts and the machine-gun nests lined up along the bank.

The fire, however, was normally fairly benign: a few shells in the morning; four more at precisely eight o'clock in the evening—no one knew why—falling one after another in the same place; that was, for the time being, pretty much the daily "sprinkling" of Port-sur-Seille. And the continuous rumble of the cannon to the north made the men appreciate the relative mildness of that favored corner. "We're peppered now and again, but it's pretty routine," was the report on the sector that the men of the tenth, before departing, had just communicated to their successors of the eighth.

The latter, about a 120 in number, assembled in the dusk in their ranks on the little square completely sheltered by the gross Medieval tower and another more modern building, in front of which the mobile kitchens were already working flat out, listened to the allocation of posts and fatigues: food supplies, sandbags, horse-grooming, barbed wire, cleaning, and so on. Then, in response to the fateful "Break ranks!" they all dispersed into the gathering gloom.

The fortunate, unoccupied or designated for night duties, went to get their water-bottles and ran for the "reimbursable"—the wine supplement, as thick and as purple as mulberry juice. In the shelters, while waiting for the soup, tins of corned beef were opened. A few, by virtue of an excess of zeal that generated mild hilarity around them, started cleaning their rifles. By the light of a candle-stub, the "artists" unpacked their materials and set about making aluminum jewelry or finding ingenious uses for cartridge-cases. An interested group watched the manipulations of the most skillful, who were occupied in inserting lice into the bezels of rings, beneath magnifying-glasses. Two inseparables, Totor and Dudule, were warmly debating the issue of the leave-roster. "Even if I get blown up, when my leave falls due, you'll see someone popping up to the head of the column at top speed..."

After casting an indulgent glance over the familiar spectacle, visiting the as-yet-deserted infirmary, watching the sapper corporal distributing picks and spades from a shed behind the church and the motorcyclist repairing his machine, the lieutenants headed for the company office, installed on the ground floor of the old tower. Beside the door, two telephonists were checking the alignment of the copper antenna that was hanging down from the top of the tower. One of them, a short thickset sergeant with a crafty expression, saluted the lieutenant with respectful familiarity.

"Bonjour, Monsieur Renard."

"Bonjour, Dupuy. Your wireless apparatus is set up in the tower?"

"In the observation-post, yes, Monsieur Renard. If you want to go up before it's completely dark, I'll join you in a minute."

The two officers went into the ancient and somber building. Going past the office, where a clerk was visible, hunched over an oil-lamp, they switched on their pocket torches in order to climb the rigid ladders linking the vaulted floors.

"Do you know that radio man?" asked de Lanselles, alias Monocard.

"Yes, that's right, you've just arrived from the two-twenty," said Renard. "You don't know. I knew Dupuy as a boy; we used to indulge in rough-and-tumble together. He was the son of the concierge in my father's workshop, at the Orange automobile factory. He became a mechanic, and then an electrician. In '14, at 25, he had just gone into the distribution factory at Issy-les-Moulineaux as a workshop manager. If he sees out the war, he'll go far."

The noise of a rapid climb shook the wooden rungs. Sergeant Dupuy arrived on the upper platform at the same time as the two officers.

"Beautiful landscape," murmured de Lanselles, parading his interested monocle around.

In almost complete darkness, only the ribbon of the Seille was still shining faintly. All the rest, whether it was allied or enemy territory, extended in vague undulations toward the forts of Metz, punctuated in the distance by rare fires. To the north, the cannonade was rumbling, and flares were describing their luminous parabolas in the sky.

"Not bad," Renard conceded. "But you'll have plenty of time to see it, in a fortnight. Come on, old chap."

Dupuy took his visitors into the corrugated iron shelter in which another radio operator, wearing earphones, was scribbling notes.

"At present, it's Lyon that's sending…a real pleasure, receiving from Lyon; clear signals and not too fast.

At midday, the Eiffel Tower. At three o'clock, Nauen, the big Boche transmitter..."

After having spent a quarter of an hour being subjected to a short course in practical wireless telegraphy, and meekly applying their ears to the receivers in which and musical modulations, mysterious to them, were drumming amid the rapid crackling, the two officers went back down. It was freezing up there, and it was nearly six o'clock. The orderlies ought to have lit the fire and prepared the meal.

As they went into the cellar, even though he was used to the cares of the unequaled Jasmin, Renard uttered a brief laugh of satisfaction—and de Lanselles, in spite of his idealism and disdain for the material, wiped the mist off his monocle and permitted himself an appreciative cluck of the tongue.

The roaring stove, laden with pans, was spreading a gentle heat and a savory perfume of roasted fowl through the subterrain. The lamp, fitted with a pink paper hood, was illuminating the table on which, on a clear white tablecloth, a blue porcelain vase ornamented with holly and mistletoe separated the place-settings. The two orderlies, standing to attention to either side of the table, completed the welcoming scene.

"Ha ha! You're surpassed yourself, Jasmin, my friend," said the lieutenant. "That vase...my word, he's borrowed it from the curé! And what's that sweet-smelling bird?"

"A teal, Lieutenant. My colleague Saucisson's been hunting. When we began cleaning up, we found two Lefaucheux, with cartridges. What wines would our lieutenants like served?"

"With game, Pommard would seem suitable to me...or perhaps Mouton-d'Armailhac. What do you think, de Lanselles?"

"Oh, I'll leave it up to you, Renard; these material details are irrelevant to me."

"All right then, Pommard and Mouton. A little glass of dry Rhenish to start, and champagne to finish. But first, an aperitif."

They did honor to the teal, and even more to the Englishman's bottles.

The next morning, as soon as their officers had left the cellar, the orderlies set about the housework. The unpolished Saucisson saw no necessity to touch the pile of furniture that, in Jasmin's words, "dishonored their masters' apartment," and would have preferred to undertake a methodical examination of the wine-racks, but a remark of Renard's on the subject of the volumes destroyed by "that stupid drunkard Loubet" had served as a pretext for the shrewd Jasmin to interpret it a formal instruction to put the "glory-hole" in order and to set aside any books they might find therein. Arguing on the basis of that order, the ex-*valet de chambre* of the Duc de Pinchefalise, obtained the support of his robust colleague in the work of clearance.

Velvet-covered chairs, armchairs, a carpet, curtains, a sideboard, even a piano—Monocard could play—gave the installation an unexpected comfort. Empty packing-cases, and whitewood tables and chairs were taken up to the ground floor as a supply of future firewood. A large trunk, whose lock scarcely put up any resistance, was full of civilian clothes: two checkered suits, ulsters, underwear, a black dinner-jacket with waistcoat and trousers.

Saucisson took the dinner-jacket and immediately put it on—and when he had completed his costume with a "stove-pipe" hat, discovered in company with several sporting helmets, he refused to continue the operation before having taken a stroll around the village in his new splendor. He did not get far, though; Sergeant Cipriani—an ill-tempered little Corsican, and a stickler for discipline—encountered him in the kitchens and suggested, in rather sharp terms, that he turn around. To cap it all, Lieutenant Monocard came in during the conversation, and the amateur dandy had to go back to the cellar with his tail between his legs.

He found Jasmin occupied in examining a black leather-bound notebook filled with lines written in a foreign language.

"What's that you're reading? Is it Boche? Where did it come from?"

"It was at the bottom of the trunk. I think it's English. I'll give it to my lieutenant. Who knows? Perhaps the document might assist the national defense."

A far more curious discovery was made that afternoon, however. The furniture having been remove, followed by three boxes of books—perhaps five hundred volumes; enough to fill the Henri II bookcase emptied by the captain twice over—they finally reached an instrument, or, rather, a machine, which was vaguely reminiscent at first glance of a van without wheels, bolted to an enormous cast-iron base. When they had exhausted the most absurd hypotheses regarding the strange device—Jasmin maintained that it was a mysterious instrument of espionage—the two orderlies attempted to get rid of it. Even though they combined their efforts, however—and Saucisson, among other professions, had been a wrestler and weight-lifter in Marseilles—the cast-iron base rendered any transportation impracticable.

"Bah!" sighed Jasmin. "We'll hide the not-very-decorative object under one of those Algerian curtains. First, though, I'll show it to my lieutenant."

At a glance, Renard—an expert in material matters—saw that the apparatus had no serious relationship to an automobile. Only the dials providing indications in English could give that illusion to laymen. In addition to the absence of wheels and even of axles, no mechanical transmission departed from the housing that might have contained something akin to an engine.

After the meal, Renard appealed to de Lanselles to study the singular device, but Monocard had a horror of anything resembling technology and declared himself incompetent. Duty was calling him, in any case; and after having rummaged for twenty minutes in the boxes of books, he left Renard plunged in his examination.

What use could the Englishman have made of this unknown machine?

Suddenly, the officer remembered the black leather-bound notebook, through which he had leafed distractedly in the early afternoon. Several inscriptions on the dials—PAST and FUTURE, among others—were to be found in the notes, where the formed chapter titles. Swiftly, he took it out of the bookcase, into which he had thrown it, and, summoning up his knowledge of English, he set about reading it attentively.

There was no doubt about it: the notebook related to the apparatus. With a disconcerting laconism, the function of each control and the purpose of each dial were specified therein...

After four pages, a suspicion of the truth dawned on the lieutenant...

Was that book by Wells he had once read, which he suddenly remembered with a singular clarity, not merely a novel, then? The machine described therein was not a pure fiction; someone—an engineer—had really imagined, designed and constructed one...

After ten minutes, in which incredulity gradually gave way to doubt, and then to persuasion, Renard, amazed and bewildered but impassioned by the discovery, was obliged to yield to the evidence. The owner of the cellar—the English engineer shot as a spy in '14—was the constructor of the machine described by Wells, and the machine that was resting here in the cellar, perhaps intact and ready to function, was neither more nor less than the famous Time Machine!

II. The Repair

As the *poilus* of the tenth had said, Port-sur-Seille was peppered with fire, but only moderately; Adjutant Etcheverry and the sergeants of the eighth were given the job of not allowing the tradition to lapse. That morning, the day after their arrival, the redoubtable Sergeant Cipriani paraded his tempestuous zeal throughout the village. His first visit was to the barn in which, the day before, he had noticed a two-twenty millimeter shell, abandoned. Two men, left behind by their squadron, were sitting on the projectile, placidly playing cards.

"What's this? I gave orders to get rid of that shell! It might be primed—you don't know one way or the other. You're part of the company lodged here. Suppose some swine comes in one night and gives it a kick— would you like your entrails soaring through the air, eh? Don't let me see that thing again. Get moving."

Then it was the dug-outs, not tidy enough for his taste, and a vengeful proclamation: "Inspection at two o'clock. Rifles taken apart, machine-guns too. Grenadiers, an exact count of grenades; the automatic pistols well greased, and their 25 cartridges. No one exempted, even the radio-operators—don't forget to tell them…and try to be ready, you load of good-for-nothings!"

The storekeeper, a little further on, was severely reprimanded. "You're going to sort out the biscuits for me, one by one, and the tins of bully beef: all the blues together, all the reds, all the greens; and you're going to count the bars of chocolate, the quarters of lard, the cans of cooking-oil and lamp-oil. Make me a list of all the provisions. Get it done inside two hours."

As he emerged on to the square sheltered by the tower and the building where the kitchens were, the sight of a seventy-five millimeter cannon with a missing wheel drew an irritated exclamation from him. "Where's the crew? The crew I ordered to get rid of this old nail for me? All playing cards, eh? Hey you, the cook, what are you doing messing about with the breech of that cannon? What? They're using it as a knife-cupboard? In God's name, what if I were to have you court-martialed for damaging armaments? That 75's still in good condition; it only needs a little work to get it back to work. And that truck over there? Those swine from the artillery haven't come to pick it up? The shells are still in it? Seven 75 millimeter shells, no? And the tarpaulin's still on top...oh, what a mess, what a mess! If we're caught on the hop by the Boche, this won't do at all! Oh, beg pardon, lieutenant—I didn't see you!"

Lieutenant Renard, seemingly preoccupied, had just come up to the sergeant and tapped him on the shoulder.

"Yes, yes, that's all right, Cipriani—but tell me, have you seen Sergeant Dupuy?"

"He's working with his crew on the bank of the Seille."

"Send someone to fetch him for me—tell him to come to my cellar, immediately."

In the first surge of enthusiasm that had followed the identification of the Machine, Renard had initially intended to tell Monocard everything as soon as the latter returned. After an hour of fruitless attempts to ensure that the apparatus was working—attempts hindered by the fear of an accident of an unknown nature, and all the more to be dreaded—he had concluded by admitting that he would never be able to grasp the precise operation of the device on his own. The notebook, a purely personal reminder kept by the English engineer, had too many abbreviations and technical terms. In order to decipher them, extensive preliminary knowledge was required, of mechanics and, above all, electricity.

Renard was not very well up in the latter branch of science. Given that, what could he possibly do if Monocard, always skeptical and inclined to deny material progress, asked him to make the Machine work, or even quizzed him about its operation? The notebook would not convince Monocard, who only knew German, not English...

No, before saying anything, it was necessary to obtain the discreet aid of a specialist, an electrician—little Dupuy, of course!—and check out the operation of the Machine with him. Then, when the operation was familiar, he could exhibit the object to Monocard and give him a demonstration. Until then, hush-hush!

Renard had, therefore, kept silent when the sub-lieutenant returned at about midnight. But the following day, in the morning, as soon as he had an hour's peace ahead of him, he set out in search of Dupuy.

Sent by Cipriani, the radio operator came into the cellar, where the lieutenant, alone and with the black notebook in hand, was waiting for him impatiently.

"You asked for me, Monsieur Renard? It is to make a repair?"

"A repair? Perhaps. I don't know yet. Let's take things in order. Have you read Wells?"

"Wells?" the other repeated, slightly astonished. "I certainly have read him. The Invisible Man, wandering naked through the streets of London...very amusing. He's an ace, that Wells! He's much better than Jules Verne."

"And *The Time Machine*? Do you know that one?"

"Yes, yes, I know it…that one, at least, is scientific."

"Well, my little Dupuy, I won't beat around the bush—I know you're discreet. The Time Machine? It was in this cellar, under a pile of debris. I've found it. Look—there it is!"

"No! You're pulling my leg, Lieutenant! In Wells, the engineer left on it, and was never seen again."

"And he landed here? Or it's another engineer and a different machine? Perhaps Wells's man didn't have a monopoly. Anyway, in brief, this is one of them. I had you come to see whether it's in working order—and if necessary, to repair it."

The lieutenant set about translating a few of the pages of the notebook, aloud. Leaning over the apparatus, Dupuy followed the explanations, verifying as he went along the situation of the controls beneath the dials. After ten minutes, he was no longer in doubt.

"Oh, but your engineer has improved it, Lieutenant! He's done better than Wells's man. This is a new model. In the book, there was talk of a little bicycle-saddle. Here, there are two bucket-seats. Oh, there's some nice tricks here. FUTURE—the control for *l'avenir*, yes. PAST—that means *passé*, doesn't it? And here's the warning-light, and the indicator that lights up—like a wireless detector—to tell you that everything's working.

"SPACE—*espace*, you say, Monsieur Renard. Why, damn it, this machine can travel in space as well as into the future or the past! Look here, at these little dials to one side, with micrometer screws, magnifying glasses and verniers to read the divisions: that's how one regulates displacement in space…a millimeter on the scale in equivalent to an actual horizontal kilometer…NORTH-

SOUTH following the line of longitude and EAST-WEST latitude, obviously.

"And this control is for altitude…it's amazing! So, if I select on the map—there's even a map!—let's say Paris…I set all the controls…one, two, three controls…and with the setting for the past…before the war, eh? That was the best time…1912… There! All we have to do is get into the seats and start it up, and we'll disembark—click!—in Montmartre in 1912."

"Be careful—no tricks. Don't go so quickly. First, we need to be sure…"

"Have no fear, Monsieur Renard: there's a safety-catch. Ah! What's this? This slide-rule thing. What can that be? Look for PERIMETER INCLUDED in the notebook."

It turned out from the notebook—on a page full of terribly complicated formulae regarding the relativity of time and space, since rediscovered by Einstein—that the Machine was capable not only of traveling in an independent fashion but also, at will, of taking under its influence and transporting with it a peripheral zone of terrain whose diameter, determined by the "slide-rule," could extend as far as 200 meters."

"What an ace! What an ace!" Dupuy repeated.

"Take care, my lad, to keep that slide-rule at zero," Renard instructed. "If we try an experiment, we mustn't displace the trenches as well. That would kick up a fuss! And the Boche would take advantage of it!"

But the experiment, all things considered, did not seem so easy to carry out. A more detailed examination convinced the electrician that, although the machine was intact in its essential parts, two things were still opposed to its functioning: firstly, the indispensable battery of accumulators had lost its charge; secondly, an aluminum component, fortunately described in the schematics in the notebook, had been corroded and rendered useless by an infiltration of acid coming from a cracked battery.

"The battery's no problem," Dupuy declared. "I can get one from the wireless apparatus—but the aluminum lever's more serious. I'll have to make another, and I don't have any aluminum to hand. Too bad—I'll find some."

Dupuy was not a man to let himself be stopped by that difficulty. The desire to try out the machine had developed in him, as it had in the lieutenant, with a tyrannical violence that silenced all scruples. The company artist, who furnished the eighth with aluminum rings, with or without the collaboration of the man with the lice, kept a good half-kilo of the metal in reserve in a satchel. Dupuy would simply steal the satchel.

But that half-kilo would not be sufficient. In his turn, Renard envisaged a heroic expedient. In order to avoid the indiscretions of the orderlies, who had caught sight of him once or twice in the process of studying the Machine with the radio operator, he had told the faithful Jasmin that there were "interests of national defense" at stake. He therefore asked him to find the aluminum necessary to repair it—and after a hour, Saucisson returned triumphantly, carrying a satchel stuffed with mugs, plates, forks and spoons that he had pillaged from the dug-outs, and rings that he had "borrowed" in order to see the effect on his huge hairy paws.

That complement of metal permitted Dupuy to reconstitute the damaged component, and to put the machine in working order, after four days' work.

III. Test Flights

It was ten o'clock in the evening. A cold January shower was falling on the tranquil village. Monocard, on duty in the observation-post, did not get back until one o'clock. The orderlies were snoring on the ground floor of the villa.

Renard and Dupuy were alone in the cellar with the Machine, on which the light of the lamp they had shifted fell directly. The copper and nickel, the glass of the dials and the ebonite controls, polished by Jasmin, were sparkling like the telephone exchange at the Palace Hotel. Two sheepskins spread on the seats offered themselves softly to the explorers, but they were in no hurry to take their places. The feverish desire and impatience of the preceding days had suddenly disappeared, and an anxiety to which they dared not admit was delaying the departure. Dupuy, oil-can in hand, had not finished oiling the axles and pivots. Renard, to maintain his composure, went to his desk and rang the three telephone posts.

"Hello, Central. Nothing new at number one? Good—all right. And number two? What! No message from two! Find out why. And three? Good. Oh, the gentlemen are deigning to reply. Nothing new from number two either. Yes, yes, we know about the cut wire. All right. *Bonsoir....*"

The radio operator, putting down his oil-can, looked for the twentieth time at the two small dials whose purpose he had been unable to discover in the notebook. "They must be for something, though, those clock-faces. One's a genuine watch, which works, but what about the other? Why that indicator-needle? At any rate, the machine works without them. Shall we get in, Lieutenant?"

"Let's have a little drink first; we don't want to get cold."

They drank—but as he set down his glass, an idea occurred to Renard.

"What about our costumes, Dupuy? What if we run into an officer in Paris in our blue horizons, in 1912? He'll have us banged up."

The Englishman's trunk was still there. Dupuy put on one of the checkered suits and a superb hat. Renard took the dinner jacket and top hat. As the latter was too big for him, he had to stuck a wad of paper under the leather, furnished by an issue of *L'Action Française*, to which Jasmin was a subscriber. The two explorers, fortified by the Burgundy they had drunk, burst out laughing on looking at one other in their new outfits, and that fit of hilarity dispelled their final hesitation. They took their places in the seats.

"Where shall we land in Paris, Monsieur Renard?" Dupuy asked, while meticulously checking the settings of the controls.

"It doesn't matter. Some not very crowded spot—put us down in the Square Saint-Pierre, in front of Sacré-Coeur. It's closed at night. The Machine will be safe there. Is the slide-rule set at zero? We mustn't take the sector with us."

"It is, Lieutenant. There—everything's in place!"

"We're only staying ten minutes, you know—no longer."

"Yes, yes, Lieutenant. A simple reconnaissance. Are you ready? First, time: I'm starting up." An oval indicator-light lit up, with a bright violet glow. There was a slight hum, a crackle of sparks, and a continuous vibration caused the apparatus to vibrate. "Look out—I'm releasing the safety catch. One…two…three!"

A kind of shock—not unlike the sensation spread through the entire body procured by the abrupt ascent of an ultra-rapid elevator, but very violent and extremely unpleasant—gripped the two voyagers and cut off their breath, at the same time as a nauseating vertigo seemed to empty their heads and envelop them in a blue dazzle, as bright as the light of a mercury vapor lamp. Choking, their ears buzzing with a noise like the static of a gigantic telephone, compressed and anguished, they both closed their eyes and clenched their jaws, crouching in the seats into which they seemed to be encrusted, crushed as of their bodies had turned into platinum, as if their weight had suddenly been multiplied a hundredfold, or as if they were at the bottom of the ocean, under a pressure of a thousand atmospheres.

That lasted for a second—or ten minutes. Then the horrible constriction relaxed rapidly; their weight became normal gain; the ankylosis and the anguish vanished; a cool wind caressed their cheeks and put the exhilarating sensation of fresh air into their lungs...

They opened their eyes...

No more cellar, no more lamp. A dark night, a wintry sky, clear and icy, where Orion sparkled before them, above the vague silhouettes of trees and tall buildings.

"Well, Dupuy, my lad…!"

"Well, Monsieur Renard, here we are. Not as difficult as all that!"

Intimidated by the suddenness of the change of scene, they peered into the darkness, chortling quietly at their success.

"Everyone descends on Paris!" joked the radio-operator, showing his companion the Byzantine cupolas of Sacré-Coeur, which stood out against the night sky, high to the left, aureoled by the luminous mist of the capital. And taking his torch from his pocket, he illuminated the gravel of a path, half-overlapped by the base of the machine, and then the lawn and the foliage of the square, He was setting foot on the ground when shouting burst out at a lower level, a hundred meters away, in the open space that was visible through the railings. Several disreputable individuals emerged into the light from a door that had been abruptly flung open, pursued by others. Gunshots resounded, knives flashed, and a furious skirmish began in the open space.

"Apaches!" Renard muttered, forcing his companion to sit down again.

"And the *flics*, for once," Dupuy added.

Indeed, four motorcycle policemen, arriving from the left, leapt off their machines and moved to surround the combatants, all too visible in the light from the doorway, still gaping, into which spectators were crowding.

In the blink of an eye, the shooting stopped. Leaving a wounded man behind them on the pavement, clutching his belly and howling, the apaches dispersed. Five or six ran to their right, but the majority ran toward the square and leapt over the railings, pursued by the policemen.

"Damn it!" Renard exclaimed, grabbing hold of the torch, which he aimed at the control panel. We're in trouble—and we don't have any weapons! Get going, my lad—get us back to Port, double quick!"

The muffled gallop of espadrilles and the thudding of heavy police boots were coming straight toward them. "Death to the pigs!" howled the bandits, pointing at the torch and the two travelers, whom they mistook for enemy reinforcements.

The electrician leaned over his controls and activated them precipitately, one after another. Fortunately, the return maneuver did not require delicate focusing. The indicator lit up; the apparatus hummed and shook...

"Hold on, Monsieur Renard, I'm letting go!"

Just as the nearest apache was aiming his Browning at the violet light of the indicator, the last lever was pulled back, and the Machine escaped in the departure's surge of vertigo, anguish and dazzlement—with the difference that, this time, the imaginary elevator seemed to be falling away beneath the travelers' feet, and the sensation of crushing was replaced by a lightening, a loss of weight, a temporary quasi-imponderability.

Nothing prevented them, obviously, as soon as they had returned to Port-sur-Seille on January 17, from hitting the road again—if that banal expression can be applied here—for a more hospitable place and moment of the past than the Square Saint-Pierre while the apaches and the police were irrupting into it. Wells's hero, or his imitator the English engineer, would not have failed to do so. The latter's opportunistic and posthumous pupils did not think of that immediately, however.

They had had their fill of excitement and shocks, and as soon as they recovered from the vertiginous semi-consciousness that accompanied the journey—or, to put it more accurately, the double spatial and temporal dislocation—to find themselves under the gross lamp and the enclosed warmth of the silent cellar, Renard and Dupuy were in no hurry to do anything but leap out of their seats and take off their tourist outfits, in order to resume their regulation uniforms. It was only after having

33

downed a glass of wine and at down face to face in the peaceful and familiar atmosphere, that they stopped speaking in interjections—furious, about their misadventure; admiring, as to the correct functioning of the machine; and joyful, for their safe return home—and were able to converse more sanely.

Their absence had only lasted thirty minutes, all told. They had left at half past ten; Renard's chronometer and the Machine's clock—whose dial was next to the other dial, function of which remained enigmatic—now showed nearly eleven o'clock. Monocard would not be back for two hours. Dupuy, now sure of the controls, was almost inclined to "have another go." Breathing the air of pre-war Paris, if only for ten minutes, had stimulated him strangely.

"Just think, Monsieur Renard, that we were in Montmartre, five minutes from the Place Pigalle, the *Abbaye de Thélème*, the *Rat-Mort*—all the nice places where one can have a bit of fun…oh, just time to drink a glass and to remember how it was before this holy mess of a war!"

But Renard, slightly thirsty as he was himself, made him listen to the voice of reason. It was necessary to check the Machine, whose batteries might no longer have an adequate charge, and think about a safer place in which to park their vehicle during their stroll to the *Rat-Mort*—still on the condition of only drinking a single modest glass...

The next day, Monocard was slightly astonished by the lieutenant's insistence that he take his turn of guard duty in the observation-post, but he agreed to it in the end—and the two accomplices found themselves back in the cellar after ten o'clock.

Dupuy had recharged the batteries, and he proposed for a landing-point, not the square, which was too risky, but the derelict ground cluttered with building-materials and rubble at the top of the butte, behind the statue of the Chevalier de La Barre.[4] The lieutenant agreed, but for further safety, on top of their civilian clothes, they both put on an ulster this time, into whose pockets they each put two grenades and an automatic pistol.

Beneath the violent electric lighting, the orchestra of the *Rat-Mort* poured out its languorous strains into the atmosphere of rooms in which a dust-cloud of luxury and pleasure seemed to be floating. On the shining parquet, couples were dancing the tango. On the tables around the periphery, painted and plumed women were eyeing up potential clients while sipping orangeade.

Among the twenty party-people, cosmopolitans and foreigners perched on high stools on front of the bar, sparkling with nickel and mirrors, Renard and Dupuy were savoring their martinis more slowly than their original program had permitted. Although they had taken care to retain their somewhat baroque ulsters, their entrance had passed unperceived, and at this hour they could see themselves in the large mirror behind the bar as a plausible pair of foreigners. The tall blond fellow next to them, with gold-rimmed spectacles and a green hat, who was talking loudly—in German! What a cheek! Dupuy observed, with a momentary flicker of amaze-

---

[4] Jean-François, Chevalier de La Barre was beheaded and burned at the stake in 1766, having been accused of mutilating a crucifix. There is a subtle symbolism in this choice of parking spot, correlated with the fact that their first one, within the grounds of the Basilica, proved direly unsafe.

ment—looked much more ridiculous. Their embarrassment and their initial timidity had melted away like sugar in a cup of tea; they were enjoying themselves blissfully, delightfully, in that atmosphere of insouciant joy, of which they had almost lost the memory...

"Why, but it's Marcel Renard! How are you, old chap!"

And a gentleman in a smoking-jacket clapped the explorer on the shoulder. The latter started with fright as he recognized a friend he had seen fall beside him at the battle of the Marne, his head blown off by a shell!

"Georges Daufresne! You! But...you're dead!"

The other bridled. "You've had one too many, you know. Me, dead! I have no desire to be, I can assure you. I've never felt better, and the fortune-teller at the Neuilly fair told me I'd live to be 90. But what's become of you since we last met?"

"Still with the eighth, with my *poilus*," the lieutenant replied, automatically, in spite of the dig in the ribs that the radio operator gave him.

"Completely drunk!" murmured Daufresne. "Go on, sleep well, old chap—another time!" And he turned back to his companions.

Having paid the bill, Dupuy dragged Renard to a table where, he said, it would be quiet—but where, in reality, he had noticed a girl in a blue toque, who had smiled at him in an alluring manner. Her blonde companion, in a pink dress, would do for the lieutenant; he liked them plump.

They offered the girls champagne. There was no urgency; it was scarcely eleven o'clock; if they left around midnight, that would be perfect. The two chicks, who also had their plans, deployed the treasures of seduction. Renard and Dupuy, gradually arming up, amused themselves with no further scruples. They even consented, at about midnight, to take off their ulsters in order to dance a two-step. But the group that Daufresne had informed about Renard's singular remarks was watching them with an ill-disguised suspicion.

"They're annoying us, those ambushers," Duput groaned. "I have a yen to go teach them to mind their own business." The chick in the blue toque held him back.

The lieutenant sighed at the idea that he soon had to leave the plump blonde. Gallantly, he summoned the flower-seller and chose a branch of white lilac.

"Keep the change," he said, taking a five-franc bill from the pocket into which he had tucked a wad of cash before leaving.

The woman examined the bill, and then looked her client up and down, her fist on her hip. "Don't try to put one over on me. If you're a forger, try to find some other mark to take your fake notes. Me, I'm not playing."

She had raised her voice. The chicks became anxious. Customers were turning round. A bouncer approached. Renard, furious about his gaffe, took back the unfortunate bill and reached into his waistcoat pocket, where he found a few pounds sterling. He held a sovereign out to the florist, who shrugged her shoulders, grumbling: "Bah! They're only English!"

Nevertheless, he had time to retreat.

Dupuy sensed a hostile curiosity enveloping them. "There's a bad smell in here—let's get out," he whispered to Renard, who consulted his watch regretfully.

"Yes, it'll soon be one o'clock. Let's go."

They settled the bill and put their ulsters back on, but the chicks, in spite of their mistrust of these singular clients, protested, half-wheedling and half-peevish: "What? You're not going?"

Renard disengaged himself from the plump blonde by means of an English sovereign. The blue toque was still clinging to Dupuy. "You're a nice boy—at least you'll give me a little gift."

"Hurry up!" called Renard, from the doorway.

The electrician took two black balls the size of oranges from his ulster. "Here, darlings—my lieutenant has given you gold; I'll give you these Easter eggs."

"Oh, they're funny, these things. What are they called?"

"They're called 'lemon grenades.'"

"And what's inside them?"

"A nice surprise."

And he decamped, following Renard.

They went back up the Boulevard Rochechouart at the double, and were about to turn the corner of the Rue Steinkerque when a muffled detonation resounded behind them, and then another, from the direction of the *Rat-Mort*.

"What can that be?" asked Renard.

"Our chicks amusing themselves," sniggered Dupuy.

On the derelict ground, amid the building-materials and the rubble, the Machine was waiting. The two tourists took their places therein.

The Machine has functioned, the return has taken place; pre-war Paris is far away, in the mysterious compartments of Relativity. Here is the cellar in Port-sur-Seille…and yet further detonations are resounding! Illusion? The memory of the grenades in the *Rat-Mort*? But to the detonations of grenades is added the explosion of shells, the crackle of rifle-fire, the rattle of machine-guns...no doubt about it, it's an attack: a Boche attack! A battle is raging in Port-sur-Seille, and neither Lieutenant Renard nor Radio-Operator Dupuy is at his post!

In the blink of an eye they are out of the Machine, throwing off their outfits, putting on their blue uniforms...helmets...

Outside. Dupuy gallops straight ahead toward his tower; Renard, crazed, runs to the right, toward the minor posts.

After ten paces he ran into the breathless Monocard, who gasped: "Finally! There you are! I've been looking for you everywhere. This has been going on for two hours. The orderlies are asleep and I've made sure that they don't suspect you. I've told the others that you were on duty in the tower, but I thought you'd been taken prisoner with the men at the post at the bridgehead. The swine had dozed off and were snoring like popes. They woke up under the pistols of the Boche, who asked them politely to follow therm. It's Corporal Venette who escaped, barefoot, and who told the adjutant to raise the alarm. Barefoot! On duty! I'll see to him! Anyway, we got out of it—it's nearly all over. But where the hell have you been?"

"My dear chap," Renard began, trotting along the communication tunnel behind his subordinate, while searching desperately for a plausible explanation, "it's fantastic—a long story...too long to tell now. I'll tell you later."

They emerged on to the esplanade of the tower, and meeting Cipriani there provided a salutary diversion. The sergeant announced that the Boche had gone back over the Seille and were retreating; we had got out of it with the loss of the prisoners from the advance post and five or six slightly wounded.

The fusillade died down, and fell silent. The two officers separated. Monocard went to draft his report, and his colleague followed Cipriani on a tour of inspection.

Thanks to skilful maneuvers, Renard succeeded in delaying a further meeting with the sub-lieutenant all morning. He took advantage of that to see Dupuy, whose absence had fortunately passed unnoticed.

"Dupuy, my lad, you've got us into a filthy mess. I don't hold it against you; you couldn't foresee the attack; but I want you—mark my words!—I want you to get rid of that wretched Machine. Dismantle it today, and fling the pieces in the Seille."

He had still not found a plausible explanation for his absence. At the midday meal, in view of the presence of Jasmin and Saucisson, Monocard did not ask him any questions, but the unfortunate tourist felt his subordinate's gaze weighing upon him, and lowered his eyes like a guilty man. Undoubtedly, his attitude and his silence must seem suspicious. De Lanselles was his comrade, but he did not trifle with matters of duty; he had the sword of an administrator of justice; perhaps he would...

No! It was absolutely necessary to say something.

At the evening meal, as at the midday one, Renard said nothing. Monocard remained equally taciturn, but a scornful curl of his lip replaced his initial anxious astonishment.

The next day, the situation became intolerable. The deadly Machine was still there, for Dupuy claimed that he had not had a minute to dismantle it. During the three hours that the two officers spent together in the office, during the afternoon, Monocard affected a mute and glacial politeness. He was about to go out when Renard made a desperate resolution. He sent the secretary away and said: "My dear de Lanselles, extravagant as this must appear to you, I want to make a confession: the other night, during the attack, I was...well, yes, this is it! I was in Paris...in Montmartre...at the *Rat-Mort*..."

The sub-lieutenant frowned, and then looked him full in the face.

"No, old chap, that's childish—try to find something else. I'm not asking you for anything, mind. Your reputation for bravery isn't at stake; it's well-enough established. You had your reasons for not putting in an appearance during the attack, that's all."

And with a frosty salute, he drew away.

Too bad! Renard said to himself. *I'll tell him everything—and I'll show him the Machine. I'll take him for a trip, if necessary. Provided that Dupuy...*

And he climbed up the steps of the tower, as fast as he could. Dupuy was alone on the platform.

"What have you done with the Machine?"

"The Machine?" the radio operator replied, in a mocking tome. "Why, I threw it in the Seille, as you told me to do, twice."

"Damn it! You're joking!"

"La la la! You're getting carried away, Monsieur Renard. It's still in its place, the Machine—I haven't touched it. Do you want to go back to the *Rat-Mort*?"

"Shut up, damn it! It's not that—it's a matter of your coming to help me put it in order."

IV. During the Attack

The adjustments were very scrupulous, and Dupuy checked the entire mechanism in detail. For additional security, he even replaced the accumulators with a battery that the motorcyclist had just brought him from Landremont, freshly recharged, intended for the wireless post. Finally, the needles, levers, handles and verniers were disposed according to Renard's instructions; in order to operate the transfer, it only remained to push the starter button and release the safety-catch.

The electrician went away, convinced that he would be called back two or three hours later to accompany his lieutenant on a new expedition.

The latter, however, was only thinking about Monocard. "If de Lanselles doesn't recover his confidence in me after this..." he murmured—and while Jasmin, hiding his curiosity, set the table with Saucisson, the waited impatiently for the sublieutenant to arrive.

At dessert—Monocard had not said a single word throughout the meal—Renard sent the orderlies away; then, repeating the previous evening's affirmation, he added: "You don't believe me, but I have a very simple means of demonstrating my good faith. That's to make you try out the vehicle of which I made use. There it is: it's the Englishman's machine. It's ready to take us away. You'll operate it—I won't touch anything. But, as I suppose that an expedition to the *Rat-Mort* in 1912 won't seduce you, I've fixed 1920 for the time and place of the arrival, at the crossroads of the Arc de Triomphe. We'll thus be informed of the outcome of the war."

Monocard's skepticism was dented by affirmations of such clarity. He was obstinate in his refusal to examine the Machine and delve into the theory that the other was ready to explain to him, but he consented to try the experiment.

Renard was getting to his feet, elated by his success, when a jovial and familiar voice with a southern accent hailed him from the threshold, and Major Thévenard, wrapped up on his goatskin, advanced toward the table.

One of the soldiers wounded the day before—all of whom were still in the infirmary at Port-sur-Seille—had developed a temperature of 38.7° during the night, and a cyclist had gone to Landremont to alert the major. The latter had just arrived on his own bicycle to visit the patient.

"A touch of fever, that's all, but no complications to fear," affirmed the senior officer, stroking his fine black beard. "He became alarmed a little too soon, your medical orderly. I could have saved myself riding half a dozen kilometers in the rain. Fortunately, it's good here, and I'm glad to see that you have a few bottles left."

While pouring him a Cointreau, the two lieutenants exchanged a glance. With this pitiless chatterbox, they were in for at least an hour of conversation. De Lanselles smile ironically, as if the major's arrival had been agreed with Renard in order to prevent the famous experiment. Renard, looking at the Machine in the corner, fidgeted impatiently.

The inconveniences of the evening were not yet over, however. As soon as Thévenard, finally put off by the monosyllabic coldness of his hosts, had remarked: "Eleven o'clock—time to hit the road," the rattle of machine gun fire became audible.

"*Zut!* An attack!"

Hastily grabbing their equipment, the three men ran outside into the rain.

The luminous parabolas of red, white and green flares were streaking the black night. A fusillade was crackling on the bank of the Seille. Shells were beginning to fall. In the village, there was a stampede of men running to their posts.

"I shall have clients," joked the jovial quack—and ran to the infirmary, while de Lanselles headed for the tower. Renard, anxious because he could not hear the machine guns—broken down again!—went into the tunnel.

It was not long before the noise of engines, approaching from the direction of Metz and mingling with the sound of detonations, momentarily gave rise to the fear of an aerial attack. The aircraft, however, did not release any projectile, and contented itself with circling, as if indecisively, during the further half-hour that the battle lasted. In the end, the Boche having given up, the shells ceased falling, the fusillade stopped, and four or five wounded me were carried away. The aircraft made its decision, and it was glimpsed in the obscurity, about to land in the open space behind the infirmary.

The lieutenants ran in that direction, guided by the shouts of the *poilus*. "A plane! A plane" they cried.

Totor ventured the historic remark: "A fine pair of boots coming down, perhaps!"

To which Dudule overbid: "And a nice waterproof leather overcoat. My brother's an orderly; he had one like it—he got it from a Boche..."

Amid the general excitement, the airplane touched down, bounced and came to a stop. A crowd surrounded the pilot, who stood up in his cockpit.

"Hands up, or we shoot!"

A guttural but calm voice replied: "English comrade—don't shoot!"

"Yes, old chap—all the Boche say that..."

Beneath the wings of the apparatus, however, it was indeed the tricolor roundels of the Allies that were displayed by the electric torches—and the head of the aviator alone, once he had taken off his helmet, was sufficient to reveal his nationality. That clean-shaven face with prominent cheekbones, the massive lower jaw and the blotchy complexion could only have belonged to a son of Albion.

In precise and laconic terms, in French that was almost correct but deformed by an abominable accent, he introduced himself—W. R. Bennsbury, lieutenant aviator of His Britannic Majesty—and explained that he had just dropped his supply of bombs over Metz. He had gone astray during the return; the flares had guided him to Port-sur-Seille and he had waited for the battle to end before descending into the open space that he had glimpsed by the light of a window—that of the infirmary, facing the French lines.

After a brief conference with the two lieutenants, he decided to leave again at daybreak. In the meantime, he would rest for a few hours on one of the beds in the infirmary.

When they went in, the major looked him over with a professional eye, and before Renard and de Lanselles could do anything to interfere, he grabbed the Englishman's wrist, learnedly, and pulled a face.

"Hmm! Pulse rapid and unsteady. Advanced arteriosclerosis. You're in a bad way, my friend. Let's see your wound."

"I'm not wounded," the islander protested, phlegmatically.

"Dysentery, then? Take two spoonfuls of paregoric elixir with meals."[5]

It required Renard's intervention to protect W. R. Bennsbury from the zealous Thévenard's medication and to procure him a simple tot of rum and a bed—after which the two lieutenants took their leave of the aviator and left the major to his patients; one of them had caught his finger in the breech of a light machine-gun and Thévenard was talking about amputation.

"I've never seen such an instrument!" he grumbled. "Another war profiteer who's succeeded in placing his shoddy goods. Enough! You're going to bed, you two? Well, I won't disturb you. I'll be here for another half-hour, after which I'll have a little nap before going back to Landremont. Perhaps it won't be raining as hard tomorrow morning. Goodnight."

After a last glance around the village, where order and tranquility reigned once again under the downpour, de Lanselles insinuated negligently: "It's too late, isn't it, for your little experiment? Tomorrow evening..."

"Tomorrow? Why? Everything's ready, I tell you—nothing but two buttons to press. And we still have enough time to convince you. A matter of five minutes in total. I only ask your permission to have a drink beforehand, for I'm literally frozen."

---

[5] Paregoric elixir, initially devised in the 18th century by Jakob Le Mort as a treatment for "asthma" (then a much broader label than now) was essentially a mixture of camphor and opium, sometimes with other ingredients. By 1917, its most popular use was as a treatment for diarrhea.

"Me too, and I hope our orderlies have prepared us a hot drink. Then…five minutes, you say? All right, then—I confess that I'd be curious to spend five minutes in 1920, at the crossroads of the Arc de Triomphe."

Since the beginning of the attack, the two orderlies had taken advantage of their officers' departure to go back into the cellar, in order to tidy up a bit, as they did every evening. They were not sorry, moreover, to go underground; during the previous attack, which they had spent in their beds on the ground floor, a shell had fallen less than fifty meters away, on the other side of the street.

"It would be truly absurd," Jasmin declared, as he began to clear the table, "when we have such a comfortable situation, to go and get ourselves killed in that manner."

"You said it!" sniggered Saucisson—who was installed in front of the roaring stove, drinking the liqueur from the glasses that the officers had abandoned. "Listen to the machines shaking the overcoat. They're making quite a racket! Yes, it's warm outside."

"It's warmer in here," quipped the witty Jasmin. "There's no two ways about it, we're lucky. We're the only two tranquil souls in Port-sur-Seille right now."

"You're forgetting the cameraman—what's he called? Oh yes—Lénac. He's nothing to shoot this time, since it's too dark."

"But he doesn't have a cellar like ours."

"And when it happens by day, he has to get busy. I've seen them during attacks, these cameramen, who aren't dug in. They're often exposed, those fellows."

After having waxed lyrical on the subject of their cushy billet, the two orderlies, having delivered the final flick of the broom, set about warming up some wine.

"Tell me," said Saucisson, "you were here this afternoon when your boss was working on that machine with the radio operator—you must have heard what it does."

Jasmin straightened up. "What it will do, rather! I was going to talk to you about that. You know that my lieutenant is an inventor, like his father, who manufactures Orange cars. Well, thanks to the black notebook we found in the trunk, my lieutenant has discovered what criminal use the Boche spy—the fake English engineer who was shot in '14—intended to make of that machine. It's a powerful engine—unprecedented statistics—that would have ravaged square leagues. Port-sur-Seille, Dieulouard, even Nancy, would have been annihilated. But my lieutenant's in the process of fixing that, with the radio operator, and turning the device against the Boche. Everything's ready. Within a fortnight, the forts of Metz will be blown up, and then it'll be the turn of the town. And in the meantime, we'll have constructed twenty, thirty, fifty of these machines—the necessary number. The whole enemy front will be overturned, smashed..."

"The Boche are finished, then!"

"...And it's the great leap forward, the great offensive, the mass attack, my dear! We're in Berlin, victorious, and my lieutenant is promoted to colonel, general, Maréchal de France!"

"Fuck! You're talking about a big brain, the fellow who found that trick. So, the war will be over in three weeks?"

And with respectful admiration, Saucisson went over to the Machine to examine it. Jasmin, proud of his importance, gave him a detailed account of the astounding engine of war.

"What's this thing?" Saucisson interrupted, pulling the cursor of the "slide-rule" along its entire course. "What does it do?"

"Can't you read? It's written above it: PERIMETER. *Pour-y-mettre*: 'put it there.' It's for launching the torpedoes, for targeting them."

The demonstration continued, and Jasmin obligingly brought a number of the levers and buttons into play.

"Me, I can't see this without getting thirsty. I'm going to have a drink."

But footsteps were approaching through the communication tunnel.

"Damn! The bosses!" And the two orderlies stood to attention in front of the stove.

Renard breathed the air in satisfaction. "You've made us hot wine? Excellent-you think of everything, Jasmin."

"It was Saucisson's idea, Lieutenant. We've driven them back, then, the filthy Boche? No serious losses to deplore?"

"No, don't worry—a few minor wounds. In the meantime, pour us the hot wine and go get some sleep. You've earned it."

Left alone, the two officers emptied their glasses as rapidly as the temperature of the liquid permitted. Monocard affected a casual smile and a complete indifference, but deep down, the delay had irritated his curiosity, and his haste to participate in the singular experiment was almost equal to Renard's.

The lamp was on its usual hook, over the table, but the lieutenant did not take the trouble to pick it up in order to illuminate the Machine as he had during the two previous excursions. The settings were all fixed in advance this time; he would be able to see clearly enough to show Monocard the two controls for the decisive maneuver. To give his triumph the maximum amplitude, he did not want to touch anything himself. As for civilian clothes, Monocard would not lend himself readily to such a disguise, and besides which, to spend five minutes at the Étoile at one o'clock in the morning, such a precaution would be superfluous. He did not even mention it,

"When you wish, old chap—the honor is yours."

They both installed themselves in the Machine's seats and Renard, guiding his companion's hands, placed one on the starter button and the other on the safety catch.

"*En route* to the world after the war!" he added, with a nervous laugh. "With your left hand, press down gradually."

More excited than he wanted to appear, Monocard obeyed.

As on the other occasions, the oval indicator lit up with an intense violet gleam, and a trepidation caused the apparatus to vibrate—but the customary hum had an extraordinary, redoubtable intensity, and the crackling sparks sprang forth visibly from the framework of the Machine, seeming to weave around them a network of effluvia that filled the cellar.

It must be because we're going into the future instead of the past, Renard said to himself, anxiously. In order not to spoil the effect, though, he immediately added, in a firm and peremptory tone: "Everything's fine. The right hand now—go!"

What a thunderbolt! They thought they had been caught in the blinding explosion of a mine, borne away, compressed, crushed in a fiery whirlwind. They thought they were dead, annihilated...

Perhaps they even lost consciousness, for an indeterminate lapse of time...

When they came round, de Lanselles took a deep breath, and then adjusted his monocle. He paraded his gaze around him, and in a tone of irritation, pierced with irony, said: "Permit me to tell you, old chap, that you have a detestable taste in practical jokes. It wouldn't have taken much for your petard of dynamite to blast us to Kingdom Come! As for 1920 at the Étoile..."

Alarmed, Renard considered the cellar, which still surrounded them with its walls garnished with bottles. The lamp was burning above the table. The pan of hot wine was simmering on the stove. To all appearances, the Machine had not budged.

"I assure you, old chap," he stammered, "that I…everything was set...you, yourself..." Then he uttered an exclamation.

The air-vent, through which the inky blackness of night had been visible before, was now open on a clear blue sunlit sky.

Together, the two leapt out of their seats, and in three bounds were out of the cellar, in the trench. The sky, profoundly blue, was above their heads, and the sun, already high, was bathing them with a dazzling light, as bright and hot as a summer noon.

Putting his hand up to shade his blinking eyes, Renard said, triumphantly: "You can certainly see that the experiment has succeeded!"

"If you say so, old chap, although we're still in Port-sur-Seille."

Collecting themselves, they climbed on to the embankment of the trench. The tower loomed up in front of them, with the kitchen building on the other side of the square, which was closed behind them by the Englishman's villa and the store-house. But that familiar sight was transfigured by the strange quasi-African light. The usual detonations toward the north had ceased; in the warm and vaguely perfumed air, they could hear birds singing.

V. The Fervent Sun

Mechanically, Monocard had looked at his watch. He frowned, examined it at closer range, put it to his ear, and shrugged his shoulders.

"Do you know what time it is?" he asked Renard. "My watch seems to be working normally, and it shows quarter past two—but that's absurd. According to the sun it's much later—at least eight hours."

Renard consulted his chronometer, with a puzzled expression. It showed two-sixteen.

"We're slow, obviously," he said. "What do you expect me to do about it? Our watches have stopped..."

"And started again. Or when we fainted...for I have a clear sensation of having fainted, when you set off your petard...we must have been unconscious for several hours..."

On hearing further mention of the petard, the lieutenant, already very nervous, became irritated. "You're wrong to deny it, old chap. The Machine worked."

Suddenly seized by a suspicion, though, he left Monocard there, leapt into the trench, went back into the cellar—and came back to the sublieutenant a minute later. The latter, still standing on the embankment, was pensive examining the kitchens and the cooks on the other side of the square. Yawning in the sunlight, the latter were setting about concocting the morning "juice" with studious slowness.

"The Machine worked," Renard repeated, his fists clenched, and staring the other in the face. "But it didn't work correctly. Someone must have touched it!"

Monocard could see that it would do no good to contradict him. He decided not to insist, for the moment—but his rancor at what he considered to be a bad joke pierced his reply: "At any rate, we're still in Port-sur-Seille, and duty still calls. Since our orderlies are sleeping late, would you care to come to the office and wait for the coffee?"

Renard, increasingly demoralized, doubting himself that the Machine had really worked, contented himself with not receiving a formal denial, and seized the pretext that the sublieutenant had offered him to raise the burning question.

Suddenly voluble and excited, he went on: "As to that, you're right, we're already late with our reports. The colonel's been on at me for a week to get things in order. I need to know whether the men have put on their second pullovers. I'm missing three sheepskins. Where have they gone? They must have been cut up again to make socks, obviously. And the parcels from the Dames de France to distribute! What odd ideas people sometimes have! There's one full of Ninettes and Rintintins,[6] and another of chessboards, with black and white confetti by way of pawns! As if the men have any need of that! They have their godmothers, twelve each at least; the famous Nénesse has twenty-three...all that can rot here. We need to write reports."

Monocard, already somewhat unsure of his companion's mental integrity, was worried by this sudden ex-

---

[6] Ninette and Rintintin were two supposedly cute but rather grotesque rag dolls, which were adopted as mascots by the French forces in the Great War, pictures of which were very widely distributed to the troops in the form of postcards.

citement. He took the other by the arm, amicably. "Come on, then—I'll help you. We'll do it together."

In the office, they found the clerk installed before his typewriter. In order to find the exact time, he had just gone up to the wireless post, where Dupuy was in despair about not receiving any messages, attributing the breakdown of his apparatus to the night's commotion.

"A mine, wasn't it, lieutenant? Or a torpedo. It can't have fallen far away. I'm still stunned, and I must have fainted—when I woke up, it was daylight. At the infirmary, where I went to look for a pick-me-up, the major was talking about an earthquake... No, he hasn't gone yet—he's taking chocolate with the English aviator."

For an hour, the lieutenants absorbed themselves in paperwork and the methodical drafting of the report for the colonel. Through the wide-open office door, however, distant voices were heard, apparently from the posts. "Good stuff, this juice!" Then there was a hubbub of approaching voices, confused exclamations and cries, getting louder all the time.

"One can't work, with these clowns!" exclaimed the lieutenant.

"It's intolerable," said de Lanselles, putting down his pen. "Let's go see what's up."

They went out. In front of the kitchens, a crowd of overexcited *poilus* was pressing around a small group of suppliers, with empty sacks on their backs but provided with inflated bags from which they were extracting and distributing oranges! Shouts of "*Valence! La Belle Valence!*" went up on all sides. They were being interrogated, and, while gesticulating, they seemed to be telling a story.

A cacophony of voices reached the officers: Yes, my friend, a camel, with two women, real ones, and six Moroccan fellows with little squeaky voices..."

As the lieutenants approached, silence fell.

"What's the matter? Why all this racket?"

Several men started talking at the same time. Furthermore, their mouths were full of slices of orange. It was all incomprehensible.

"Put down those oranges for a moment," said Monocard. "Where have they come from, by the way? Have the Dames de France sent parcels? But first, why haven't you brought the supplies? Just you, corporal!"

The corporal launched into confused exclamations. A mine had blown up the communication tunnel and half the village. The road beyond had disappeared. The little wood had got strangely closer...to the extent that they hadn't found the supply depot..."

"What are you talking about?"

But it was necessary to interrupt the investigation. Sergeant Cipriani came running from the guard-posts, angrier than ever, out of breath, sweating and red-faced.

"It's insane Lieutenant! The men at the guard-posts haven't had their juice yet. There must be punishments. This can't go on. Since that mine-blast...the cannon have stopped, the little hamlet opposite has disappeared, the Seille's dry. Metz is only half the usual distance away; the Boche trenches can no longer be seen, nor the forts. The juice hasn't arrived...there have to be punishments, Lieutenant!"

Without seeming to attach any importance to Cipriani's bizarre and incoherent news, Renard tried to calm him down.

"There'll be punishments, Sergeant Cipriani, there'll be punishments—but please put a bit of logic into what you're saying. Go have your juice. Cooks, get on with it, instead of standing there sucking oranges."

An exclamation from Monocard distracted him, however. Monocard had just caught one of the men who had gone for supplies occupied in secretly showing an unexpected object to his fellows: a scimitar. A superb, damascened scimitar, brand new, and with a sharp cutting edge. Renard came closer.

"It wasn't a Boche you took that from, was it?" Monocard demanded.

In the midst of whispers and sniggers, the embarrassed man, exhorted by his comrades in low voices, suddenly came to a decision. "Lieutenant, it's a paper-knife that I rescued from one of the Arbis."

De Lanselles shrugged his shoulders, but Renard wanted to get to the bottom of the affair.

"It's 'Arbis' now! I heard mention of Moroccans and a camel just now. What's the story? Was it the 'Arbis' who gave you the oranges, perchance? Come on, tell—you, Dudule."

Dudule started to speak, assisted by the inseparable Totor, who sometimes reminded him of a detail or suggested and expression.

"Well, it's like this, Lieutenant. After the big explosion of the mine in the night, we slept late, and we left to get supplies in broad daylight—eight of us, with four donkeys. Then, when we set off to get out of here by the tunnel, after a hundred meters, we came out into the sun. No more tunnel, no more trenches. It was the mine—had to be…nothing but open country, or, rather, a sort of ravine, but as we couldn't hear any *zinzins* any more, we went on all the same, toward the little wood. It seemed to be a lot closer than usual, the little wood, and it had leaves—beautiful green and shiny leaves, but we weren't sorry to get into the shade, because the sun was blazing down on our noggins. We smelt a funny odor of orange-blossom—you might have thought we were at a wedding. When we went into the wood, what did I see on all the braches? Oranges! The lads must have worked hard, I thought, to hang the oranges on the branches—but they were real oranges, with leaves and everything, and we stopped to pick them. While we were doing that, we heard the voices of two chicks. That was a bit much, we thought, chicks in the lines…and what did we see coming? A camel—a live camel, with the chicks on top, in a palanquin. They came close. Then there were six negroes, who seemed to have sprung out of the ground in front of us…"

"Then," Totor continued, "I ask them: what are you doing here? They jabber at me in some argot that no one can understand, and they have little shrill voices more piercing than girls. Then Bec-d'Ombrelle, the donkey-boy, tries to get fresh with the chicks on the camel. An Arbi gets annoyed, and wants to knock him down. Me, I jump the Arbi and land him with a kick in the solar plexus. But other Arbis turn up. They have clubs, spears, shields, and as we didn't have any weapons, we couldn't go any further, and we beat it, at the double…but I grabbed my Arbi's paper-knife all the same…"

The men of the supply-party expected a severe reprimand, but the two officers, who had listened to the amazing tale until the end without interrupting, exchanged singular glances.

"What do you think of that?" asked Monocard, in a low voice.

"Well," said Renard, "I think…come back to the cellar, where we can talk more freely. You, the cooks, distribute the juice to the men on watch, and everyone get back to his dug-out. Sergeant Cipriani, I don't want to see anyone outside before they're summoned to roll call, understood?"

Monocard and Renard headed for the cellar. They did not find anyone these, but the coffee was ready.

"Well?" Monocard queried, as soon as they were sheltered from indiscreet ears.

"Well...the sun, the heat, the oranges, the camel, half the village disappeared, the landscape transformed, and all the rest? We're in Africa."

"And in Port-sur-Seille at the same time?" Monocard riposted, not wanting to yield to the evidence.

At that moment, Jasmin made his reappearance, followed by Saucisson. Both looked away on seeing their bosses occupied in examining the Machine, and set about dusting in a sheepish and furtive manner.

"Yes, and in Port-sur-Seille at the same time," Renard replied to his colleague's ironic question. "It's not my fault if someone touched the controls."

Jasmin began trembling under Monocard's stare, the latter having been alerted by their suspicious behavior.

"And I preset the guilty parties," de Lanselles pronounced "Remember their expressions when we came in last night, after the attack."

"God damn it, that's right!" cried Renard, marching upon the orderlies. "It's the fault of these wretches that we're in Africa!"

Jasmin had thrown himself to his knees, theatrically. The vigorous Saucisson, his eyes wide, bent his back, brutalized by fear.

"We didn't mean to do it, Lieutenant!" the latter stammered.

"Mercy, Lieutenant—I put all the levers back in place myself, ten minutes ago," Jasmin added, raising his arms to the heavens.

"Villains!" howled Renard, brandishing his fist. "You ought to be shot!"

But de Lanselles intervened. "What good would that do, old chap? Leave them be. At any rate, the damage is done. They've been punished enough. Rather than come down on them, it would be better to try to find out where we are, and get back as quickly as possible."

"That's true," Renard concluded, darting one last wrathful glance at the orderlies. "Get up, Jasmin, you idiot, and go fetch Sergeant Dupuy."

Jasmin did not need to be told twice, and hastily made himself scarce, escorted by Saucisson.

"Are we even in the future?" Renard murmured, collapsing into the seat of the Machine.

"In any case, we're deserters," said Monocard, in a stinging voice, having ceased to doubt. "It's nearly nine o'clock—our absence must already have been notified to GHQ!"

After three minutes, Dupuy arrived. He listened to Renard's confession regarding the experiment in a bad humor.

"And you didn't take me, Monsieur Renard? That's not very polite."

"Alas, if only I had taken you…too bad!"

"Good God! I do believe you've pushed the PERI-MITER indicator all the way—a diameter of 200 meters. You've carried off half the sector!"

"It wasn't me who touched it…someone altered your settings…but that doesn't matter. The thing is to get back. Put the machine in order, old chap, and let's get back right away!"

The accumulators, indispensable for the return, were, however, flat, and those in the wireless post no better. Just before the displacement, Dupuy had sent his two radio operators to fetch a fresh battery from a shed situated beyond the ruins of the church. They had remained in 1917, with their accumulators!

"Damn and double damn it! We're in a fix!" Renard moaned. "What are we going to tell the *poilus*, if there really isn't any way to get back?"

"Bah! You can demob the enlisted men, Monsieur Renard—there doesn't seem to be a war on here."

"The war must have been over for a long time if…if we really are in the future, at least? Take a look at the dials, Dupuy."

"How do you expect him to figure it out?" Monocard put in. "They've been fiddled in all directions!" He began pacing back and forth, with a somber expression.

Renard, overwhelmed, looked at Dupuy, who was trying in vain to obtain a spark from the dead batteries.

"They're only flat, Monsieur Renard. I'll try to rig up some makeshift piles, to recharge them, but they won't be ready today or tomorrow. In the meantime, there's nothing to be done. Look—the second little dial has moved!"

Captivated by that technical problem, he absorbed himself in the study of the said dial.

The officers started arguing. Monocard wanted them to reveal the situation to everyone without further delay. Renard declared that it would be untimely, and even imprudent, since they still did not know whether they were really in the future, or in Africa. Nothing had been decided when they emerged from the cellar, and found the major and the English aviator walking by the tower. To them, at least, they could tell the whole story;

they would understand. When they had exchanged greetings, the major commented on the weather.

"Unexpected, this sunlight—incomprehensible. Damn it, I could believe that I'm in Toulouse in midsummer. This can't have been seen often, in Port-sur-Seille in January."

Renard seized the opportunity. "We're no longer in Port-sur-Seille."

"Eh? Where are we, then?"

"Africa...perhaps. Let's see, Doctor, what would you say if I told you that last night...you had aged four years...or more?"

The major looked at him with anxious solicitude. "My poor friend, the sun's not doing you any good this morning. Offer us a Pernod instead—Monsieur the aviator and me—and then I'll get on my bike to go back to Landremont. I've a little chick waiting for me—I don't want to miss the boat."

"No, Doctor—Landremont is a long way away. It's serious, what I'm telling you..."

The explanation was laborious.

The major was willing to admit the scientific possibility, and even the existence of the time machine, but he had formed a very different idea of the "dirty little automobile" he had seen in the cellar. Most of all, he could not resign himself to believed that it had worked to his detriment, had aged him by four years and transported him some five hundred leagues from Landremont and his chick. According to him, everything could be explained by an earthquake.

"But what about the camel and the Arabs?"

"Tch! You haven't seen them, and nor have I!"

"And the oranges? The scimitar?"

"Parcels from the Dames de France..."

The English aviator, for his part, listened to Renard's explanation phlegmatically. At the name of Wels he smiled wanly, and declared: "I know him. I've seen him drinking whisky in Folkestone harbor." After rendering this homage to the great novelist, however, he did not open his mouth again. Did he believe in the transfer? Did he disbelieve? His face gave no clue to his intimate sentiments.

While chatting, the four men had advanced as far as the kitchens, and, by means of a side-street descending toward the Seille, they discovered the new landscape that had replaced the gray undulations of Moselle with a yellow-tinted plain parched by the sun, strewn with meager brushwood, with no trace of forts or trenches. Five or six kilometers away, there was the silhouette of a white town, from which trees spread their branches against a blue background above terraces, domes and minaret. All of them, except the English aviator, took out their binoculars.

"They're palm trees," de Lanselles declared.

"Damn it!" exclaimed the major. "The Boche have certainly done a good job of camouflaging the terrain!"

"Africa?" murmured Renard, dubiously. But the binoculars told him nothing more.

"We need to go and see," Monocard declared. And turning to the impassive Bennsbury, he added: "Monsieur Aviator, would you care to do us the favor of going to cast a glance over that town?"

"Yes, I would," said the Englishman. "I'll take gander at *Metz*." And, turning on his heels, he headed for the store-house, behind which his apparatus was garaged. The other three officers followed him.

"Send the cameraman with him, so that he can bring back a few snaps," Monocard whispered to the lieutenant. "That aviator's capable of coming back and telling us that it's still Metz."

Renard had spotted the photographer Lénac in front of the kitchens; the latter had extracted a magnificent beef bone, and was delicately extracting the marrow to spread on a slice of bread.

"Do you have your apparatus, Lénac? Leave that bone and go with the aviator."

Lénac went pale. "It's just...I've never been up in a plane, Lieutenant. I'd be afraid of coming a cropper..."

But he had to obey the order, and the unfortunate Lénac was green with terror as he approached the aircraft, whose engine was already turning over, with his camera slung over his shoulder.

"Strap me in tightly, Monsieur Englishman," he begged, as he climbed into the cockpit.

"Call me Lieutenant," Bennsbury replied, severely.

The propeller roared; the aircraft rolled away, took off, and soared into the sky, heading north.

VI. Orange Picking

Meanwhile, thanks to the initiative of Duranton, the chief cook, and the tacit authorization of Adjutant Etcheverry, a new supply party had set out, half an hour earlier—well-armed, this time—in order to bring back a few oranges from the little wood that had sprung up so opportunely south of the village. Its return was to procure new subjects for astonishment.

Attracted by the preparations for the aircraft's departure, a certain number of men emerged from the barracks to which they had been ordered and spread around the square in front of the tower. There were also emissaries from work-parties and the guard posts, armed with mess-tins.

Cipriani was running around, exasperated. "What are you doing? You were forbidden to come out!"

"It's ten-thirty, sergeant; we've come for some soup!"

"No excuses! Go back in!"

Renard, who was talking to Monocard and the major not far away, intervened.

"Let them be, Cipriani; it's not important, for the moment. And you, Duranton, why isn't the soup ready?"

"Because I haven't received any supplies today, Lieutenant. I've sent out a scavenging party..."

"No matter—don't wait for them. Open the tins of bully beef..."

On the far side of the square, however, exclamations overlapped.

"It's the Moroccans!"

"Arbis!"

"It's a circus!"

"What are the troopers bringing back?"

In fact, a singular procession appeared, coming around the corner of the infirmary. Behind the six men of the supply party, whose bags were stuffed with oranges and whose rifles were shouldered, some twenty white-clad horsemen were advancing two by two. Their swarthy faces, with serious masculine features, mostly bearded, were framed by the flaps of vast burnooses fastened around the temples by ornamental metal bands, and which hung loosely over the rumps of the black or bay chargers with long tails. By way of weapons, some carried bows and the others, equipped with shields of painted wood, had naked scimitars or long bamboo spears with triangular iron heads, each ornamented with a ribbon of green silk.

Having arrived in the square, their leader raised his bare arm, where silver bracelets clinked together. The lined up in the sunlight, saluting the nonplussed officers and re-sheathing their scimitars. Not a single slap was heard.

"Lieutenant," said Nénesse, coming forward from the scavenging party. "We found these fellows in the orange wood."

And, in the midst of a dazed silence scarcely troubled by whispers and the furtive footsteps of newcomers hurrying in response to the news, Nénesse, a veteran of the African army, related the adventure.

While their companions were picking oranges, he and another man had advanced as far as the edge of the wood. Instead of the familiar landscape—devastated fields and villages, then the forest, and Dieulouard in the distance—they had the sea before them "as blue as a telegram form," and also, to the right, a vast bare yellow plain, in which, two or three kilometers away, stood a host of white tents. There were perhaps two hundred of them: an entire camp, with fires lit and horsemen cutting capers. A nearby patrol had spotted them and come running, at a gallop. Confident of their Lebels, the six men had closed ranks in the shelter of the orange trees and stood their ground. The leader of the "spahis" had seemed astonished to see them and, speaking Arabic, had demanded to know whether they were enemies or friends of "the people over there"—presumably the Boche in Metz. Nénesse, who knew Arabic, had replied with an invitation to bring his troop to visit his mates in Port-sur-Seille, and the other had brought his "spahis" trustingly.

For the *poilus*, the interpretation of this arrival was simple: a reinforcement of Moroccan cavalrymen. The sub-officers had a difficult job holding back the crowd of curiosity-seekers who were pressing around the horsemen, while Renard, de Lanselles and the major, sensing a new mystery, continued the interrogation, with Nénesse as translator. The leader with the silver bracelets had dismounted, and greeted Renard in the Oriental style—index-finger to the forehead, then the lips, and then the breast—replied to him while looking him in the eye.

"Who are you?"

"I am Ali, and I command these men for the glory of my master and Allah."

"Who is your master? General Gouraud?"[7]

Nénessse had to make Ali repeat his worrying reply before being able to translate it correctly.

---

[7] Henri Gouraud was the general in command of the French Fourth Army in the latter half of the Great War.

"My master is Abful Khan, the noble Emir, who is himself obedient to the holy successor of the Prophet, Caliph Haroun-al-Djézir.

Renard shook his head despondently and continued: "How many men do you have at your disposal?"

"Four thousand horsemen—the finest army on Earth. We're going to lay siege to the infidels, and with Allah's aid, reconquer the city our forefathers possessed."

"Tch!" the major put in. "The Moroccans possessed Metz now? At any rate, they're not very well armed. I'm afraid they'll run into a firestorm."

De Lanselles told him to be quiet, and Renard continued.

"What do you call that city?"

"Don't you know, O stranger who has come to join us in the Sacred Cause? It's Valencia—Valencia the Beautiful."

The three officers looked at one another.

"So we're in Spain now!" said Monocard.

"Yes, but not in 1917—in 1920…at least," Renard replied. "Anyhow, it's very strange! The Spaniards have allowed themselves to be invaded by Moroccan Riffs? The division of Morocco hasn't done them much good. Just as long as the French have held Casablanca. So tell me, Ali…"

Questions followed about Morocco, Algeria and Tunisia—but the Arab leader did not have any idea that France had ever possessed any colony in Africa.

"We must be much further in the future than I thought," the lieutenant murmured, in a low voice. "What revolutions and catastrophes can have occurred? Do you have artillery?"

Incomprehension on the leader's part.

"Rifles, at least?"

As Nénesse strove to make Ali understand that they were talking about firearms, a sudden crackle of Lebels was heard from the direction of the Seille, and then, almost immediately, the rattle of machine guns.

"It's the Boche! We're firing at them..."

An effervescence ran through the crowd of *poilus*. The Arab horses pranced and whinnied, and their riders, while restraining them, seemed scarcely more reassured.

The attentive officers lent an ear to the fusillade, which had already ceased.

"That's odd," Monocard mused. "The Boche haven't fired a single shot."

"Ha!" Renard replied. "There are no more Boche— there are only Valencians. Go and see what's happening, Cipriani."

Reassured as to the outcome of the attack, the men crowded around the cavaliers, and established friendly relations by means of gestures. Five or six Arabs accepted cigarettes, but it was obviously the first time they had smoked and seen lighters. They seemed to have fallen from the moon, and the simplest things amused them like children. They plunged their fingers into a tin of sardines that Duranton offered them and gobbled them down; the oil ran into their beards. Suddenly, clucks of joy erupted from the *poilus* around the apprentice smokers; one of them, manipulating a kerosene lighter, had just set fire to his burnoose. The soldiers hastened to put it out.

The hilarity continued, and the two officers deigned to smile at the grotesque incident—the major laughed out loud. Then Monocard frowned, and uttered an irritated exclamation, on seeing two armed *poilus* appear, who were joking and herding before them a dozen individuals dressed in strange outfits.

"Oh no!" the sublieutenant fulminated. "I've had my fill of these masquerades. I said nothing the other day to the oaf parading around in a dinner-jacket and a top hat, but this is too much! If the colonel...Go on, hurry up and take that off."

"But lieutenant, they're prisoners!" exclaimed Cipriani, who was marching behind the little troop. "We've just disarmed them."

No ordinary prisoners, at any rate! Their faces were covered by some sort of steel-mesh hood, allowing nothing to be seen but their glittering eyes and formidable black moustaches; their torsos were enclosed in pale leather cassocks garnished with iron plates, with similar gauntlets and boots.

Mocking gibes burst forth on all sides.

"Their new helmets aren't much good."

"They're mad, these Boche! They no longer have anything to wear."

Carried away by professional habit, Monocard interrogated them in German. Who were they? From what corps? "Come on you load of Ostrogoths—what language do you speak?"

They limited themselves to rolling bewildered eyes, their expressions terrified at the sight of the Arab horsemen, who had gathered together and drawn their scimitars, ready to fall upon them. The officers had to intervene to hold them back—but, furious at seeing their prey escape, the Orientals set about insulting the newcomers with grand gestures. The latter, realizing that they were being protected, replied in kind, and for five minutes there was an interchange of invective above the heads of the troopers, who were bellowing to make them shut up.

In the midst of the frightful din, Adjutant Etchever-ry, a Basque, came up to Renard and shouted in his ear: "Lieutenant, the prisoners speak Spanish!"

They would be able to interrogate them, then. But first, when the noise had died down, one of the armed men who had brought them described their capture.

Twenty men had advanced from the distant city on reconnaissance. As they were not carrying rifles, but bows and swords, they had been allowed to approach as far as the Seille—the barbed wire on the other bank had vanished—and then the French had opened fire. When they had all fallen, there was a charge—but only four were dead. The others got up again, and seven were able to run off, while the nine here present were captured.

The arrival of the airplane, the drone of whose en-gine had been approaching for several seconds, mingled with the distant tolling of bells, caused the interrogation to be forgotten. The apparatus wheeled over the square in such a fashion as to land on the esplanade, behind the presbytery. At the sight of it, however, the Arabs and the Spaniards, abandoning their invective, uttered a com-bined howl of fright. The riders leapt of their horses, frightened by the sound of the engine, and invoked Al-lah. The others, on their knees, made the sign of the cross repeatedly, imploring the Virgin and all the saints.

"Well," said the major, "they're a bit behind the times, your men of 1920. One would think they'd never seen a biplane."

The cameraman was the first to climb down from the cockpit into the middle of a gathering crowd. He was radiant. "It's charming, my friends! What a beautiful trip! We caused a sensation: all the inhabitants were cheering us, all the bells were ringing! Above the mar-ket, though, we were attacked. A volley of projectiles..."

And he pointed to a dozen arrows hanging by their barbed tips from the fabric of the apparatus.

His mates joked: "But they have wooden tips, your arrows, Crab-face!"

"All the same, they could easily have wounded me. I hope you'll mention me in your report, Lieutenant!"

Renard sent him to develop his photographs right away, and, having ordered Cipriani to clear the vicinity of the airplane, he walked over with Monocard and the major to the Englishman, who was methodically stuffing a pipe.

"Well, Monsieur Bennsbury, have you seen Metz?"

Without turning a hair, the Englishman declared: "That's not Metz. It's a cinema town, like Hollywood—but they play hard; they fire arrows. There are mountains, great rivers and the sea, with distant islands. It all looks very similar to Spain."

"It is Spain—and Valencia. The Arabs told us that."

"Valencia, yes—but I didn't see the railway, or the station, or steamships in the harbor."

"Of course!" muttered the major. "There's been an earthquake."

No one cleared up his misconception, but they followed his suggestion that they take advantage of the shade of the office, for the sun was becoming increasingly ardent. Five minutes later, Lénac, stimulated by the prospect of the *croix de guerre*—nothing less—brought them his photographs, developed and still moist.

They were passed from hand to hand.

They confirmed what the aviator had said. De Lanselles, who had traveled in Spain, recognized on one of them the silhouette of the Balearics on the marine horizon; the mountains—the Sierra de Cuenca, the Sierra de Gudar—the Guadalaviar and Xucar rivers, and the coast, corresponded tell to the environs of Valencia. It was, however, impossible to recognize the city itself in that city in the Moorish style, from which radiated, instead of a railway and highways, vague tracks streaking an arid countryside, rocky to the south, dotted with gardens and woods to the north.

"All the same, it's Valencia. No doubt about it."

"But what year are we in?" muttered the lieutenant. 1920? 1930?"

"Let's put an end to this confusion," declared de Lanselles. "The Arabs must know the date, and the prisoners too."

They summoned Ali, with Nénesse as interpreter.

The question seemed to astonish the man in the silver bracelets. He replied nevertheless, out of politeness.

"He says," the old African warrior reported, after having him repeat it three times, "that's it's the year 719 of the Hegira."

"719?"

"Yes, yes. 719."

Renard wiped his forehead, astounded. "Thanks," he said. "Take him back outside. Send the adjutant in, with all the prisoners."

"We're not in the future, then!" exclaimed the sub-lieutenant. "We're in the past! I can't remember the exact date when the Hegira began, but it was around six hundred and some. Six and seven are thirteen. Thirteen hundred and something. We'd be in the 14th century!"

"Oh, that sun, that sun!" said the major. He was no longer talking about earthquakes.

The aviator smoked his pipe, without saying a word.

Etcheverry brought in the prisoners, already half-reassured by the conduct of the *poilus*, who had fed them and give them something to drink. Several of them, caught in mid-swap, were already wearing the regulation helmets of the trenches instead of their mail head-dresses.

The oldest one was asked first, then the other eight—and the adjutant, rolling his incredulous eyes, reported their invariable replies. It was the year of grace 1341, Wednesday, June 29.

The two officers had difficulty concealing their disturbance. The aviator choked on his pipe smoke. Thévenard launched a resounding: "God damn it! What about my chick? She's in the genitals of her remotest grandfather!"

Monocard was the first to pull himself together. "We need to send a reconnaissance party to the city," he declared.

"That's what I was about to propose," Renard replied, going out of the office in order to give the necessary orders.

He stopped momentarily on the doorstep. In the furnace-like atmosphere, dominating the voices of the *poilus* in the square, the north wind was bringing the sound of bells. In Valencia, that Medieval Valencia frightened by the airplane, the tocsin was still sounding.

Part Two
THE JUNCTION

I. Tortorado & Co.

The curfew had sounded an hour ago. Valencia was resting beneath the warm night, and the sleepers, fleeing the mosquitoes, were breathing on the terraced roofs, for no breeze agitate the long palm fronds falling back into the gardens like foliage of bronze—like the minarets and domes of the cathedral. In the entire area enclosed by the ramparts, only two lights were shining: at a window in the University near the Eastern Gate, and on the first floor of the fortress-palace that rose up in the center of the city like an acropolis. Constructed long ago by the Moors, in the times of their splendor, modeled on the Alhambra in Grenada, in order to serve as both a fortified tower and the Emir's residence—with gardens, arcades and fountains—since the Spanish reconquest, the tower had sheltered the personnel of the Holy Office: Dominican monks and their hirelings, torturers and executioners, notaries, scribes and archivists.[8]

---

[8] What we nowadays think of as "the Spanish Inquisition"—which was established by and answered to the monarchs of Aragon and Castille—was not founded until 1480. The infamous Tomás de Torquemada was appointed its Inquisitor General in 1483 and held the position until his death in 1498. The Inquisitorial method of persecuting heresy, with the aid of torture, had been instituted by the papacy in the 12th century,

In the little room whose window was emitting one of the lights that we have just seen shining, three individuals were assembled. A stout green wax candle—the color of the Inquisition—illuminated four walls, once gleaming with mosaics but presently whitewashed with chalk, like everything in the edifice that might be reminiscent of the dissolute luxury and superstitions of the pagans. Its only ornament was a crucifix in black wood, on which a life-sized Christ displayed wounds painted with a realism that modern sensibilities would have found hideous.

The individual sitting beneath the Christ in a wicker armchair, whose enormous pimply nose spoiled a white ascetic face, wore the tonsure and the black and white robe of the Dominicans. He was the Grand Inquisitor of Valencia, Fray Luiz Alcover de Tortorado. His eyes lowered and his hands inside his large sleeves, he was listening to the police reports that were being read, in a high-pitched and monotonous voice, by the notary Fernando Arcos. Their companion, the clerk Martinez, sat at a table in front of a leaden inkwell and a sheaf of parchment, ready to write.

The first report came from Cristobal Alvarez, secretly affiliated to the Holy Office. Cristobal Alvarez

---

and was entrusted to the Dominican Order in the 13th century, but Inquisitorial tribunals tended in those days to be *ad hoc* affairs set up to deal with special circumstances, like the infamous "Cathar crusade" that united France by means of vicious slander and mass slaughter. It is, therefore, extremely unlikely that there was a permanent Inquisitorial organization in Valencia in 1341, let alone that it could wield tyrannical power as this one does. The novel is, however, an extended apologue rather than a historical reconstruction, so it is fully entitled to its poetic license.

had been accepted as a domestic by Fray Geronimo, Master of Arts at the University, and had succeeded in winning his confidence. He deposed on oath that the day before last, his master had taken him outside the city two hours before the gates were closed. The said Geronimo, accompanied by Alvarez, had waited for nightfall reading his breviary in the little orange-grove that was about a league to the south of the Puerta del Sol. When darkness fell, he had headed, still in the company of Alvarez, toward the Moorish camp a league and a quarter further away. After an exchange of kabbalistic formulae—in Arabic—the sentinel had taken them to an officer. The officer had taken them to the tent of the Emir Abdul Khan. There, Geronimo had gone in alone, but Alvarez, left at the door, had heard his master talking for a full hour with the Emir in a tone of the most amicable familiarity.

Impassive in appearance, the Grand Inquisitor drank in the notary's shrill voice like a celestial harmony.

This would do it. This evidence, so long awaited, was sufficient—even if it had been the only evidence—to prove the Franciscan Geronimo guilty of heresy and have him thrown into the prisons of the Holy Office this evening, where torture would extract further confessions from him. If he denied it, he would be condemned anyway, for obduracy. Either way, he would perish on the pyre—and his Order would never recover from the blow. Tortorado and the Dominicans would be triumphant...

Behind the hatred that the Grand Inquisitor had borne Fray Geronimo for many years, however, there was something other than a question of discipline, a rivalry between Dominican and Franciscan. In the eyes of his enemies, Geronimo was guilty of a double sin that

77

was inexpiable: not content with eclipsing all the scholastic doctors in Valencia with the power and brilliance of his genius, of sustaining propositions with a heretical odor and extracting from the books of pagan Antiquity a science corruptive of youth, he scarcely concealed his sympathy for the civilization of the Moors, of which one of the most refined representatives was this Abdul Khan, now Emir, and formerly his disciple here in Venice— before the king of Castile, Alphonse XI, *El Vengador*, had expelled the hereditary enemy from the city, forced Grenada to pay tribute to him, and blockaded the pillars of Hercules with his fleet to prevent the arrival of reinforcements from Africa.

A refined civilization, the inheritor of an ancient tradition less complete but more alive than that of the Byzantine Emperors, at the other end of Europe! The Caliphs still ruled in Cordova, in their Alhambras with golden mosaics, where jets of rose-water, and even of quicksilver, fell back into lapis-lazuli bowls supported by marble lions, with carbuncles or amethysts for eyes, amid slaves and concubines, naked beneath their silver lame gauze, with hair sprinkled with sequins and anointed with rare essences; amid choirs of handsome children and sweet music.

The Caliphs, enthroned over guards of Emirs constellated with jewels, over the sons of the desert in white burnooses, ready to fight to the death at a sign from the Master...

The people, obedient to the simple and undogmatic faith of the Prophet, devoting themselves to ritual ablutions and reciting the verses of the Koran at the hours when the muezzins chanted their appeals from the height of minarets perforated by arabesques in stone lacework...

And, in the Universities, crammed with students, the Sages of Islam transmitting the sacred fire, in the expectation of a renewal, of a luminous awakening of the thought of the world, asleep for seven centuries, since the invasion of the Barbarians and the dismantling of the Roman Empire...

Certainly, Geronimo would not go so far as to deny Spanish patriotism the right to take back from these African invaders the captive lands of their ancestors; he did not prefer Mohammed to Christ, and he invested his hope for the regeneration of the world in the Catholic faith—but his high intelligence reproved the brutal method of merciless warfare adopted against the Moors by the kings of Spain, who went so far as to dream of a general castration of their Muslim subjects!

Before his most reliable disciples, the bold innovator advocated, along with the free exercise of the Christian, Islamic and Judaic religions, a political alliance: a fraternal fusion of the two peoples, whose qualities would thus be completed and their faults attenuated. In his generous utopia, a new Spain, to which Portugal would be joined, would emerge from that unanimous collaboration: from the Pyrenees to the Pillars of Hercules, and from the Ocean to the Interior Sea, everything would blossom in joy and prosperity; on the plateaux of the Sierra as within sight of blue waves among the orange groves, there would only be one people at work, cultivating an immense garden punctuated by cities in which concord, wisdom, elegance and just freedom would flourish.

That would require—and Geronimo almost admitted it—the crushing of the Monster, the origin of all the evils in which Spain was then struggling, of the somber decline into which it had sunk, and from which it would emerge five hundred years later, for an era of unprecedented but temporary era of material prosperity. He abhorred, with all his luminous genius, that octopus with a thousand atrociously vigilant tentacles, which garroted minds and stifled every generous or new idea—heresy!—by means of the *san benito* and the auto-da-fé. He detested the Inquisition.

With the immeasurable power that it had gradually wrenched from the weakness of popes and usurped from the bishops previously charged with pursuing heretics and delivering them to the secular arm, the Holy Office—omnipresent by means of its spies, omnipotent by means of its hirelings, its tortures and its executioners, and even the royal troops that the inquisitor could requisition at will—exercised over consciences a frightful terror. It had gradually lowered upon them a monstrous candle-snuffer that had eventually brought them to the level of an egalitarian ignorance, which would soon enthrone the immobility of stupor and death in all the brains of the unfortunate Peninsula!

Tortorado raised his eyes toward the bay-window open to the night, and stared with a smile of hatred at the distant light shining in a high window of the University. There, leaning his orange-colored hair—already marked with an infernal glow, for alert eyes!—over the studious lamp, the Franciscan Geronimo was lunged in accursed sciences. Oh, he had no suspicion of what awaited him!

The Grand Inquisitor's nose quivered when the notary passed on to the second report.

This one, Tortorado knew by heart; he had dictated the terms to Myriam himself…and in his dark soul, the image of the young Israelite was evoked. He saw her again as he had the first time, naked on the torture rack;

he saw that virginal body once again, striped with blood by the whip: that body which had immediately set him ablaze with desire...

She denied the participation of her father—Melchisedech, the chief rabbi of Valencia—in the ritual assassination of a Christian child and the profanation of a consecrated host. But seven of her coreligionists, witnesses to the crime, had confessed: the father and daughter were doomed...

Exercising his authority, Tortorado had stopped the procedure, saved the father and saved the daughter. The latter, seemingly converted and baptized, had become his mistress, his slave, body and soul. No resistance possible! He held her by means of the trial, permanently in suspense; at any moment, he could have her thrown into prison again and burned for having relapsed. Meekly, therefore, she spied for the Holy Office. Every Friday—she was just a trifle thin, thought Tortorado, with the same frightfully jovial smile that he had when killing flies (his favorite pastime)—under the pretext of confession, she came to make her report to him.

The last time, she had reported this: She had already retired to her bedroom at dusk the previous evening, when someone scratched at the street door and a visitor came in. She recognized the tread of the Franciscan from the University who passed beneath the windows every day: the red-haired monk. Getting up with one bound, she went down the stairs stealthily, and through a gap in a door-curtain that she parted slightly, she saw Geronimo seated at the table with her father, in front of a large book illustrated with magical symbols.

"You recognized him? You're sure that it was Geronimo?" Tortorado had said, when she described the scene. And when she hesitated, he had grabbed her by the hair and brutalized her, with a pleasure preliminary to other criminal carnal delights.

And while listening to the notary of the Holy Office read him the official version of the report, he closed his eyes and saw the young woman again as he dragged her across the floor and tore off her tunic and chemise, in order to beat her more effectively on her bare flesh—that demonic flesh for which he had damned his soul, the precious soul of a Grand Inquisitor!

"That's good, Don Arcos. The Holy Office is enlightened. And you, Martinez, write:

"The Franciscan Fray Geronimo, Master of Arts at the University of Valencia, is accused of maneuvers prejudicial to the safety of His Majesty, of Spain and its Catholic faith. He is accused of participation in the Kabbalah and satanic evocations. He will have to answer for these crimes and other minor heresies before the sacred tribunal of the Inquisition. To that end, the order is given to the captain of the guards of the Holy Office, Juan Cabramontilla, immediately to take possession of the person of the said Geronimo, and to take him, duly enchained, to the prison of the Holy Office, from which he will be extracted tomorrow in order to be interrogated by the Ordinary, submitted to questioning by water[9] in case of his denial of the crimes imputed to him by witnesses worthy of faith, and in case of confession, burned at the imminent auto-da-fé: all for the benefit of his immortal soul.

---

[9] One of the most common tortures employed by the Inquisition (because it required no special apparatus) was to force interrogatees to drink enormous quantities of water, which distended their gut painfully, threatening ruptures.

"Written in Valencia, in the palace of the Holy Office, this Monday, June 27 in the Year of Our Lord 1341, at eleven o'clock in the evening.

"Clerk: Martinez.

"Inquisitor of the Faith: F. Tortorado."

When the document was signed and sealed with a large cachet of green wax with the arms of the Holy Office, Tortorado struck a gong. In the corridor, heavy and rhythmic footsteps approached, and a halberdier in a tight-fitting leather jacket appeared, coming to a standstill on the threshold.

"Take this order to the captain," the inquisitor said, handing the arrest warrant to Martinez, who passed it to the soldier.

The latter took it, saluted, turned round and disappeared. His footsteps drew away over the floor-tiles. A minute later, on the floor below, there're was a sound of command being issued and the clink of weapons. A patrol left the palace, and could be heard crossing the square and heading toward the University.

Impassively, Tortorado, with his hands in his sleeves but his infamous bulbous nose quivering in his ascetic face, watched the distant high window, in which the studious light was about to go out.

"We'll save the soul of that stray lamb," he murmured.

"With God's aid," Fernando Arcos added, piously.

"And the executioner's," Martinez concluded.

"Amen," chanted the others.

In the window in the University, two shadows passed in front of the light. A feeble cry of indignation carried all the way to the palace, in the vast silence of the night...

The light went out.

II. The Capture of Valencia

It might have been midday when the little expeditionary company traversed the dry bed of the Seille and set off across the sun-drenched plain, on the far side of which the silhouette of Valencia was tremulous in the hot air. Ali, the Moorish leader, had appeared astonished at first to see Renard send his men off at that scorching hour, but he had had rapidly come to a decision and, having ordered two of his horsemen to return to the camp, where the Emir might be becoming anxious, he and the other eighteen joined the reconnaissance mission.

The nine Spanish prisoners marched at the head; then came the principal force, commanded by Adjutant Etcheverry: ten troopers armed with Lebels, two light machine-gunners, and two sappers, revolvers at their sides and picks over their shoulders. To safeguard his dignity with regard to the cavalrymen who were following in good order, Lieutenant Renard had installed himself in the motorcyclist's side-car. By his side marched Nénesse, very proud of his new importance as an interpreter, and the cameraman Lénac, sweating beneath the weight of his apparatus.

Although it was not far—five or six kilometers at the most—the journey took a good hour. The terrain was rocky, encumbered by low and stunted vegetation— kermes oaks, the adjutant declared—and impenetrable thickets of Barbary figs with grimacing profiles and prickly pears, which it was necessary to go around.

In Valencia, where the bells redoubled their tintinnabulation, an extraordinary effervescence reigned. In the crenellations of the ramparts and the towers, warriors were crowded, their weapons glinting in the sunlight. On the terraces of the edifices that loomed up behind them, framed with palm trees, on the minarets of the churches and the cupolas of the cathedral, confused and variegated crowds had gathered.

Two hundred meters from the hermetically-sealed gate, with its iron-barred and nailed battens, Renard called a halt.

These hostile dispositions disrupted his plan, which was not to attack the city but to confer with its governor. By way of precaution against a possible sortie, however, the two light machine-gunners were positioned in readiness. Three Spanish prisoners, waving a white flag—constituted by a handkerchief—went forward as negotiators. They were warned that, at the first sign they gave of running away, their companions would be put to death.

On the tower overlooking the closed gate a party of bare-headed black and white monks could be made out, carrying banners and crucifixes, grouped around an individual with a miter and crosier in a gold-spangled dalmatic. The crowd fell silent. The disordered clanging of bells had ceased, and one alone, grave and raucous, continued to toll like a knell.

When the three negotiators appeared in the open space at the foot of the walls, a powerful voice rose up from the tower, in a funereal chant that the monks punctuated with responses: "*Vade reto! Vade retro Satanas!*" The bishop, brandishing his crosier in his left hand, launched his right in a gesture of malediction, and the final words of the anathema vibrated in the tragic silence:

"*...In ignem aeternum cum haereticis et daemonibus!*"[10]

From the entire city, a formidable modulated "*Amen!*" rose up; ten thousand voices roared: "*A muerte los Moros!*" and immediately, a volley of arrows and arbalest darts departed from the battlements, and felled the three negotiators, instantaneously transformed into huge porcupines. Other arrows fell a few meters short of the troopers arranged to either side of the machine-gunners. One, more vigorously launched, pierced the shoulder of one of the Moorish cavalrymen who were watching the bare-headed and bound hostages with their scimitars drawn.

Reprisals were not long delayed. With howls of rage, the men with the burnooses took hold of the wretched captives by the hair and cut off their heads with two sweeps of the blade. Meanwhile, the machine-gunners and Lebels fired a salvo, without waiting for Renard's order. The latter had stood up in his side-car with a grand gesture.

On the ramparts, the brief silence of stupor was succeeded by cries of agony and the clamor of a frightful panic. The bishop and the monks disappeared. In the crenellations, the last archers, firing with frenetic obstinacy, were felled in their turn, and in less than sixty seconds, the silhouettes of the ramparts and terraces, previously swarming with people, stood out empty of human presence against the indigo of the sky.

---

[10] This formula is not part of the standardized exorcism ritual, but is an instruction to the (alleged) heretics and demons to go back to Hell permanently. Most of the Latin speech is improvised by the authors, although a few familiar formulae are included.

Frightened by the detonations, the Moors' chargers had reared up, and were carrying their riders away at a gallop, but the latter had already had time to finish their work, and it was while brandishing the severed heads of their enemies that they launched themselves toward the ramparts. There, one after another, they whirled the hideous projectiles around, and with guttural exclamations of effort, sent them like missiles for a slingshot over the walls, behind which cries of rage and vengeance rose up. Then they came back and a moderate gallop, and, with smiles of satisfaction on their bronzed faces, wiped their scimitars with their fingers and shook the blood on to the sand.

Renard had succeeded in ordering a cease-fire, but war had now been declared. It was not sufficient to have cleared the battlements and scared the population. It was necessary to enter the city and impose themselves upon it by force if they wanted to stay in Port-sur-Seille.

The *poilus* discussed the situation.

"What do you think of the new war?"

"It's a funny business!"

"I think it's devilishly hot, and there's aren't any bistros so far."

"No, the aviator was right, it's the cameraman putting one over on us."

"Bah! We just have to act; we don't need to understand."

"If we can just nab the city...

"There are nice tarts there, and even more priests."

"But there aren't enough of us!"

"They've only got arrows and spears, and we've got the Moors with us..."

On Etcheverry's advice, the motorcyclist was dispatched to Port-sur-Seille to get the sticks of dynamite with the aid of which the two sappers would be charged with blowing up the gate. While awaiting his return, as the heat was becoming abominable, the expeditionary force went to take shelter in the shade of a clump of palm trees, which formed a sort of small oasis a few hundred meters away in the direction of the sea, provided with a delightfully cool grass-bordered spring. They dipped wine-bottles into it and relaxed, collars unbuttoned, in their shirt-sleeves, repeating the fateful: "We just have to act; we don't need to understand."

The Moors, having stripped the Spaniard's corpses and abandoned them on the sand, naked, tied their mounts to the palm trees and distributed a few gold pieces from their booty, in a spirit of fraternity.

These auxiliaries were found to be generous, but a trifle over-keen, and not very interesting, all things considered—but they regained their popularity thanks to a minor incident. Corporal Venette—the aptly-named[11] individual caught barefoot by the attack—discovered a large scorpion under a stone, longer than his middle finger and as yellow as an amber pipe, and started poking it with a palm-twig. People came running.

"Damned spider!"

"No, it's a crayfish."

"A sand-lobster."

"But it's not red!"

"Be careful," said Nénesse. "I've seen those little beasts in Africa—they can kill a bloke in five secs."

Laughing silently, a Moor insinuated himself between the huddled troopers and deposited around the strange arachnid a circle of dry twigs. Then, borrowing Nénesse's lighter, he set fire to them. The surrounded

---

[11] Aptly named because his name is a slang term for fear.

animal ran rapidly around the flaming circle, its claws and tail raised threateningly; it seemed to understand that it was hopelessly doomed. Then, in order to flee the ardent bite, it stopped, arched its venomous tail in reverse, and with two furious thrusts implanted the sharp sting in the joint in its carapace, level with its front legs. It was seen to fall, thunderstruck, and someone extracted the moral: "The fellow's had enough of war and committed suicide!"

By virtue of this humorous trick, the Moors rose in esteem again. Their example was followed and everyone lay down on the grass beside the spring.

Renard, preoccupied, was smoking cigarettes while walking with Etcheverry, who brought him up to date with the true situation.

The sputter of the motorcycle engine awoke the sleepers.

"It's the mech, Vidal. He was quick."

"Shut up—we've been resting here more than half an hour."

"Hey, Vidal, give me some fuel for my lighter."

"We're going to take the town, then?"

"Are there bistros inside, at least?"

"Is it true that they're Spaniards, Lieutenant?"

"Silence!"

And the attack on the city began.

Under the protection of the machine-gunners, who cleared the battlements, where heads had surged forth again, the two sappers went to place a stick of dynamite under each batten of the gate, lit the fuses and came back. A double explosion thundered; stones flew up volcanically; the tower collapsed—*en bloc*, so to speak—filling the ditch, and when the cloud of smoke dissipated, the two battens of the gate were seen lying flat on the rubble in the middle of an enormous breach. People were fleeing in disorder along a street.

The Moors rushed into the breach at a fast gallop, and Renard, in order to support them, raised his arms and gave the order: "Charge!"

For the moment, the *poilus* were greatly amused.

"Come on, lads—let's have them!"

"Get on with it—there's glory enough for all!"

"Kill! Kill!"

"To Berlin!"

Stumbling over the debris in the breach, the bayonet charge surged into the city—but not a single warrior was to be seen. The Moors had swept away the last resistance; already, their horses reuniting at the fountain at the crossroads a little further on. A few had set about looting the houses, from which cries of agony or fury and the screams of women emerged. Under the pretext of moderating their actions, five or six *poilus* joined in.

"Try to take prisoners!" Etcheverry shouted at them.

The others, spotting a *posada* at the entrance to the street, on the left, asked the lieutenant for permission to have a drink. Renard gave permission, went in with them, and accepted a glass of rosé wine from the abjectly-trembling innkeeper—which was delicious, but too sweet for his taste. Then adopting a vast earthenware jar as a writing-desk, he scribbled a note to de Lanselles, which Etcheverry took to the motorcyclist, who had stayed with his machine outside the breach.

The adjutant thought he saw a blue uniform disappear behind a door that reclosed immediately—that was Lénac, who, having filmed the explosion of the door and the Moors' charge, had noticed a discreetly-raised curtain at a window, and a pretty feminine face with an alluring smile. And the cinematographer, heedless of other adventures, received the hospitality of a robust *fille de joie*, who began by modestly veiling the image of the Madonna in front of which a small lamp was burning. Their love-making was silent, but at the far end of the street, the shouts rising up became more numerous, mingled with spasmodic laughter—for, having absorbed a glass of wine, the troopers had quit the *posada* in order to rejoin their mates and the Moors.

Renard waited for Etcheverry, alone in the middle of the street, and they both climbed the slope of detritus, in which dogs were beginning to root around. The noise of the battle—cries for help and howls of pain—guided them to the next crossroads. There, near the fountain, in the crenellated wall of an enclosure, a door opened into a courtyard. They went in. Five or six Moors were finishing running through a black-clad man with the appearance of a sacristan, whose fingers were still clenched on a bunch of large keys.

A few paces away, two *poilus*, leaning over an air-vent, were calling out jovially: "Is anyone down there?"

"Hey, it's Latude!"[12]

In the shadow of a subterranean cell, a person in a monkish robe could be seen, chained at the waist. He raised toward the light a face with keen eyes and noble features, aureole by bright red hair. A Moor had ap-

---

[12] Jean-Henri, or "Masers" de Latude, incurred the displeasure of Madame de Pompadour for some minor offence to her dignity, and was imprisoned, first in the Bastille and then in the Châtelet and at Charenton; although he escaped several times, he was always recaptured and remained locked up for a total of 35 years, thus acquiring a legendary status he would presumably rather have avoided.

proached with Renard; he uttered an exclamation on recognizing the prisoner, addressed a few words to him in Arabic, and called out to his companions.

They all came running. "Geronimo! Geronimo!" they exclaimed. They set about trying to open the grille. Ten strong arms soon put paid to it, and the red-haired monk was brought out into the daylight. The Moors bowed to him with demonstrations of respect, and then drew away, uttering cries of vengeance.

The red-haired monk, pale and weak but dignified nevertheless, adjusted his robe. He paraded an astonished gaze over the *poilus*, Etcheverry and Renard, identified the leader, and addressed the lieutenant in Latin. Renard had not entirely forgotten his Classical studies, and was able to understand him, with a little effort. His interlocutor thanked him warmly, and asked who he and his companions were—from what unknown country the Lord had sent the Moors these auxiliaries in blue uniforms: the angels who had just pulled the claws of the Inquisition.

An embarrassing question! With a gesture, Renard vaguely indicated a remote distance, spoke about champions of liberty, named himself, and, in a Latin that would have made Cicero wince, interrogated the monk in his turn.

The latter was Fray Geronimo, prior of the Franciscans of Valencia, Master of Arts at the University. His love of progress and Enlightenment, and his acquaintance with Moorish and Jewish scholars, had caused him to be accused of heresy by his rivals, the Dominicans. Arrested in the middle of the night the previous day, he had been subjected a few hours later to questioning by water...

Recalled to reality by Etcheverry, however, Renard was obliged to interrupt him. In order to avenge their fiend Geronimo, the Moors had just set fire to the stables on the far side of the courtyard, and behind them, from the battlements of the fortress, Spaniards appeared, throwing water on the flames and becoming bold enough to fire arrows. The lieutenant became anxious; the two troopers had taken advantage of his conversation with the monk to rejoin the others, occupied in pillaging, but the city would not remain prey indefinitely to the terror of the firearms and the abrupt invasion. There might be a backlash...

Leaving the Moors there, he drew the monk and Etcheverry away, to set out in quest of his men, whose conduct sickened him.

Slightly disconcerted by their overly facile victory, almost intimidated by seeing the streets so absolutely deserted and only finding women and "civvies," paralyzed with fear, inside the houses, the conquerors of Valencia had not ventured very far. The second crenellated enclosure, the fortress of sorts whose courtyard they had invaded before breaking into a cell and setting fire to the stables, marked the limit of their advance.

Only a few Moors had gone beyond the crossroads with the fountain and penetrated into the labyrinth of the ghetto to the left. Having explored the main street, the majority of the horsemen and all of the Frenchmen had flooded back into the adjacent side-streets, breaking into houses, knocking down young women, and raiding the savings of that eccentric quarter, specializing in prostitution and petty commerce.

The *poilus* of the eighth, intoxicated by the sun, the shouting and the triumphant gaiety as much as by the wine, and wearied by the heat, thought it unnecessary to press on. They would have all the time in the world methodically to exploit the resources of the conquered city. For the moment, they were hot and thirsty, and a brief pause in one of the numerous taverns of the quarter would be welcome.

Leaving the Moors, blinded by lust and carnage, to get on with it, Little Charlot, Nénesse and a few other adherents of system D[13] made for a *bodega* just off the crossroads, populated by pretty girls who were a little scared, but welcoming, where they organized a party. When the two men who had assisted in the liberation of the monk came out of the postern, they were hailed by their mates, occupied in laying in supplies of figs, melons, oranges, cheeses and pickles.

"Hey, lads! Little Charlot has unearthed some nice Cointreau. Rally at the *Beau dégât des Soles*." (The *Bodega del Sol*, apparently.) "Stop pestering the locals and bring whatever you want to keep. We're going to paint the town red, and no mistake! There's going to be a big blow-out!"

This, when Renard appeared at the crossroads, with Etcheverry and the monk, they only found Corporal Venette in the process of passing solitary judgment, in the shade of a porch, on the contents of a bottle of mulled wine, which he was drinking in gulps.

"Ah, Lieutenant, what do they put in this stuff?" asked the brave corporal, with naïve affection.

---

[13] *Système D* [System D] is a euphemistic derivative of the verb *se démerder* [to get oneself out of the shit], referring to actions employing initiative and improvisation—often of an illicit nature—to get out of trouble.

Already dissatisfied with everything he had seen, the lieutenant berated him roundly.

"Where are the others?"

"The others? They're somewhere around, having a booze-up, Lieutenant. Except for the darkies..."

"Enough! You don't even know where your men are? It's anarchy here. It can't go on, I warn you, Corporal Venette. You'll lose your stripe if you haven't reassembled your platoon in five minutes and formed a guard-post at the entrance to the town, in the bistro where we first had a drink, and where we left the machine-guns and the sappers' tools. I'll wait for you there."

Venette, extremely discomfited, drew away muttering: "There you go! More duty. Can't have any fun. It wasn't worth the trouble..."

He spotted two troopers with hams stuck on their bayonets, then another laden with a fishing-net stuffed with melons—contributions to the "big blow-out"—who were attempting to head for the *Bodega del Sol*.

"Not there, you lot—the lieutenant's on to you. Drop that and came with me."

At the end of the street, in company with the monk, Renard was waiting. Etcheverry had just brought Lénac back, having collected him as he made his exit from his beauty's house.

With a cold rage, the officer examined the four drunkards. "Nothing to be done with these swine!" he groaned. "It's vile! You're behaving like Cossacks. Hurry up and set up a guard; try to find your comrades, have Nénesse alert the Moors, and all reassemble here before nightfall. We don't know what's being plotted in the city—we haven't taken a single prisoner. Instead, you've been chasing women and wine! Enough! Keep watch as necessary, okay? I'll have you relieved tomorrow, and between now and then the motorcyclist will come to fetch news. Make sure you give him a report."

He listened momentarily to the distant clamors and the sounds of galloping, which gave evidence of the exploits of the Moors. He darted a final glance at the crossroads, where the other seven *poilus* were showing no signs of life. Then, utterly disgusted, anxious as to the fate of the four drunkards who were about to guard the city gate, and also anxious about what might be happening in Port-sur-Seille in his absence, Renard sent Etcheverry to the crossroads to fetch four horses saved from the fire in the stables, and gave his final instructions to Venette and his worthy acolytes.

"If there's a serious fight, of course, you'll have to send a rider to warn us, and dig yourselves in properly."

The mounts having been brought, he took one of them; the monk, Lénac and Etcheverry bestrode the others, and the little caravan, going through the breach, headed for Port-sur-Seille, where the tricolor as flying over the tower.

The four horses trotted between the Barbary figs and giant thistles with yellow flowers. The heat was declining. A sea-breeze had got up. Behind them, against a background of immaculate azure, Valencia mutely outlined its palm trees, terraces and deserted battlements against the redness of the setting sun.

III. Thévenard, Skull-Stuffer

During the journey, Renard and the monk got to know one another better. From the first stride, the gait of the horse had provoked a violent nausea in Geronimo, accompanied by liquid vomiting.

"It's the effect of the torture to which I was subjected yesterday," he explained, between two retches. "I was put to the water torture. They wanted to make me confess monstrous and absurd crimes—but my conscience is clear!"

The sympathetic Lénac offered him a melissa cordial,[14] a flask of which he always carried with him, having long suffered from indigestion. The monk took the flask, uncorked it, sniffed it approvingly and took a large mouthful, which caused him to cough, choke and go red in the face, but the eventual result seemed to him to be excellent. Sitting upright in his saddle thereafter, he attempted to decipher the label of the marvelous elixir, and asked Lénac in Spanish to let him have the recipe. There was a brief misunderstanding, sorted out by Etcheverry.

Then, studying the printed label again—such neat calligraphy!—Geronimo recognized a Christian dialect akin to that of the Franks: the northern language he had learned to read in the *Chanson de Roland* and the more recent and almost-contemporary chronicles of the Sire de Joinville,[15] but which he did not speak for want of prac-

---

[14] Melissa, in this context, is a plant in the mint family cultivated for use as a balm.

[15] Jean de Joinville (1224-1317) accompanied Louis IX on one of his crusades, and was persuaded to write his chronicle by

tice. He renewed his questions. Renard had to admit that he was not a Moor but, in fact *Gallus vel Francus*—a Gaul or a Frank, and that he had come directly from his homeland.

The monk seemed quite astonished.

"I've seen Franks before, from the north and the south," he said, "but none of them resembled you either in their voice or their costume. The Gauls are tall, it's true, and of various mores...but what are you doing here fighting with the Arabs? Your people have been the declared enemies of Moors and Saracens for centuries—your kings led crusades against them. But for the war against England, your present sovereign, Philippe VI... Even though you're a warrior, and scarcely accustomed to meditation, are you, like me, enlightened enough to understand that truth, justice, progress and a better future for humankind lie not on the side of those who are persecuting me but rather, setting questions of religions and patriotism aside, among their enemies?"

Renard judged it too difficult to explain the true situation to his guest, which it would be probably impossible for him to grasp. Perhaps later. In the meantime, he admitted that his civilized preferences inclined toward the Moors, and that he would willingly support them against the backward-looking Inquisitors.

Geronimo, delighted to find himself in such intelligent society, was enthusiastic to elaborate his ideas regarding "outdated institutions" and the tyranny of the

---

the king's widow; Joinville thus became a major factor in establishing the posthumous reputation of "Saint Louis," and in consolidating the myth of the crusades as a saintly endeavor rather than an epic adventure in terrorism, massacre, pillage and rape.

Holy Office—for his rancor was still fresh; he still hard the marks of the chains in his flesh and the memory of the torture that the sacred tribunal had inflicted upon his stomach for having dared to think freely.

Renard was curious about that formidable institution, which was about to be, so far as he was concerned, no longer an object of facile jokes and literary allusions, but a living enemy against which he would need to defend himself and fight for his life. Nevertheless, it was more urgent to obtain information about the man he already considered as a useful, and almost indispensable ally: the Emir.

"What?" the monk exclaimed. "I've seen you with his soldiers. Don't you know him?"

"I don't know him yet. I've only just landed with my troops."

"So you aren't taking me to his camp?"

"I'm taking you to my camp, which isn't far from his—look, there it is!"

Until that moment Geronimo had been riding without paying any heed to anything except for his traveling companions, whom he had not wearied of examining. He raised his eyes, and distinguished for the first time the tower and village of Port-sur-Seille, which the officer was pointing out. He started in alarm, commenced a mechanical sign of the cross, then collected himself and smiled understandingly.

"That was what the jailer meant this morning when he talked about a town sprung from Hell!" he murmured. Then, in a louder voice, he added: "You have powerful Spirits at your disposal, Man of Gaul! Skillful and rapid builders! And the madmen who invoke their paltry and cruel God won't forgive you for knowing how to command the forces of nature in this way—but I bless the true God for having met you. You're indubitably his emissaries; you'll liberate the world from the monsters who want to stifle intelligence. You think like my friend, the noble Abdul Khan, but your power surpasses his by a hundred cubits. No matter—I'll introduce you to him, and. thanks to your alliance and your combined efforts, this unfortunate land of Spain will finally experience regeneration, liberty, justice and truth!"

Renard experienced a moment of melancholy in thinking that, the day before, he had been fighting for the same ideals, against the same oppression, exercised by other monsters. 1341 or 1917…after a six-century interval, humankind was still at the same point!

He shook himself out of it. They were approaching Port-sur-Seille. This was no time for philosophy—and, without disabusing the monk of his generous illusions, he asked him to negotiate the proposed alliance with the Emir as soon as possible.

As they crossed the bridge of planks that had been established over the Seille in their absence, Etcheverry pointed out to Renard that a trickle of water was running along the river bed again. The lieutenant rejoiced in that, for if it had remained as dry as it had been in the morning, it would have been necessary to dig a well or obtain supplies from some distant source. He had no time to ponder that stroke of luck, however. The sentries had alerted the garrison to their return, and it was in the midst of an effervescent crowd of *poilus* that the four horsemen dismounted, in front of the kitchens.

De Lanselles, the major and the aviator came to shake Renard's hand.

"Well," said the sublieutenant, "things have moved on, so the motorbike courier tells us."

"Yes, that's right—we've taken the town. And here—anything new?"

"No, everything's fine."

"What about your troopers?" Thévenard asked. "They're not dead?"

"Oh, don't talk to me about them. They're dead drunk, the swine! They let themselves be drawn by our allies into an almighty rampage. They've gone on the spree, Nevertheless, I've succeeded in establishing a small base with the least drunk, and tomorrow morning we'll go to occupy the town properly. But let me introduce you to the Reverend Father Geronimo, Master of Arts at the University of Valencia—a noble victim of the Inquisition, gentlemen! Can you imagine..."

Among the troops, the boasting of Jasmin and Saucisson concerning the mysterious "torpedo machine" in the cellar, the indiscretions of Dupuy and the doctor's tall tales regarding the nocturnal "earthquake"—all deformed, embellished and confused by others—had sufficed until two o'clock, along with the fatalistic "We just have to do it, we don't have to understand it," to nourish curiosity and explain the unusual phenomena, more or less: especially the camel, the "chicks" and the eunuchs (fairground performers), the arrival of the Moors (Moroccan reinforcements) and that of the Spanish prisoners (Boche spies). No one was unduly astonished by the temporal perturbation and the passage, without transition, from the depths of winter to Mediterranean summer. Even the disappearance of part of the village and a third of the company personnel, and the replacement of the usual surroundings by that exotic landscape, had been put down to profits and losses. "We just have to do it, we don't have to understand it." They rejoiced in the good weather and the cessation of the Boche fire, and they stuffed themselves with oranges—*la belle Valence!*—without bothering too much about their origin.

The comings and goings of the motorcyclist, however—his first trip to fetch sticks of dynamite, then his return with the news that the town had been taken—had excited the imagination. When Vidal had recounted what he had seen and heard; when they knew that "the others" were occupied in freely looting an entire enemy town, taken without resistance or any losses; when they imagined the booze flowing in rivers and girls dressed up to the nines—the murmurs began.

There was naked envy of the comrades selected for the expedition. "It's always the same ones who get the nice jobs—we know who they are. They make a semblance of calling for volunteers, but that lot were decided in advance!" The vigorous intervention of the NCOs was insufficient to calm the effervescence. As time for soup approached, anxiety grew regarding the lack of new supplies and the broken communications with Landremont. When Duranton served corned beef for the second time that day, indignant protests went up.

They had not calmed down by the time that the return of Renard and his three companions furnished a new pretext for discontent. The lieutenant's indignant words regarding the conduct of his *poilus*, and the less virtuous but ultra-seductive amplifications added by Lénac, made the mouths of the men of the eighth water. They imagined their comrades surrounded by *houris*, plunged into the bliss of a Muslim paradise, and they reflected bitterly on their own lot.

In an exquisitely warm dusk, the crowd around the officers became agitated. The latter were occupied with the monk, the object of bewildered comments—was the fellow a Boche, the new chaplain, or what? Cipriani jostled a few men and tried to shove them away.

"Go on, turn around—you don't have any business here. Go back to your bolt-holes."

"But Sergeant, the lieutenant hasn't said anything."

The Corsican became angry. "What's that? Answering back now! Whether the lieutenant's said so or not, I'm ordered you to go back to your bunks. It's getting dark."

And as the troopers went away, murmuring, to reform into groups a few meters away, Cipriani ran to Renard.

"There's no means of calming them down, Lieutenant. I don't know what's up with them. They're talking about a torpedo machine that has sent them into Bocheland. They think they're near Berlin. I've had the most loudmouthed thrown in the lock-up, but one can't have them shot."

De Lanselles, who had been listening to what the men were saying, without appearing to, since two o'clock, whispered in the lieutenant's ear: "I didn't want to talk to them without your authorization, but I think it's time to do so. Better to tell them the truth."

The lieutenant was reluctant to explain the operation of the Machine, in which he felt that his responsibility was seriously engaged. How should he tackle the matter? He looked at Monocard doubtfully. "Do you think they're capable of grasping an explanation? Well, if that's your opinion, so be it. That's all right, Cipriani, let them be. I'll talk to them shortly."

But the major had his own ideas. When the sergeant had turned on his heel, he came over to Renard. "Well, I can see that you're worried about telling them. Would you like me to do it? I'll get it in to their thick heads.

They know me." And without waiting for a reply, he headed for the truck with the seven 75 millimeter shells, which as still parked in front of the kitchens, climbed on to it and, standing in the back, he hailed the *poilus* with his stentorian voice.

"Hey, lads! Listen to me for a minute. I have to talk to you."

In spite of his affected rudeness toward the wounded men he medicated with paregoric elixir, his good humor and brusque familiarity made him universally popular. The men of the eighth hurriedly gathered around the truck.

The doctor began: "You know me, eh? It's me, your major, Père Thévenard, and I've always looked after you. You trust me, and you've never had to regret it. When you have the colic, or a bullet in the bum, it's me you come to, and I do what I can to make you better—and I make you better, if there's a means; no one can say otherwise. Well, today, it's the same thing—I'm going to give you a remedy.

"Oh, you're not happy! Oh, you're murmuring, you've got complaints? I'm telling you—me, who's had my finger in your eye up to the elbow. You're pissed off because you've had bully beef twice today? You won't be pissed off any more when you've listened to me, and you've drunk a cup of *gnôle*[16] before you go tuck yourselves up in bed. Do you know what the Golden Age was? Well, tomorrow, the Golden Age is opening up for you..."

In the increasing darkness, the troopers listened, seduced by the major's truculent glibness. The latter interrupted himself, had one of the truck's lanterns lit, took it

---

[16] Crude eau-de-vie.

and set it down in such a way that he was fully illuminated on the improvised platform, while his shadow on the kitchen walls repeat his gesticulations in a grotesque fashion, to the *poilus'* amusement. Conscious of that effect, he continued;

"You've heard mention of a Machine, that you're annoyed about not having seen? Tomorrow, it'll be shown to you. It'll be shown to me too, for I haven't seen it any more than you have—but I'm not complaining, and I'm your major! Tomorrow, we'll all see it— you'll be there along with Père Thévenard, and I promise you a good time.

"In the meantime, I can tell you one thing, and that's that you won't have any cause to complain about the Machine. Thanks to that, the war is over for you, and the Golden Age is beginning! As you've already been told, it's a splendid machine. You've been told that it's powerful—very powerful—and that it can send you from Metz to Berlin? You weren't told the half of it. It's sent us much further than Berlin. We've left the Earth behind and we're…on a planet!"

He paused, his arms widespread, magnificently.

Timid voices rose up. "What planet?"

"What planet?" he thundered, folding his arms. "Do I know any more than you do? What does it matter? You've all read in the papers that there are planets. That chap Flammarion has seen the inhabitants of Mars with his telescope. For the planets are inhabited; the planets are like the Earth, but on this planet, they're six hundred years behind the times—they haven't yet discovered gunpowder, or cannons, or matches. You've seen that for yourself, with the Darkies. I haven't invented anything. And since his morning, since we arrived, which of you has been wounded? Which of you has heard a *zin-*

105

zin? Which of you has seen a Boche? I repeat, the war's over for you, unless you make an easy sort of war here, in which you'll always be victorious. You'll have wine, and women and all the rest, as you please, like your mates in Valencia now. Tomorrow, that will be you: everyone will get a turn. Here, you're at rest, as in the rear—better than in the rear. I can't tell you any more—it's a professional secret—but I give you my word that…that you're going to be heroes, all of you, and …extraordinary heroes, since you'll have all the advantages without the inconveniences!"

He was out of breath, and bombast. He saw that his listeners had been subjugated by his vehement speech, and concluded, *ex abrupto*: "Now, no more talking—everybody take your mugs to Duranton's, and off to bed when you've had your cup of *gnôle*."

And, leaping down from the truck in the midst of enthusiastic cheers, he called out to the chief cook: "Give these lads some rum, Duranton—a good dose, as for an invalid!"

Opinion had been won over; and like an ancient co-ryphaeus,[17] Dudule summed up the general sentiment: "Talk about a bloke with the gift of the gab! How he can turn you around!"

Only the men in the advance guard-posts were perhaps less than content, but Cipriani took responsibility for wetting their beaks.

Gathered in the company office under the lamp, de Lanselles, the major, the aviator, Dupuy and Lénac were listening to the lieutenant. The monk, quite unable to

---

[17] Literally, the leader of the chorus.

comprehend what was going on, had been installed in the clerk's armchair, in front of a light snack.

"Gentlemen," Renard began, "I'll get straight to the point. You all know what's what. You've learned individually what combination of circumstances had transported us from the 20th century and the Lorraine front to the 14th and...let's say the Moorish front. For an indeterminate lapse of time, we're constrained and forced to live in this new milieu, and to make a choice between two irreconcilable adversaries in whose presence we find ourselves. On the one hand, the Spaniards, otherwise known as the Inquisition; on the other, the Arabs, whose alliance we have virtually secured. In these exceptional circumstances, I can't make the decision alone. We have to form a kind of General Staff. To begin with, I'd like your opinion as to which side to take."

A discussion began between the officers. Monocard opted for the Moors—"the true custodians, in this dark era, of civilized traditions." He was carried away by the prodigious renovation that they would be able to impose on the world, by serving as a lever to accelerate the course of History.

The aviator, who was in the lay ministry of the Anglican Church, cordially detested the "instruments of the Inquisition," but similarly refused to treat with the Moors—"those negroes." The English, he proclaimed, in India...

The major simply laughed, and could not be drawn out of his buffoonery. Dupuy and Lénac, in their corner, listened without saying a word. Etcheverry made the modest observation that they had already, in practice, declared war on the Spaniards, and that the side of the Moors had already been implicitly adopted.

"We're all of the same opinion, then," Renard concluded. "The first thing to do is to render our occupation of Valencia, presently unstable and precarious, complete and methodical. The second is to procure an effective alliance with the Emir...and the Reverend Father Geronimo here has offered to negotiate it.

"Thanks to our weapons, thanks to the science of our era, we've arrived here, rather like Captain Cook on an Oceanian island, among savages. Supported by the Moors, we'll be invincible. We'll be the masters of the world, the kings of the Earth...

"In sum, I don't think that have anything to regret in this scarcely-banal adventure...and after what we've been though these last three years, the prospect of having to conquer half of Span shouldn't give us pause."

During this debate, the monk, left to himself, had explored the marvels that he found within range. The studious scholar and bold innovator, whose boldness of thought had made the Franciscan colleges and his disciples at the University tremble, the luminous brain that enclosed all the science of his era, was bewildered and distressed by this first, somewhat intimate, contact with a new civilization.

The cold meal that Jasmin served him on a corner of the table began a series of astonishments: he examined, and carefully tasted, corned beef, biscuits and chocolate. The aluminum mug intrigued him with its lightness. He studied the fork curiously, and finally decided that it was a backscratcher, like the one the voluptuous emir possessed. The oil lamp fascinated him. He switched an electric pocket torch on and off fifty times. Then it was the turn of the office equipment: the pencils, the steel-nibbed pens and the typewriter—which he was very eager to try, with Etcheverry's help.

His keen sense of observation informed him of the use of the tobacco-jar and the old "Jacob" left there by the clerk. He stuffed a pipe for himself, but was astonished not to be able to light it by means of the electric lamp as the others had by means of their lighters. The obliging Lénac struck a match for him, however—another prodigy!—and it was with the pipe in his mouth that he admired, once again, an alarm-clock and the bracelet watch of which he had been made a gift, before plunging into an examination of newspapers and books.

He swore to himself that he would soon be able to decipher the strange "manuscripts" fluently. The saucy images in the *Vie Parisienne* and the *Culotte rouge* disturbed him, as did the inevitable photographs of naked women pinned to the office wall. A date in Roman numerals that he encountered at the foot of the title-page of a novel—MCMXIV—bewildered him. What calendar did these singular Gauls use, then?

The black notebook, however, which he found close at hand—that grimoire full of kabbalistic formulae—troubled him even more. His vigorous rationality saw nothing but nonsense and illusions in the occult sciences—astrology, magic, sorcery—and in so-called pacts with Infernal spirits, but he believed in the spagyric art[18] and in a possible domination of all the natural forces by the man who discovered the Great Arcana...so did his new friends possess the secret of the Philosopher's Stone?

---

[18] The spagyric art is the concoction of herbal medicines using alchemical principles; in the 14th century almost all medicine was so based.

In spite of the attraction of these marvels, he did not want to delay his mission to the Empire any longer. A letter in Latin was composed under his direction and typed by Renard, then authorized with the Company stamp. He slipped it into a bag with a few truly royal presents: the alarm clock, a gasoline lighter made from two Boche cartridges welded together, a tin of sardines and one of corned beef, and an aluminum flask full of rum. And at eleven o'clock in the evening, refusing any escort but accepting a pocket torch for the journey through the orange wood, he set out for the Moorish camp, beneath the stars that would serve as his guide.

At the same time, at the other side of the village, the motorcyclist set off for Valencia to obtain news.

IV. Nénesse's Booze-Up

By force of habit, the troopers had gone to be in their bolt-holes, but they were stifling there. At daybreak, all the *poilus* went outside to breathe the air that was arriving gently from the south-west, laden with the perfume of orange-trees.

The major's speech had satisfied curiosities, and even the thorny question of furloughs, which had been indefinitely postponed and relegated to secondary status in the presence of the advertised Golden Age and the perpetual booze-up. Anyway, planet or not, the promised leave had come, since they were at the rear! In spite of everything, excitement was running high; the proximity of Valencia had a deleterious effect on discipline.

Cipriani tried to organize the relief of the guard-posts, but no one wanted to go. The priority of tours of guard duty was contested. He was obliged to issue formal orders, in spite of the murmurs and protests.

"Why aren't they sending us to relieve the men in town?" demanded Corporal Moreau, ordered to a listening-post. "That would be more useful, since there are no more Boche."

"We'll get there," the Corsican condescended to reply. "Patience. We need news. The bike's gone to fetch some."

"We could still set out before he comes back."

"The lieutenant hasn't said anything. I can't send you just like that." And to save himself from having to argue with an inferior, Cipriani shouted angrily at an idler who was in the process of sucking fresh oranges: "Who's been to the orange grove? I forbade anyone to leave the sector. There'll be trouble, damn it! It's like that cannon, which I told you to move..."

The members of the new General Staff formed the previous evening in the office had, for the most part, accepted the situation and were sleeping blissfully after the final grog. The idealist Monocard, however, overexcited by the grandiose prospects he had glimpsed, had spent the night smoking cigarettes and pacing back and forth feverishly outside the kitchens.

After two hours' sleep, Renard had joined him. His responsibilities were weighing upon him. Soon, he became anxious, not having seen the motorcyclist return, and communicated his fears to the sublieutenant. At two o'clock, Etcheverry having not reminded him in time about the existence of an acetylene searchlight, he had two fires lit on the tower. When daylight came, he gave Cipriani orders to repair the 75mm cannon—it only needed a new wheel fitting—and to make an inventory of the munitions: shells, grenades and cartridges of every sort.

"Yes, lieutenant. Should I send a cyclist to the artillery, for the cannon?"

Renard stared at him in amazement. The artillery! It was a long way away! But the worthy Cipriani wasn't joking. The true situation escaped him, that was all. There was no point in disillusioning him.

"No need," Renard said, simply. "We have a wheelwright in the company to improvise a wheel, and a few former artillerymen to get the piece into working condition if it's needed. Get on with it right way. Check that the truck has fuel in its tank too. There's stock of cans in the storehouse."

The sergeant hastened away. Duranton, who was waiting for him to leave, came over to the officer.

"Lieutenant, I still don't have any new supplies. The men have already had bully beef all day yesterday. I don't know what to give them."

"Do you have potatoes?"

"Yes—as many as we need."

"Well, make fries then. And for fresh meat, take the horses that we brought yesterday. Two of them are practically ponies; there's no reason they can't be slaughtered, if you have a butcher available."

"I was a butcher myself in civvy street. I'll get on with it. I'll make a stew—they'll be licking their chops."

The major and the aviator arrived, having already downed a morning whisky. On being told that the bike had not returned, Thévenard mocked the anxieties of the two officers. "He'll be having a party, your lascar—he'll have done the same as his colleagues and found a pretty girl to spend time with..."

The aviator thought that it was a simple matter of a breakdown. He agreed, nevertheless, that if there was no sign of the man in another half an hour, he would go in search of him in the airplane,

As the officers strolled around in the square in front of the office, watched by the buzzing crowd of *poilus* who were hoping for the promised exhibition of the Machine and for the departure for Valencia, the acoustic screen of the tower and kitchens prevented them from hearing two distant gunshots to the north and the sputter of the approaching motorcycle. There were, in consequence, only the sentries on duty in the guard-posts when the motorcyclist arrived, rolling awkwardly. He dismounted in order to cross the plank bridge over the Seille, and it was then seen that his rear tire was flat.

Someone called out to him jovially: "What's new, Vidal? Everything okay over there?"

He was scowling, downcast and exhausted, however; scarcely responding to the questions he pushed his machine along. "You can talk! I've been out in the cold all night...and that's not good for a chap. Is there still juice at the cookhouse?"

Finally alerted to his arrival by rumor and the general movement of curiosity, the two lieutenants, the major and the aviator collared him as soon as he arrived in the square. He was only given time to drink a mug of coffee and immobilize his machine on its stand. As soon as he mentioned revolver shots and arrows in the tire, Renard shut him up and took him into the office, with the Genera Staff, to hear the rest.

His report was as brutal as a cudgel-blow.

A magneto breakdown had stopped him half way to Valencia in the dark. Having succeeded in repairing it, at two o'clock or thereabouts, he had lost his way in the brushwood, in spite of the fires lit on the tower, which showed him the location of Port-sur-Seille but not that of Valencia. At daybreak, he had reached the ramparts of the city, but it was impossible to get in; the breach in the gates had been sealed with the aid of faggots and padding; the battlements were garnished with archers and arbalesters. Arrows had been fired at him, and one had punctured his rear tire. He had fired revolver shots, and had made his engine roar, which had frightened the horses. Of Corporal Venette and his men, no trace. He concluded: "That's your lot, Lieutenant. I can't say any more."

Renard was the first to break the consternated silence that welcomed this news.

"Damn it! A dirty shame! My men must have been murdered. The Spaniards have had another go, and finding them drunk..."

"You're going too fast," said the major. "They're merely prisoners..."

"Provided that we have the Emir's reinforcements this morning..." De Lanselles hazarded.

"We can't wait for them," Renard replied. "Whether they're here or not, we need to attack the Spaniards within two hours, as soon as we've had breakfast."

They went out to organize the expedition. Sniffing the bad news, the men pressing around the vicinity of the office had already stopped envying their mates who had stayed in Valencia. When Renard asked for volunteers to go and rescue them, however, they all offered themselves without hesitation. Half of the contingent got ready to set out on campaign. The aviator placed two cases of fifty grenades in his cockpit. The wheelwright, having found an old wheel that was usable, fitted it to the 75mm cannon. To haul it, they still had two horses—Duranton had already killed and butchered the other two—but the major advised hitching the piece to the truck, which could also carry a machine-gun and a trench-mortar, and his plan was adopted.

All the preparations had been completed before ten o'clock, and it only remained to eat the soup when a rumor started and spread, and the shout went up from the guard-posts: "It's the lads! They're coming back!"

But "the lads" were only two in number: Nénesse and Ali, mounted on a pack-mule, with no other weapon than a scimitar, and both ragged, dirty and in distress—undoubtedly escapees.

Leaving the *poilus* perplexed by this disquieting arrival, Renard dragged the two men away. "Well?" he demanded, as soon as the office door was closed. "You let yourselves be taken by surprise?"

"Oh, Lieutenant!" Nénesse exclaimed. "You're spot on! You could say that they put one over on us, the filthy monkeys. As you can see, I think the *sidi* and me are the only ones who were able to dodge the nutcracker, and we had to slip away and leave our mates in the shit!"

"Go on, tell me everything."

"Well, this is how it as, Lieutenant. I have to tell you that after the attack, we found a nice enough little eatery where they had everything necessary to ring the bell good and proper: peppered wine, ham, fruit, cheese, etcetera, etcetera. Not to mention what the other lads brought by the by. We even had a dozen old tarts to serve us. We didn't speak the same language, them and us, but we finished up understanding one another quite well all the same..."

"Good—get on with it!"

"Okay. In the end, you understand, with the heat, the dust-up, hunger, thirst…in brief, after a certain time, everyone was pissed out of their heads and didn't know what was going on any more. Some had already gone to sleep, others were having it away with the tarts, others having a laugh at some old mole who wanted Venette to give her a good time."

"What! Venette? He wasn't at his post, then?"

"Can't have been, since I remember that he finally arrived, with Sauvage and Peltier. He came to tear us off a strip, but we soon took care of that with a nice mug of cider. In brief, after that I went out to have a slash and noticed that it was pitch dark outside. There was no one in the streets but dogs. Have to admit that I was as drunk as the mates. Then I went back in to have a nap in a corner, and I'd no sooner lain down than I dozed off, just like that.

"I don't know how long I'd been out when I suddenly woke up trussed up like a sausage. At first I thought it was the mates having a joke. Then I started shouting: 'Get up, Moors!' to make a joke about the *sidis*—but I hadn't yet shut my trap when I got a crack of a whip on the head and saw stars. 'Fuck,' I said to myself, 'that hurt. Either I'm nuts, or chances are we've been done over by the locals.' Then, it was a matter of shutting up, curling up and pretending to be out for the count while keeping an eye on what was happening.

"The only light was a miserable candle, and I saw shadows in some sort of priestly get-up strutting around as if they were at mass. All the mates were in the same state as me, and at least half the Africans were bleeding like stuck pigs with their throats cut. The priests were going through our stuff and gathering up all our weapons. There were even some of them reciting prayers over them and blessing them.

"When all that was finished, they picked us up and carried us into the yard, then along corridors, down stairways and through tunnels, until we finally arrived in a sort of big cellar, well-lit but with the air of an assize court or a gym. There was a raised counter with another beneath it and two to the sides, with a big table in front, all filled with black and white monks, and on the other side and in the middle of the room all sorts of machines and gadgets like those acrobats use in the circus. Me, I was thinking in pessimistic terms, and I could see that some kind of reckless judgment was about to be passed. You can imagine that that sobered me up double quick, and I began to look out for anything that might be useful for me and the mates.

"I'd been put with the remaining *sidis*, so I was separated from the other *poilus*, who'd been put with the

117

chicks, although the poor lads were scarcely thinking of having fun, any more than the girls, who were mewling so much that the junior priests were oblige to roll up their scarves to make gags. We were untied, but civilians with swords in their fists were keeping us under close guard, and there was nothing to be done, for the moment, except try to turn into a gust of wind.

"Immediately afterwards, the fellow at the counters started jabbering away to the ones who had brought us. That went on and on—they were all rolling fearful eyes and pointing at us, waving their arms. Then the one who seemed to be the president—the others called him *Tarte-au-Ragout*—called for silence, and the bastard started by having all the girls dragged by the hair to attach them by the feet to wooden crosses of some sort, while the other monks rooted around in their clothes, doubtless looking to see what their numbers were.[19] In the meantime, they gathered around the big table where our weapons and the things they'd fished out of our kitbags had been piled up.

"You should have seen the gaping mouths of all those guys passing everything in detailed review and recoiling from the pictures of naked women they they'd found in Little Charlot's wallet. Others were trying to read newspapers while passing their fingers over them, but it was obvious that they couldn't make head nor tail of them. One of them got hold of a Browning, which he was turning every which way. I said to myself: 'That fellow will do himself an injury before long.' No sooner had I thought so than the idiot put the end of the barrel to his eye and *bang*—the gun went off a splattered his

---

[19] In 1917, French prostitutes could work legally, provided that they were registered with the local police, and were issued with serial numbers for identification purposes.

brains all over the floor! Talk about a fuss! The one called Tarte-au-ragout stood up behind his counter, cursing and chewing out the monk, who was no more than dead meat.

"Then the guards surrounded us more tightly, and they looked as if they were going to finish us off. It was a near thing, but the old guy stopped them and started jabbering away to his acolytes again, and they went back to examining our stuff, but without touching anything and blessing them all the time. Only there was a little fat chap who seemed more excited than the rest, and they all started arguing nineteen to the dozen. Me, I jogged Ali's elbow—he was beside me—and whispered in Arbi: 'Look out, old son –this could be the time to make ourselves scarce!'

"The little fat chap was shouting even louder, and waving his arms around like crazy to persuade the others, and then, suddenly, would you believe that he picks up a grenade from the table to give it a closer look, and bangs it down hard on the table? Bloody hell! That put paid to him and no mistake—not to mention the others! It wasn't a time to stand on ceremony. I yelled: 'Every man for himself!' and snatched the cabbage-chopper from one of the civvies, who was busy shitting himself. I headed for the exit without looking to see if anyone was following me.

"I was racing through the corridors when I heard galloping at my heels. I turned round to settle the hash of whoever was following me, but I recognized Ali! 'Shift your butt,' I said to him, 'and let's move.' Talk about a business! We climbed stairs, we knocked over two monks who tried to bar our way, and finally arrived in a courtyard the opened on to the street. There, we fell upon some soldiers who were chatting, and took to their heels when they saw us. We grabbed a mule that they'd left behind, and it was off to Port-sur-Seille at top speed!

"But Lieutenant, as for the mates who stayed behind, I don't think there's anything we can do for them, for the swine must have skewered them after the last grenade went up!"

V. The Pernod Alliance

There was no longer any need to hurry. Since it was no longer a question of rescuing, but of avenging the mates, and for exacting that vengeance to the full, it was better to act in concert with the Emir's forces.

As soon as the escapee had finished his story, therefore, a cyclist was sent to the Moorish camp with a message for the monk, briefly relating the misfortune that had overtaken the twelve Frenchmen and the nineteen Moors, and asking him to hurry the Emir along.

Renard feared the effect that the drama might have on the troops, for the order given to Nénesse to keep his mouth shut did not prevent him from talking, and even Ali's gestures were only too eloquent. He therefore saw the cyclist return with unconcealed satisfaction, after half an hour, announcing that the Emir and his retinue were close behind. He had met them some ten kilometers away.

"I recognized the red-haired priest, the new chaplain. I gave him the piece of paper. He read it, gave me a sign that everything was okay. I saluted him and came back. They aren't moving quickly, they've got a whole Arab camp with them. They won't be here for another hour, at least."

A fortunate diversion! Enough to occupy the men and prevent them from dwelling on the drama in Valencia. In order to impress their new ally, it was appropriate to welcome him with great ceremony. They had time to arrange things, but only just.

"Quickly, Etcheverry—everyone outside and in battle-dress. Kit out the half of the contingent that's going to stay here. Tell the sergeants and the corporals to make the men hurry up. At the trot, as if for a review..."

Cipriani went into top gear. He was everywhere at once. He was the one who unearthed six tricolor flags, organized the parade, had the trumpets polished and the trench-mortars loaded. It was thanks to him that they were ready. Taking advantage of the circumstances to stimulate the zeal of that loyal watchdog, whose services had probably never been as valuable as they would be in the new period that was beginning, Renard entrusted him with the role of standard-bearer and, under the pretext that he had just assembled the company in ten minutes—a record—promoted him to adjutant on the spot.

A tear that he tried in vain to retain rolled down the brave soldier's wrinkled cheek. "This is the best day of my life," he stammered, incapable of thanking his leader in more fitting terms—and, in honor of his new rank, he put on white gloves and the beautiful belt of an English officer, from which a sporran was dangling, into which he fitted the shaft of his gold-fringed flag. With the cannon's bayonet-guard he took up his position to the right of the General Staff grouped outside the presbytery, in front of the company formed up in the sun-drenched square—which comprised Renard, the major, Etcheverry, de Lanselles and Dupuy, in blue horizons and helmets, the Englishman in khaki, plus Nénesse, wearing for the first time the sphinx-like insignia of a sergeant-interpreter, clean-shaven and wearing the aviator's boots.

The hoofbeats of the numerous cavalry troop drew closer, mingled with neighing and the guttural bellowing of dromedaries. A makeshift orchestra struck up, comprised of tambourines, drums, fifes and cornets. Green standards and multicolored pennants appeared. And on a gesture from Renard and his "Ten'shun! Pre...sent arms!" the sergeants and the bayonets immobilized themselves, glittering.

The two trumpets sounded, the mortars thundered three times, and in the resplendent glory of his damascene armor the Emir surged forth, holding back his gold-clad palfrey. In the first rank of his officers, sparkling with precious metals and gems, the monk made a dark patch with his dark brown robe. Behind them, the horsemen's lances bristled confusedly.

On a word from the monk, the Emir shouted an order, which brought the cortege to a halt. He got down from his horse and advanced toward Renard, who stepped forward to meet him, his hand extended. But the Emir nobly gave him the accolade. The orchestra stopped playing, and in the religious silence of the two armies, the French leader addressed the Moorish chief in his best Latin.

"Noble warrior, valiant prince by whose side I shall be glad to fight, our friend Geronimo, here present, must have told you that we have come from our distant land with the sole aim..." The expression of his idea became too difficult, however, and he had recourse to the interpreted Nénesse, who set about—God alone knows how!—translating the rest, which he pronounced in French, into Arabic: "...With the sole aim of defending progress and civilization, apart from any partisan spirit, and to bringing about the triumph over obscurantism of liberty of thought..."

He went on in the same style for five minutes, but the Emir listened distractedly. De Lanselles' monocle, which caught the sunlight as his head moved, was darting fascinating flashes at him and his neighbors, who were commenting on the prodigy between themselves and baptizing Monocard "Eye of the Sun." Discreetly, the monk recalled the Emir's attention, and he replied to Renard's speech in Latin.

With a few Oriental flourishes, he declared that he accepted the alliance. They were friends already; his cavalrymen, welcomed fraternally by the Gauls, had fought and perished with them. They would avenge them together. As a warrant of his trust he had come with a small escort of five hundred warriors—the bulk of the army would follow tomorrow—and, as a pledge of friendship and gratitude for the magnificent gifts brought by the monk, he had brought a few modest presents, which he begged the Gallic chiefs to accept.

During this speech, the horsemen of the escort had spread out quietly into the open space behind the church and the infirmary, and when the Emir fell silent, the procession of presents was set out in the square, in front of the *poilus*, facing Renard and the General Staff.

First came seven camels bearing hermetically-sealed cages, led by the halter by black men in scarlet trousers and turbans. Behind them came black mules with red leather harnesses and red pompoms over their ears, drawing four brightly-painted carts carrying pyramids of fruits and vegetables, live chickens and confused heaps of foodstuffs. Closing the parade, a veritable flock of sheep kicked up dust, all their feet making a noise like rain.

"We do not have your science," the Emir went on, smiling delicately in his benzoin-perfumed beard. "Our friend Geronimo and my cavalrymen have told me that you can enclose an entire ox in a little iron box. I offer you these gifts as nature has made them, but if you wish, our cooks will prepare them in our fashion, and a fraternal feast will bring your men and mine together this day."

On an order from Renard, the *poilus* spread out and mingled with the Moors, making contact cheerfully and noisily. A canvas tent had been erected by the Mors with marvelous promptitude, beside the Englishman's villa, and the two orderlies set up a trestle table laden with the wines of honor destined for the two General Staffs.

The presents were not yet finished. The carts of victuals and the flock of sheep had continued their progress as far as the kitchens, where, amid the curiosity of the *poilus*, and even that of Duranton, playing the idle critic for once, the Moorish cooks lit big fires under their pans of couscous and commenced the methodical slaughter of the desperately bleating and clucking animals. The camels remained, however. The eunuchs made them kneel in front of Renard and his companions; the green silk curtains at the sides of the ages opened, and women appeared, clad in pink, white, blue and yellow veils that revealed pretty faces—blushing, smiling or affronted—with eyes magnified with kohl. The Emir, delighted by the effect produced by his "surprise" pointed out that these slaves—Greeks, Circassians and Italians—numbered fourteen: two for each member of the allied General Staff!

With the exception of the aviator, who was apoplectic and scandalized, their eyes devoured these forms exhaling a rare and voluptuous Oriental odor. The major was already taking liberties; he pinched the chin of the nearest one and called her "My little chick!"

Fearful of regrettable scenes and faithful to his role as leader, Renard removed the temptation. He thanked the Emir warmly for his royal gift, but declared that the division would be made at leisure that evening. Between now and then, it would be better to lodge the ladies in the former town hall under the vigilant guard of their eunuchs—and the harem, veiled again and remounted on the camels, were guided to the retreat by Dupuy, who was ordered to provide them with a box of chocolates.

Wines were drunk—or rather, in view of the reluctance of the Moors, who were good Muslims, to taste the juice of the vine, the honorary Pernod. The opaline liquor was a big hit with the Emir and his officers. Even the monk accepted a glass, and in spite of the linguistic difficulties, gesture and broad smiles supplied a rather animated conversation.

The men, for their part, fraternized around cooking-pots in their tents. They too were soon exchanging presents: uniform buttons, matches, lighters. Aluminum rings—especially those ornamented with lice—were at a premium—and, competing in generosity to win the friendship of a *poilu*, the Moors did not hesitate to part with their gold rings in exchange. "That's super, mate!" one of them sniggered. "It really suits me!" And there were handshakes all round, and embraces thereafter—for the wine and rum were flowing feely around the plates. The *poilus*, out of deference to the manners of their hosts, plunged their fingers into the steaming couscous just like them and attempted the same position, sitting on the ground with their legs crossed.

Gradually, the feast warmed up; the orchestra was added to the hubbub of joyful voices filled the square. Corporal Meunier took out his ocarina; a taciturn Limousin fetched an accordion; the Moors' drums, pipes and cymbals played a prelude, and then the orchestra joined in, and songs rose up in a pleasant cacophony. The General Staffs, in their tent, did not want to be left out. With the aid of many strong arms, the piano was extracted from the cellar and Monocard started to play—with all his energy—to drown out the din. Lénac, endowed with a fine tenor voice, sang the *Madelon*[20] and *Marseillaise*. The Emir, who had passed on from kummel to whisky and from whisky to Benedictine, was jubilant.

They were reminded of serious business at about five o'clock in the afternoon by an emissary from the guard-posts. A troop of approximately three hundred men was approaching slowly from Valencia.

It was a superb opportunity to demonstrate the superiority of firearms to the new allies. The Emir sent his officers to assemble the Moors; the trumpets sounded "boots and saddles." They were about to charge the enemy! Renard asked him to keep his troops on this side of the Seille; then he went with the French General Staff to a mound near the tower from which the entire plain could be seen, all the way to Valencia.

The company of Spaniards, whose helmets and weapons were glinting in the sunlight between the bushes, was still some two thousand meters away.

"Hand you binoculars to our friend," the sublieutenant whispered in Renard's ear. The latter had not thought of it.

---

[20] "The *Madelon*," whose actual title, *Quand Madelon*, comprises the first two words of the song, was composed in 1914, with music by Camille Robert and lyrics by Louis Bosquet; it became extremely popular during the war, partly because it is about soldiers chatting up a girl and partly because it is one of the few songs with that subject that is not obscene. It became a kind of patriotic anthem, considered worthy to be coupled with the *Marseillaise*.

With remarkable sagacity, Abdul Khan grasped the purpose of the instrument and the operation of the focusing mechanism at the first try. When he had located them in the field of the Zeiss, the martial figures of his enemies suddenly moved a hundred paces closer and he uttered a little cry of joy, removed the lenses from his eyes for the sake of comparison, replaced them, and started spitting out a stream of insults at the Spaniards, as if they could hear him.

Pale with enthusiasm, the monk, who was experimenting on his own account with the major's binoculars, stammered halting sentences which featured the names of Ptolemy and Averroes, and that of Aristotle, accompanied by epithets that were obviously unflattering. Out of deference to his hosts, he communicated a part of his reflections to his former pupil in Latin. "You see how far superior this crystal is to the eye alone? Well, it appears that it's by an even greater margin that our friends' weapons surpass the javelin and the arrow. In spite of your treasures, your genius and the science that I've shared with you, we're like little children compared to them."

"Nine hundred meters!" Renard said, and commanded: "Etcheverry, have the machine-guns open fire."

The crepitation of detonations frightened the horses, but the Moorish cavalrymen, forewarned and reassured by Nénesse, only manifested a brief nervous start. They restrained their prancing mounts, and reformed their lines almost immediately. The Emir scarcely trembled, without quitting his binoculars—but he exclaimed with astonishment and joy, and his troops roared with triumph, as he saw the ranks of the enemy column collapse one by one, like scythed-down ears of wheat, under the invisible thunderbolts. Within two minutes, not one was left standing.

"Cease fire!"

Then, roused by their chiefs, to the bellowing of horns, with frenzied shouts, the Moorish squadrons departed at a great gallop, shaking the ground, in a vast palpitation of burnooses and a flamboyance of lances and naked scimitars. With his eyes glued to the magic crystal, the Emir stamped his feet, urging them on with guttural monosyllables. He breathed out, his jaws clenched in a rictus, his red lips pulling back to display his white teeth, as he watched them lean over the recumbent bodies, decapitating the dead and wounded indiscriminately, and come back brandishing scalps in a triumphant fantasia, pursued by the curses of the Spaniards who had watched from the heights of the ramparts, to the dismay of their fellow citizens.

Judging that the performance was over, Abdul Khan prepared to get down from the mound.

Renard retained him. "You haven't seen everything." And, addressing Etcheverry. "Have the 75mm aimed at the city. Just one shell...we don't have that many. An incendiary shell."

The shot thundered. Almost immediately, from the roofs of Valencia, on the left of the city—the quarter where the *poilus* had been taken by surprise—a column of smoke rose into the sky. The silhouettes of archers on the ramparts waved their arms at the heavens tumultuously, and the sound of the tocsin rang out, shrill and multiplied, in the hot and limpid afternoon air.

Instinctively, as a true warrior, the Emir understood the relationship between the cannon-shot and the fire lit in the distance, in more than one place. He exhaled his enthusiasm, in Latin to the Frenchmen and the flabbergasted and admiring monk, and in Arabic to his General Staff, who had come to meet him. For the Moors, that final flick of the thumb was superfluous; they lavished respectful salaams upon the machine-guns and the re-formed ranks of Lebels.

Interrupted by this martial episode, the feast got under way again with a new zest. The couscous had been eaten some time before, but there were still fruits to gnaw and pickles; there was still drinking, smoking and singing... Above all, there was still the alliance to be sealed. The *poilus* did not think that indispensable, but they did not want to sadden such generous guests and cavalry so skilled at cleaning up battlefields. The Moors, already wonderstruck by the practical demonstration of firearms, could no longer see any means other than the alliance to thank such powerful and modest collabora-tors, for they had refused the gift of the severed heads, and those trophies were already ornamenting the little camp to which the horses had been relegated, behind the presbytery.

The sun was setting. The tents were relocated in or-der to take better advantage of the sea breeze, and the two General Staffs appeared in public view. With loud shouts, the men in the burnooses clamored for their prince to give the signal for the ceremony.

The Emir stood up. Pulling back the sleeve of his tunic, he laid bare a slender arm, as firm and polished as bronze. With the point of his dagger he pricked the crease of his elbow. Renard, warned by the monk, im-itated all his actions. For want of a dagger, he used his pen-knife.

"Hey, watch out!" muttered the doctor, passing his lighter, ready lit. "Cauterize that!"

In a liquor-glass still half full of gin Abdul Khan collect the generous trickle of his blood and held it out to Renard, who did the same.

"Drink!" proclaimed the Emir. "It is the sacred libation, more binding than all the most terrible oaths."

Amid the hearty cheers of the Moors, the two leaders drank their mingled blood.

On seeing that it would be necessary for him to carry out the same ceremony with a tall young man with long black hair, the major pulled a face. "It's not very antiseptic, you know, that procedure," he said. "If one or other of these chaps has the..."[21]

"You're forgetting that Christopher Columbus hasn't yet discovered America," Monocard observed.

It was necessary to do it. Ritually, the two General Staffs—even the aviator, furious at being obliged to lend himself to "pagan maneuvers"—completed the exchange of blood. Among the *poilus*, this was a pretext for enormous merriment. In view of their small number, and as they could not bleed themselves white to satisfy the six or seven Moors that surrounded each of them, soliciting the libation of fraternity, they thought of diluting a few red droplets in a full mug of rum and passing it round. The Moors accepted the new rite without demur.

The Emir explained his plans to his "brother." The following day, when the bulk of his army had arrived, he

---

[21] The missing word is "clap" (as in syphilis), which was a major problem reducing the effectiveness of the armies involved in the Great War. Monocard's interjection reflects the common belief that the disease had been introduced to Europe by sailors returning from the Americas; it now seems more likely that different strains of the spirochete were endemic on either side of the Atlantic, and that the reciprocal importation of the exotic strains, to which no immunity had built up, wreaked havoc in America and Europe alike, but that hypothesis had not yet been advance in 1917.

would begin the siege of Valencia; within a month, by virtue of famine or otherwise, the city would fall.

Renard smiled. "Tomorrow, noble brother, with the aid of your warriors, we shall be in Valencia."

The prince, already excited by the unaccustomed beverages, was overcome by this prospect, which surpassed his wildest hopes. He stammered a few inconsequential words and was seen to go pale, and then his head fell back on the back of his armchair. The major hurried forward to catch him, in the midst of exclamations and general distress.

"It only needs him to pop his clogs—we'll be accused of poisoning him! Jasmin, run to the infirmary and ask Paincarat for a flask of ether!"

The ether reanimated the Emir. He took a deep breath from the handkerchief steeped in the strange perfume. He plunged his face into it delightedly and demanded a second dose. Then raising a visage radiant with ecstasy, he paraded his shining and intoxicated eyes over his entourage.

"Victory, my friends!" he murmured. "The Prophet has just revealed the victory to me! I've seen..."

In the darkness, beneath the fabulous eye of the large acetylene searchlight that Renard had ordered to be lit on the tower to give warning of any new incursion by the Spaniards—for troops had come out of the city and lined up under the walls—the two fraternal armies continued drinking for a long time...

VI. The Battle

All night long the Spanish troops continued massing in front of the ramparts. New detachments hastily summoned from neighboring towns had joined the garrison decimated two days earlier by the first attack, demoralized by the explosion of the gate, which had taken refuge in the fortress and had then taken Corporal Venette's *poilus* by surprise. In all, there were between five and six thousand. Evidently the Spaniards were making a supreme effort to rid the land of the diabolical intruders.

The superstitious dread of the infernal "nocturnal sun" aimed at their concentration, however, paralyzed the Spaniards. While it was shining, they had not dared to advance.

Renard was not displeased, for that respite gave the bulk of the Moorish army time to arrive. To be sure, he did not need such reinforcements to put five or six thousand enemies to flight, but if they did not capture the runaways, the war might drag on at length. On the other hand, with a numerous and well-organized cavalry, no one would escape and the battle would be conclusive.

Emboldened by the advent of daylight and the extinction of the searchlight, the Spaniards advanced, in an order inspired by the ancient phalanx, in tight deep columns, presenting a front of five hundred meters at the most. Bristling with long pikes, their squares were unintimidated by the danger of being surrounded by Moorish horsemen. Their intention was to bring down the French gathered in the center, to annihilate that handful of men and to turn their attention thereafter to their old enemies, incapable of prevailing in formal battle against the pikes and arbalests.

Preceding the two General Staffs on horseback, the truck, hidden behind a curtain of troopers, advanced slowly with its two machine guns, the 75mm having remained in Port-sur-Seille, aimed at the city. To the right and the left, the two ranks of cavalry, still swelling, were more widespread than the Spaniards. Intoxicated by the certainty of their victory, the latter mingled prayers with war-cries and, once they had recovered from their initial alarm, howled insults at the airplane that was circling above them inoffensively. Eleven or twelve hundred meters still separated them from the *poilus*.

Suddenly, the truck was unmasked, and the machine-guns and Lebels opened fire.

It was more a massacre than a battle—a mere shooting match—and the *poilus* enjoyed themselves tremendously in creating that epic collapse.

"Your turn, Guillaume!"

"That won the egg-cup!"

"Chalk up the one on horseback to me—that was a least a general I shot just then!"

"It was me, not you, you clown!"

"Sock it to them, lads!"

"It's better than the fair at Neuilly!"

"It's thirsty work—pass me your bottle."

"Fuck! My rifle's hot!"

"Piss on it!"

The Spaniards, literally mown down, initially fell without understanding what was happening. Their ranks had lost half their personnel when the panic commenced and the remaining three thousand men turned round and fled toward the city. But the crackling truck launched forward in pursuit, spitting death from left to right and right to left; the Lebels were still firing without sparing cartridges; the aviator launched his grenades on retreating groups of bewildered men, who threw away their weapons in order to run faster. On the crowd of spectators swarming on the ramparts the 75mm shells inflicted somber blows.

In its turn, the Moorish cavalry charged, irresistibly, in a whirlwind of dust. It was necessary to cease fire. Already, though, no more than five hundred men of the Spanish army were still standing, and the Moorish charge quickly completed the extermination, at the price of five or six horsemen killed and a dozen wounded.

From the city, on which the aircraft's grenades and the shells were still raining down, a frantic clamor of despair was audible.

The victory was crushing, absolute and definitive.

At the top of the palace-fortress overlooking the city a white flag was unfurled; another floated on the ramparts, and a third appeared in the breach of the blasted gate.

Fortunately for the deputation, the Moors were busy with the cadavers with which the plain was strewn, and the officers did not have to protect the negotiators against their fury. The latter were brought to Renard, the Emir and their entourages.

A lamentable procession! In chemises and bare feet on the sharp stones, with lighted wax torches in hand, there were a dozen individuals of venerable appearance, but defeated, white-faced and tremulous in the legs. Amid the jeers of the *poilus*, greatly amused by the underdressed procession, the leader of the postulants, the governor, Don Pedro Casanova himself, darted a glance of unspeakable hatred at the monk and knelt down before the Emir to set down two enormous keys of polished steel on a green velvet cushion—the keys of the city and the fortress. He surrendered them unconditionally, but implored the conqueror's mercy.

"The conqueror is this man—my brother the Gaul," said the Emir, nobly. "He holds all our lives in his hands."

There was a brief deliberation. Abdul Khan thought that they should make an example and cut off the heads of the twelve notables, as he had done in similar cases. The monk advised adding Tortorado and the principal inquisitors, in order to ensure the tranquility of the city. Monocard, by contrast, wanted to win hearts by a general pardon. The major, supported by Etcheverry, was in favor of punitive taxation.

"With the cash, we'll have all the partisans we want. Come down hard on the treasury, Renard."

That was, indeed, the most judicious course of action. Life was granted to everyone, but a ransom of five hundred kilos of gold—a weight that the monk was charged with translating into Spanish coinage—was to be delivered an hour after the entry of the allied troops; otherwise, the city would be looted.

The governor, heartbroken, returned to his fellow citizens to have this dolorous condition fulfilled, and his eleven companions were kept as hostages, while a squadron of Moors went forward as scouts, in order to prepare for the allies' entrance.

That took place via the same street where the *poilus* had fallen into the trap two days before. Either by virtue of fear of reprisals in spite of the pledge given or authentic horror of the foreign devils, the Arabs of the city, who came to cheer their brothers and liberators, the Jews and the Christian converts who had high hopes of the new order of things, were alone, with the riff-raff, in lining the streets along the route. There was no one to be seen but tavern-waiters, grooms, tent-makers, market-traders with bare arms, children in rags and prostitutes in yellow mantles and red stockings—but behind the peep-holes of doors and the slats of shutters, and on the heights of terraces, an invisible crowd, hate-filled and wonderstruck, was watching the progress of the procession.

Two trumpeters headed the march, filling the narrow Medieval streets with their blasts. Then, on the rattling and jolting truck—the truck chosen by the Emir in preference to his customary elephant as a triumphant vehicle—Abdul Khan was enthroned with the monk by his side, between the two machine-guns and their gunners, shaded by green palms. Renard, the true conqueror, followed modestly on horseback, amid the two confused General Staffs, to which the interpreter Nénesse had been added.

Then came the motorcycle, with Lénac in the side-car; the cyclists, juddering at slow speed over the cobblestones but objects of terrified admiration nevertheless; Adjutant Cipriani, the bearer of the tricolor standard; the *poilus*, in fours, with their arms shouldered, helmeted, grey with dust, but superb and exceedingly amused; the elephant, the glory of the Emir; the Moorish orchestra, tambourines, cymbals, pipes and horns; the standards and smaller flags; the cavalry, draped in burnooses, lances in hand, grim-faced; and, finally, the army's retinue, the camels of the harem, the eunuchs, the grooms, the cooks—the vague and variegated host of Moorish foreigners, with whom the city's Moorish inhabitants immediately mingled.

At the crossroads of the fountain, the palace-fortress raised up its high crenellated walls. They went alongside them on a street to the right, finally emerging into a large sloping square. The palace formed the upper side of it with the cathedral, decorated with gold and mosaics; on the far side stood the somber and massive façade of the Convent of the Incarnation, and then, opposite the palace, the vast buildings of the University, in the Arabic style, in pale stone, as if gilded by the sun; a little further away was the government building.

The troopers and a few hundred cavalrymen formed up in the square. Renard, the Emir, the monk and the two General Staffs gathered on the steps of the palace, and the deputations filed past them, in order.

Don Pedro Casanova and the Corregidor, in a black velvet costume with a gold chain around his neck, successively introduced the magistrature and the University, in black, red, mauve and green togas; the brotherhoods of penitents in blue, white, grey and violet; then came the guilds of jewelers, weavers, coppersmiths, tanners and twenty others, with their banners, who came spontaneously to implore the grace of protection for their markets, storehouses and shops, or an exemption from billeting, and to deposit their particular gifts, in addition to the gross taxation—which was collected in the meantime.

At the feet of the conquerors, in two esparto baskets, gold coins were heaped up: doubloons, quadruples, dinars, piastres, cruzados and escudos. The Jews, alerted to the fact that freedom of religion was about to be proclaimed, came forward, with yellow roundels on their maroon robes, to offer the "blue-helmets" lodging. The students, pupils of the monk, and the Franciscans in their brown robes introduced themselves as friends, congratulating Fray Geronimo on having escaped his torturers and having returned among them. They succeeded in obtaining an exemption from the taxation for their convent.

With a reluctance that was only too visible, and only after repeated summonses, the temporal clergy followed. The bishop, at the head of the canons of the cathedral, had the boldness to present himself with an aspergillum in his hand, and, under the guise of a blessing, performed an exorcism. He was threatened with the confiscation of his cathedral, in addition to the four churches already designated to serve as mosques and synagogues.

Geronimo, however, his voice hoarse from serving as an interpreter, along with Etcheverry, to the delegations that expressed themselves in the vernacular, insisted that the Dominican inquisitors be compelled to appear. A patrol, dispatched into the palace-fortress that they habitually inhabited as soon as the city was entered, had not found any of them. Even the archives of the Holy Office had disappeared; the prisoners were lying in their cells with their throats cut; all that remained were the coffers of gold and the instruments of torture, which had been too heavy to carry. According to Casanova, the Dominicans and the entire personnel of the Inquisition had left Valencia. Geronimo wanted the city to be searched methodically, in order to discover their hiding place, but Renard had other things to think about and the matter was postponed.

The five hundred kilos of gold having been collected and duly weighed, one bag at time, and then stored with the treasures of the Inquisition, the session was ended, to the great joy of the *poilus*, who had been standing in the sun for two hours. Shouts went up: "To the big booze-up!"

But Cipriani—Adjutant Cipriani—was on the lookout for the squall. "A booze-up?" he shouted. "All in good time! In the meantime, you're going to come with me, in good order, and get your billets, and duty-rosters. You know what happened to the others. We have to make sure that you're not nabbed in your turn."

And the seventy obedient *poilus* went into the palace, into which the General Staffs had already retired. Squads of Moors, under the direction of Lénac, were busy scraping away the monastic whitewash in order to make the marble and mosaics shine again. The splendor of the place and the comfort of the apartments brought forth cries of admiration.

"It's not bad, here!"

"It's nice and cool."

"And the beds! We can have one each!"

"We'll be in clover!"

"Look—he's already taking his photos!"

Nénesse, who was all too familiar with the place, guided a squad to the torture-chamber. His indignation, still fresh, was reanimated. "This is the mates' tomb. Look—that's where I was. There's just enough left of the table to make kindling. That's where they pulled the poor girls by the hair. And that door, that's where I made my escape, with that fellow Ali…"

The palace-fortress thus became the barracks and general headquarters of the French. Two machine guns placed on the steps guarded the entrance. Another defended the postern by the stables burned during the first occupation.

The Emir was lodged in another, smaller palace. Some of the Moors were billeted in the Puerta del Sol quarter, others in tents outside the walls. They took charge of guarding the city gates. They also formed the police force. To replace the alguazils, immediately disarmed, four hundred elite cavalrymen, scimitars by their sides, clubs in hand and each additionally armed with two grenades, went around the town maintaining order and protecting the dwellings of the inhabitants who had paid the ransom and were displaying tricolor insignia.

They could not abandon Port-sur-Seille, which remained an arsenal and place of safety in case of misfortune, nor could they leave it to be guarded by Moors alone. In order to overcome the reluctance of the troopers to leave the conquered city, where they awaited all pleasures, even for half a day, Renard decided that the men on duty over there should have the services of six harem women—to serve as cooks, of course—and Cipriani took responsibility for organizing a duty rota.

On the first day, the motorcycle and the truck made several trips back and forth, bringing to the palace boxes of cartridges—few of which remained, alas, in view of the excessive consumption made during the battle—a few barrels of rum and almost all the bottles from the cellar, removed under Jasmin's surveillance. Renard personally supervised the placing of the precious Machine under lock and key. It was transferred to the tower a few days later.

After the siesta, toward sunset, the party recommenced in Valencia. To impress the population, the aviator performed some remarkable acrobatics over the rooftops: loops, spiral descents and the "dead leaf." Lénac, charmed by his previous flight, had offered himself as a passenger; he climbed out of the cockpit green around the gills, and threatened to lodge a complaint against Bennsbury—whose evolutions, he affirmed, had put his cinematic apparatus out of order.

Then, while the Moors and the troopers banqueted in the cool air of the square, with the aid of provisions offered by the inhabitants, and the General Staff dined for the first time in the Lion Hall, a firework display organized with the aid of red, white, blue and green flares brought the terrified admiration of the Valencians to a peak.

During the night, however, on the battlements of the Convent of the Incarnation—which Renard, in spite of the urging of the monk, had neglected to have searched—a shadow leaned over: Tortorado, with his hand on his chin, somberly contemplated the city delivered to the foreign devils, the demons who played sacrilegiously with the stars in the sky!

VII. The Blue Helmets' Triumph

Naturally, there was some excess in the early days. The Moors and the *poilus* remembered their murdered comrades, and affirmed their authority as conquerors harshly. Under the slightest pretext, for an insulting glance or on a whim, the new police forces did not hesitate to unsheathe their weapons and break heads, and to loot the houses in the vicinity of the disorder. Several *poilus*, having seen the regulatory salute refused by haughty individuals, forced them to come to the palace every morning to render them menial services. They boasted of their Neronian exploits in the Unicorn Hall, which served as a refectory.

"The civvies? Me, I treat them to kicks up the bum!"

"Me, I've got a genuine archduke for a flunkey—a hidalgo, as they say. I make him polish my boots. And they have to shine!"

"Me, I do better than that. I have my feet washed by some sort of priest. I think he's a bishop. And when he doesn't do it to my liking, I make him lick the soles. He crawls like a dog! Here, Azor, I say to him..."

Two whims of this sort had a tragic outcome.

Titi-la-Vache came home one evening triumphant. "Oh, you can talk, lads—the fun I've had...I've been having a nice time with a chick who's been doing turns on my knob for a couple of days, and I was in the middle of humping her when her husband turns up. 'Don't move,' I say to him, without stopping, but taking out my revolver, 'or I'll blow your head off.' The bugger doesn't make a squeak. Me, I finish my little business, and to complete the joke, I make him serve me refreshments afterwards. He was hopping mad, and I think the little wife must have got a good hiding when I'd gone—but the station-master's wine was excellent."

It was so excellent that two hours after this wonderful adventure, Titi-la-Vache rendered his soul to God in atrocious agony—poisoned, the major declared.

To set an example, the husband and wife were duly shot—not to mention all the other inhabitants of the house, who were set ablaze along with the building by a more or less official delegation of *poilus*—and the typed judgment was attached to the doors of the churches, mosques and synagogues.

The second victim of a similar vengeance, Rousselet, nicknamed Haricot, was found one morning in the harbor area, strangled with a rosary and frightfully mutilated. This time, the guilty parties escaped, but a state of reinforced siege was proclaimed and the Moorish police lent themselves to it with a joyful heart, along with their grenades.

The vigor of the repression eliminated any danger of revolt. Valencia no longer put up any resistance, and the conquerors reigned over an enslaved people. In any case, since the day when five hundred of the most notable inhabitants, requisitioned to dig long trenches on the battlefield, had buried the six thousand lime-covered cadavers of the defeated army with their own hands, it seemed that all hope of deliverance had been buried with them, forever. They might perhaps see the last of the Moors one day, but the Devils had the power of Hell behind them; they were invincible by terrestrial arms; only the spiritual arms of the Holy Inquisition, when it decided to act, could prevail against them. It was necessary, in the meantime, to suffer them and bow down to them.

For three days, Renard turned a blind eye to the excesses of his men, but on the fourth, at Monocard's instigation, he gathered the troopers in the courtyard of the fountain and made a little speech.

"My friends," he said, in substance, "we're not here simply to amuse ourselves. You're aware that I've given you much more freedom than in the past, but it's necessary that discipline is maintained, and that you make yourselves as useful as you can. A civilizing mission is incumbent on all of us: that of giving the benefits of 20th century progress to the backward peoples of whom fortunate circumstances have made us the masters. And the first condition of arriving at that goal is not to make too many enemies among the inhabitants..."

A daily wage of three "quadruples" of gold allotted to each man contributed greatly to taking some of the tension out of their relationships with the populace. Besides, the personal attractions of the French gradually conquered feminine sympathies, and the civilians found a singular charm in the alcohol that was distributed randomly along with blows.

The *poilus'* frequentation of the taverns and outlying districts—where lively hostesses taught them the fandango, not to mention the Andalusian dancers who performed in the nude to the accompaniment of castanets—became less tumultuous. By way of reciprocity, in the ex-torture chambers of the Holy Office, which had, in response to Nénesse's suggestion, been converted into dance-halls, the local young women were initiated into the subtleties of new dances, from the waltz and the boston to the tango and the two-step, to the accompaniment of an accordion.

While waiting for the work of civilization to be organized, and in order to give the men something to do, other diversions were also organized that were more appropriate to the hot climate: bathing in the thermals of the palace or on the beaches; boat-races; gymnastic competitions; bull-fights, and so on.

Among the General Staff, it was the monk who took his work most seriously, and communicated impulsion to the others, thanks to his rapid progress in the French language. The boxes of books found in the cellar had been gifted to him, and he devoted himself to their avid study. He read Rabelais and Montaigne almost fluently; he extracted from Calvin the desire to reform the Church; and at the same time, he was already attacking the moderns, with a marked predilection for the reformist tirades of Voltaire and Rousseau in favor of the humble and the oppressed.

Fearing the total subversion of his reason, Monocard had given him a few vague explanations of the mysteries of future dates, but his genius perceived the greatness of the task in which he was collaboration, and he lived in a perpetual fever, aided by the alcohol of which he made liberal use at the General Staff's table. The civilization of the 20th century, which he discovered *en bloc*, carried away his enthusiasm, and with mad impatience, the seething fervor of a neophyte, he tried to assimilate it in order to apply it to his surroundings, to impose it on his compatriots—to the human race, of which he would be the regenerator.

For the moment, named Grand Master of the University, he had resumed his courses, and transmitted his innumerable discoveries to his students at random. A dozen *poilus*—including the motorcyclist Vidal, holder of a baccalaureate—seduced by regal rewards, were teaching the students French. Monocard promised lectures on philosophy when the young students were able to understand them. The major, in spite of the burdens imposed on him by his hygienic ministry, accepted the title of Professor of Surgery, Anatomy and Obstetrics, and, as his demonstrations did not necessarily require oral commentaries, he began his course immediately with a few operations and elementary dissections.

The aviator, also solicited by Geronimo—for the latter held him in high esteem during the fortnight that the reformational crisis lasted—refused to initiate pupils in the aeronautical art, but he took it into his head to teach English to some of the children in the cathedral choir, with the baroque design of making clergymen of them. In addition, under the pretext of reconnoitering the locality, he used up a lot of fuel in long excursions, on which he took a collection of small British flags, for mysterious reasons, which he did not bring back.

Renard, the "Director of Operations," was overwhelmed by work. All the practical care of organizing the conquest devolved on him, for his worthy "brother," the Emir, in spite of his new title of "Generalissimo of the Allied Troops," was primarily occupied in completing his harem with the aid of a few pretty Valencian maidens—and in spite of the keenness of his intelligence, the gifts of civilization that pleased him most, for the moment, were Pernod, Chartreuse…and ether.

Even the Moorish functionaries who had replaced the Spaniards in all the administrative positions were dependent on Renard. He had to direct the finances, the food supplies and the police. In addition to the typist, two secretaries were continually busy under his orders.

Etcheverry, in charge of counter-espionage, seconded him as best he could, but the over-zealous Director of Operations bitterly regretted the old routines of the Lorraine front, where there was certainly less comfort and more danger, but also less anxious harassment. He sometimes wondered whether it might be better to give the *poilus* immediate orders to return to Port-sur-Seille, where Dupuy would activate the Machine to rejoin the mates left behind in 1917, in the part of the village that had not been displaced.

For the urgency of the return no longer existed. A new fact had reassured the officers as to the consequences of their involuntary desertion. While effecting the transfer of the Machine to the tower in Port-sur-Seille, where it would be safer than in the cellar, Dupuy had finally discovered the purpose of the two mysterious dials. Their controls permitted the reduction—the compression, so to speak—of the duration passed outside the initial epoch, and the return, not merely to the exact place but to the exact moment of the departure.

In practice, and in the present case, if they remained, for example, for a month, that month, thanks to the manipulation of the dials, would only represent a single minute of time—and an absence of one, two, three, or even ten minutes would not create any grave inconvenience.

In the joy of his discovery, Dupuy had communicated it to the entire General Staff at table, who had unanimously decided to stay for as long as circumstances permitted. It was sufficient to have the Machine ready to function—and within a week, Dupuy had assembled the zinc and other ingredient required to manufacture a battery of rudimentary piles quite sufficient to recharge the accumulators.

Everything was therefore in readiness, and the return could henceforth be effected at any moment—but Renard knew only too well that no one on the General Staff had the slightest desire to leave the delights of a Capua that became more seductive every day. Even Monocard wanted to bring his civilizing labors to a satisfactory conclusion.

As for the men of the eighth, not one would have consented to go back to the sector; life in Valencia was too beautiful!

The dirty and exhausted *poilus* of the triumphant entry had give way to potentates with the salaries of senators. The blue uniform, at first enlivened by gilt and embroidery, was soon reserved for duty, in the narrow sense. Outside tours of duty, the men of the eighth wore a uniform of fantasy more appropriate to the torrid climate: a sort of colonial costume in white silk, secured at the waist by a tricolor sash, and completed by a cork helmet and espadrilles. And the power of the "demons" was so well-established that the people of Valencia feared them no less, and continued to call them Blue-Helmets.

Gathered in the Unicorn Hall, around a table refreshed by jets of water, they savored the fine ratatouilles that Duranton served to them—a newly-ambitious Duranton who had an entire ministry of culinary aides, scullions and slaves, both male and female, under his orders—and they rejoiced collectively in their good fortune.

Nénesse opened fire:

"I was idling in a little street in the Arab quarter when I spotted a nice lace veil on a railed balcony, which took my fancy, and two nice little chicks blowing me kisses. I took out my revolver and slipped quietly upstairs. They salaamed, brought me jam and pastries, sugared wine, while jabbering away and smiling. I tucked in, but I knew right away where they wanted to go when they started chattering at me, and undressing me, and making me lie down in a marble bath full of patchouli. After that, a little massage session all over—I was like a little Jesus. Talk about a party…I'll spare you the rest, but I came home on my knees."

"That's all right!" retorted Marloie. "It's the usual. Me, I was passing through the Jewish quarter behind the University. A juicy little chick grabbed me and took me into a drawing-room. I made no bones about it and had myself served on a sofa that was there. Immediately afterwards, though, in comes a lovely bookworm who makes herself at home and starts to tell me tall stories. I carry on, and she has a good time, like the serving-girl. But that's not all, it appears, for after that one another one arrives, dressed like a duchess…and I got my prick well-oiled, old chaps, I can tell you. Each of them even gave me a gold ring, and I gave them aluminum rings in exchange, since I was fortunate enough to have a batch of them in my pocket…"

"Shut up!" said Bidart. "You're boring us. To begin with, it's not necessary to try to introduce us to women of the world; we know them, we've been there…haven't we, lads? That's not as good as the little intrigue to which I treated myself not long ago near the docks. Cudgels…oh, my friends! She didn't smell of patchouli, but she delivered, she delivered! It was me who was obliged to give thanks!"

"Possibly," said Garrigou. "But that's not as good as what we got from the kind sisters."

Everyone knew what the situation was with regard to the Convent of Santa Cruz. Some time before, on the

150

first day of the occupation, the Mother Abbess had come, in tears, to beg Renard to give the Lord's brides protection from the enterprises of his *poilus*. The major himself had gone to inspect the damage, but had found no trace of a break-in. Since then, no further complaint had emerged from the holy dwelling. On the contrary, the postern of the convent, in the garden, opened at certain hours to permit the penetration of men of good will...not to mention others. Even Cipriani, the chaste Cipriani, who had ventured there, had seen his virtue succumb to the assaults of a troop of maenads.

"Oh yes, the nuns!" sniggered Souplet. "You know them even better than we do, Professor Debray."

"What? Debray's a professor? Of what?"

"Of cycling. He gives lessons to the kind sisters on the garden paths. That's why he's so pale."

"That's true—he's getting thinner."

"It's wearing me out—I can't cope any longer. Anyone who wants to come to help me out...I'll hand over."

"Okay, I'll come—and my bike too...and my saddle."

"What, you? But you've forgotten your eight whores this morning, you stuffer!"

The governor's wife, an Italian—perhaps a Corsican; at least she pretended to be—was one of those insatiable Messalinas who, disguised as a woman of the people, tasted the pepper of sun with the subaltern demons. First Jasmin, then Cipriani—a compatriot in that foreign land!—and then Lénac secretly received her favors. By a singular casuistical scruple, however, she remained aloof with the officers, and the latter scarcely suspected what she was for several of their men when they saw her sitting motionless, pale beneath her thick black hair, presiding over the governor's table. For Don Pedro Casanova, among others, had received secret orders from the Inquisition opposite to those given to the people, to attract the principal Devils to their homes in order to try to discover their plans and to obtain certain alleviations of the weight of the conquest. On several occasions, Renard, de Lanselles, the major, Etcheverry, Geronimo and the Emir had been invited to magnificent feasts at his sumptuous dwelling.

The hidalgos, in black velvet with golden chains around their necks, and their wives constellated with diamonds, welcomed the conquerors with a politeness that was both obsequious and glacial. "By order of the Holy Office" was readable in all the faces, in every smile, and the difficulty of conversation—in spite of the Spaniards rapid progress in French—completed the congealment of the audience beneath the gilded ceilings, while the lackeys in armorial livery passed the silver plates and filled the glasses with sherry and amontillado.

The conquerors, although flattered by these receptions, found them immeasurably tedious. The major, especially, was bored by such sessions, which terminated in concerts of guitars and plaintive violas, and he tried to introduce a little zip into them by bringing the accordion-player, who performed his most brilliant repertoire—but the result was pitiful; three great ladies fainted under the excessively sonorous strains and Thévenard gave up.

To those gala evenings, the major greatly preferred his escapades in the Emir's palace with Lénac. The latter, commissioned by Abdul Khan to procure new recruits for his harem, had adopted the major as a collaborator, in order to carry out medical examinations of the subjects, whose plastic aspects he also photographed.

The Pernod ran freely during these little sittings and no one ever got bored.

The simple daily meetings of the General Staff around the mess table in the Lion Hall were of considerable interest in themselves, by virtue of the lofty speculations that were indulged there.

Served by women of the harem—who had not been divided up, in view of the difficulty of an equitable division—the leaders of the eighth never failed to get stuck in, over dessert, to the subject of their civilizing duties. Over the alcohol, they all waxed lyrical.

"We're really doing something for these ostrogoths," proclaimed Thévenard, one day, "in spite of them! Valencia's almost in step, but this only a beginning. It's a matter of doing something to extend the benefits of progress further."

"That's easy," opined the monk, who now spoke French with a certain elegance that was literary and familiar at the same time. "It's merely a matter of silencing the Inquisition."

"Well, we've closed it down in Valencia," Monocard replied, "but elsewhere? Toledo, for example?"

"Bah!" Renard interjected. "We'll conquer Toledo too."

Etcheverry made the observation that they had expended a great deal of ammunition, and that they did not have enough for another battle.

"We'll make some," Dupuy put in. "The same with black powder, guns and machine-guns."

"I don't doubt it," said the major. "But before making gunpowder, we'd do better to think about alcohol. Do you know that the cellar's terribly low? Isn't that so, Chief Cupbearer?"

Jasmin, who was attempting to merit this new rank by means of an even more dignified manner, declared that the fine liquors extracted from the cellar would run out in less than ten days.

"That's your fault, Thévenard," de Lanselles remarked. "You've lavished a bit too much Pernod on your chicks, with Lénac."

"Don't complain! Since it procures you the pleasure of examining our collections of photographs...and even the originals!"

"All right, all right, gentlemen," Renard put in. "Tomorrow, we'll look into the problem of alcohol, gunpowder and a few other manufactures. I have an idea. It won't be these details that stop us. In a month, two at the most, we'll be entering Toledo—that's a done deal."

"Then it'll be the turn of Madrid, Salamanca, Burgos..."

"In six months, Spain will be ours."

"We could leave Andalusia to the Emir. He's a good bloke."

"I claim Gibraltar," interjected the aviator, who was swilling whisky in his corner."

"You've already planted a few too many of your little flags," said de Lanselles, severely. "We'll have to be careful not to use as much fuel with your aircraft."

"Let it be—it'll run on alcohol when the manufacture's under way. Its flights are preparing the populations for our coming."

"And when we pass the Pyrenees...what shall we do in France?"

"In France? Why, we'll proclaim the Republic...more than four hundred years in advance. It'll be a famous progress—a great leap forward for history."

"The Republic? Damn! You're going too fast. I doubt that they're mature enough for that, our ancestors—they're scarcely out of the Crusades. They're just starting the Hundred Years' War with England. In parentheses, Bennsbury, watch out—we might take you prisoner."

"Not at all, since we're going to prevent the Hundred Years' War. It'll be necessary to aid Progress, to fulfill our civilizing mission."

"All those are long-term projects, which it will be necessary to realize by force of arms. We have to hand a means of acing on the consciousness of all Christendom. That means is to make our friend Geronimo pope. Nothing prevents us from proclaiming him pope in Valencia. We can enthrone him in a Rome later..."

"The papacy isn't in Rome at present," Monocard sniggered. "You're forgetting that Benedict XII is in Avignon, busy building his famous palace.

"All the more reason to elect Geronimo," the major said. "The popes at Avignon aren't real popes." Tapping Geronimo on the belly he continued: "Well, what do you say, Brother?"

The latter, congested by Martell, started and became even more red-faced. "Oh, personally, I don't care," he declared. "But for the good of my Order..." Then, struck by a sudden idea, he added: "Yes, yes, my dear friends—that's it! Make me pope! I'll crush the swine! I'll suppress the Inquisition everywhere!"

"Granted! That's another job done! Next...but first, Chief Cupbearer, fill the glasses. I'm thirsty tonight!"

And, over another round of liqueurs, the division of the world continued.

VIII. "Adversus Diabolos!"

To R. F. Fray Esteban Segura, Inquisitor-General of Toledo and superior of the Order of Dominicans, from R. F. Fray Juan Tortorado, Grand Inquisitor of Valencia and Provincial of the Dominicans.

My Most Reverend Father,

The power of God is infinite, but that of demons is great, and God permits it to be exercised in full plenitude on those who have sinned. Alas, in spite of the vigor that put the Holy Office into the hands of the glorious Order of which you are the venerated leader, to pursue heresy and bring back stray lambs to the flock, Valencia has sinned greatly. Today, Valencia is receiving its punishment.

Hell is unleashed, and demons reign as masters in Valencia: such is the unprecedented, frightful news that has plunged all the faithful here into sadness, and which will make the heart of Your Paternity bleed. As in the times of Nero and Domitian, the Faith is reduced to hiding away: the Holy Office—I weep as I write—has seen its treasures dilapidated by odious persecutors, and it has been constrained to suspend its activity and to take refuge out of human sight, in the crypts of the convent of the Incarnation!

But to help Your Paternity to understand the full extent of an evil that threatens to surpass in gravity the most famous heresies, to show him the anguishing situation to which we have been reduced and what need we have of spiritual and temporal assistance, it is necessary for me, overcoming my legitimate dolor, to offer a detailed account of events.

You know already, my Most Reverend Father, that in answer to the appeal of the heretic Geronimo, an annex of Hell surged forth on Earth on the morning of June 29 in the vicinity of Valencia; that an airborne Vampire which came to our city was repelled, not so much by our archers as by the ringing of our bells and the prayers of the faithful. You know that, two hours later, a small number of demons, guided by some Moorish horsemen, vanquished our warriors by means of invisible bees launched from metal tubes with a loud noise, felled the city gate with two thunderbolts, along with the tower above it, which we had only just left, and freed their protégé Geronimo. You know, too, by what artifice we surprised them, plunged in debauchery—without, alas, being able to lay our hands on the impious monk, whom they took to their infernal City.

When I sent you the courier bearing that report, we believed the city to be purged, without any reprisal from those reprobates. Alas, I repeat—the power of demons is great!

In order to ward off a further attack by the Moorish forces that had theft their camp to join the demons, we had gathered in the city all the royal troops from ten leagues around. Our valiant soldiers, duly confessed and provided with blessed medallions and scapulars, recovered their courage and massed in front of the city, notwithstanding a fire suddenly lit by magic in the Puerta del Sol quarter and the unexpected prodigy of an artificial sun that the sacrilegious imitators of Joshua had brought forth to dissipate the darkness.

My pen is incapable of the description necessary to enable you to see all the horror of the disaster in which our troops perished. I shall limit myself to reporting the pure and simple fact with a brutal dryness: our army was annihilated by the fulminating bees and thunderbolts of the infernal militia, and the cadavers mutilated by their allies, the Moors. And while we watched this catastrophe unfold from the top of the battlements, and addressed our prayers to Heaven, which did not heed them, the Vampire, from high in the air, harassed us with its thunder and multiplied the victims among the unarmed crowd.

We took pity on our unfortunate fellow citizens and authorized the governor, our faithful and devoted Don Pedro Casanova, to surrender the city.

In all haste, I had the sacred vessels and the archives of the Holy Office moved out of the palace; the prisoners in the cells were executed; and I ordered our brothers to seek shelter in the secret floor of the Convent of the Incarnation, for I anticipated that the apostate monk would pursue us with his hatred. But time was pressing and the greater part of the treasures confiscated from heretics in the last ten years by our vigilantes fell into the hands of the invaders. An irreparable loss, in the present circumstances, when gold is more necessary to us than ever!

The entry of the Satanic hordes—I saw it with my own eyes, under a disguise—justified the belief, widespread among the people, that the end of the world was nigh. But it was demons in blue helmets, not archangels, that sounded the trumpets in front of a chariot in which the image of the Antichrist, the apostate monk, was enthroned, alongside his ally, the Emir. That chariot was an object of fear and admiration to us all. No horses drew it; it climbed the slope of the street under the sole impulsion of the damned souls who were contained within it, and whose presence was attested by their howls, their flatulence and the din of their charms. Another chariot of the same species, but much smaller, with only three wheels, came after the horde of the principal demons and their standard in the three colors of blasphemy: blue, to symbolize their power over the air; white, over the Earth; and red, over Hell. Other vehicles with two wheels placed one behind the other, were each mounted by a single demon, who toyed thus with weight and equilibrium.

Before disappearing, we had fulminated an anathema against the invaders—demons, properly speaking, Moors, and the apostate Monk in particular—and an excommunication against anyone who trafficked with them. But already, when the demons on foot, or "blue-helmets," and the innumerable Moorish cavalry filed past, I saw that many had eluded our defenses and I looked at them with avid curiosity. Our necessary eclipse, the all too evident power, the threats and violence of the strangers, quickly multiplied disobedience to our orders. Deputations of all the professional guilds, not content with having furnished their quota to the enormous ransom of the city, went spontaneously to offer the conquerors gold, more gold and yet more gold—the better part of which would have reverted to us one day, in the form of tithes or confiscations; gold lost to our Order, which I had the dolor of seeing engulfed, by a bitter irony, in the Palace that had been the Palace of the Faith, where Hell will henceforth hold its assizes, and exact tithes in our stead.

This gold, which they subsequently distribute to the people, is for demons the primary means of recruiting adherents to their infamous cause. The second means is the influence that the apostate Monk has retaken over the youth of the University, whose intelligence he is corrupting, in concert with other demons who are teaching science and an accursed language. The third means is a magical beverage, which they cause their victims to drink. Thanks to the skill of our spies—although they are still too few, as we lack gold to stimulate their zeal and increase their number—we have been able to procure two bottles of this beverage, and try it out on a Moor secretly captured in a tavern kept by one of our affiliates, Alfonso Escobar. The fire of Hell, liquefied, constitutes this beverage, which—a frightful prodigy!—burns like a torch if ignited!

Under the influence of this fire, the condemned began to proffer voluble and insensate speeches, blasphemies and obscenities. When he had absorbed two pints, Hell took possession of him; furious and foaming at the mouth, he broke his bonds, fell in convulsions and expired, strangled by invisible demons.

But the demons in human form, the "blue-helmets," as they are known here, distribute this fire in small doses, and in small doses it excites gaiety and urges the flesh to voluptuousness. Prostitutes, women of the people, and even a few well-born ladies, attracted by this lure and by an unhealthy curiosity, have delivered themselves to it and to daily fornication with the blue-helmets. And it seems that the latter procure frightful delights for their succubi, for the number of these debaucheries is increasing every day, and the excesses of Sodom and Gomorrah will soon be equaled by those of Valencia. The women of the people are forgetting all their duties, great ladies are delighting in their crime, and instead of devoting to the good of the Faith the jewels that they were able to save from the requisition, they are going so far as to make gifts of them to their monstrous lovers.

One noble lady, whom I dare not name, has already weakened in the embrace of a blue-helmet supposedly born, like her, in a foreign land. And to complete the abomination, it extends as far as the Lord's brides, the pious Daughters of Mercy. The gardener at the convent of Santa Cruz has reported orgiastic scenes to us—angels of the Lord, veil your faces!—in the course of which the nuns, not content with abandoning themselves to fornication, try to imitate their incubi in the use of the magic wheels, on which they sustain themselves and roll around the garden by virtue of the power of Hell. And it saddens me to add that their Mother Abbess only intervenes mildly.

If the women of the city were only yielding their bodies to these Satanic incubi! But several virgins of the best families, forcibly dragged into the Emir's seraglio, have denied the faith of their fathers and embraced Islamism. All the young women in society, moreover, whether or not they are chosen concubines of the Emir, are subjected to an examination accompanied by impure touchings, and *see their souls stolen*.

That last point may seem obscure to Your Paternity, but you will find in the documents attached to this report, in appendix A, two specimens of this animic theft. With the aid of an apparatus that, unfortunately I have not yet seen, the young woman, put in a state of nature, is subjected to the aphrodisiac beverage and stripped of a part of her spiritual substance, which is fixed on a square of diabolical papyrus, which reproduces her features instantaneously, including the most secret details of her body, more accurately than the most skillful artist could achieve in a month. This apparatus is called "photo-graphic" by the demons.

Appendix B contains:

Item 1. An papyrus ornamented with stamps, written with an inconceivable regularity and perfection. The title, EXCELSIOR, is the sacrilegious motto of these fallen angels. The text, which has taxed the sagacity of our best linguists, seems to relate to an infernal war that will happen in the year 1917 of an enigmatic era. But that to which I call Your Paternity's attention is one of the stamps, on which I can discern several individuals in red ink. It is THEM! It is the demons of Valencia, figures with their helmets and bee-lances, in their primitive costumes.

Item 2. A volume entitled *The Mysteries of the Inquisition*, the atrociously blasphemous character of which is evident, although we have only been able to make an uncertain and incomplete translation. (See Appendix C.)

I have limited myself to sending these few justificatory pages and I shall not extend and further the list of prodigies produces by the stranger, with the aid of which they fascinate the popular imagination. I shall say nothing about the quasi-miraculous cures operated by their therapeutics, nor the daily magical spells that they realize with the aid of fire, nor the stars that they are able to make rain down from the sky. Their demonic origin is sufficiently proven without that.

The important thing, for the moment, is to prepare for a secret war against them.

The situation is grave, the peril excessive, but I now have several reasons to hope for a better future:

Firstly, in addition to the documents collected by our spies, other information from an unknown source has begun to reach us, written on papyrus analogous to that of item B in Latin—exceedingly incorrect, denoting foreign origin—and deposited by an unknown hand in the alms-box for the Faithful Departed in the cathedral. Might we have a secret ally among the demons?

Secondly, Your Paternity will perhaps recall that during the defeat of the demons taken by surprise in the Puerta del Sol quarter, we took possession of a certain number of their infernal weapons—large and small bee-lances and thunderballs. With God's aid, it might be that these weapons, in our hands, can one day be turned against our oppressors.

Thirdly, the rage of fornication that the demons inspire in the feminine fraction of the population furnishes us with a means of investigation, and perhaps of action, that I have resolved to put to work. Several subjects of incontestable good will have been acquired.

Fourthly, the demons are not invincible. In addition to the few surprised and massacred with the Moors before the great battle, two have expiated their abominable sins, one by means of poison, the other by strangulation. The people believe blindly in their power and their invulnerability, but if these examples are multiplied, we shall be able to disabuse them.

Before obtaining that preliminary result, however, we need gold, the sinew of war, to encourage wavering good wills—and we lack gold. We are plunged into the most complete destitution; our palace is in the profane hands of Demons, and the defenders of the Faith, reduced to eating onions and black bread, have a dark and damp crypt for a refuge, while the abomination of Sodom and Gomorrah triumphs, while the Moors have transformed four of the city's principal churches into mosques and synagogues and the blue-helmets mock the priests who administer extreme unction to the dying and throw tomatoes and rotten eggs at them!

Spain cannot remain indifferent to our peril, which is also its own, for our invaders dream of extending their domination and the winged Vampire has already taken flight, several times, to mark with a sign the lands that they intend to conquer. Moreover, even if they were alone, the Moors, emboldened by the recapture of Valencia, will attempt to regain everything that Their Catholic Majesties have taken from them.

Toledo, advised by Your Paternity of the news that I have the dolor of sending him, will understand. It is not just a matter of Valencia: it is Spain and the Faith that are in danger. *Adversus Diabolos!* Take up arms against the demons! It is necessary that the Faith be alarmed, from the Manazares to the Pyrenees, that by means of an untiring propaganda, a new Crusade is being prepared by Your revered voice—perhaps even on the order of His Holiness Benedict XII, to whom I have sent a reliable courier.

I shall not have the audacity to say any more about this subject and to appear to dictate Your Reverence's duty; I shall leave to Your Reverence the care of organizing matters, and rendering us prompt aid—initially by sending us some subsidies.

We shall redouble or zeal and vigilance, and I shall not fail to keep Your Paternity up to date with the result of our efforts.

From the depths of affliction, I bow my unworthy head and humbly solicit Your Paternity's blessing.

In nomine Patris, et Filii, et Spiritus Sancti.

FRAY JUAN TORTORADO.

Part Three
THE COUNTER-ATTACK

I. Civilization!

Things went on in the same sleepy vein. They drank, they feasted, they amused themselves, they sweated, they gave themselves to all the pleasures—but they also worked hard, making every effort to introduce progress to the ignorant.

They all did so with good intentions, under the impulsion of Monocard and the monk, drunk with apostolicism—and those who had followed the movement with the least conviction were now the most enthusiastic.

For it was no longer a matter of commanded service, of vague duty, of fatigues; it was a matter of earning good money, every man for himself, since Renard, in consequence of one of his projects born over drinks in the General Staff's mess, had recruited the skilled workers and organized the management of the factories by means of which civilization could be imposed on Valencia, as a prelude to the conquest of the 14th century by the 20th.

Assembled in the Court of Myrtles, all the men were interrogated in turn.

"You, Debray, what did you do in civilian life?"

"I was a foreman at a factory in Saint-Étienne; I made bicycles."

"Well, you'll continue that here: find assistants, and make bicycles."

"But I don't have any metal tubing."

"It doesn't matter—make wooden ones. And you, Loustalot?"

"Me, Lieutenant, I had a rather haphazard education. I was at Clairvaux, I made espadrilles."

"Good—we need them; it's still summer. Make us espadrilles. Marloie?"

"Present, Lieutenant. I was a compositor at the Imprimerie Nationale."

"Then you're going to build us a printing press. That will be indispensable, for proclamations—the typewriter isn't sufficient. Lénac, you'll show the local engravers how to engrave letters. Bousquet?"

"Me, I'm from Angoulême."

"Excellent. You can make paper."

"But I only sold manila envelopes."

"Well, get help. Use your initiative—learn. Cendron?

"Distiller at Pantin."

"Perfect. You can distill in Valencia. Is there anyone who can help him?"

"Me, Thomassin, Lieutenant. I was a waiter in a café. So was Domec."

"No, I was a dishwasher at the Brasserie Gruber on the Boulevard de Strasbourg."

"It doesn't matter. Thomassin and Domec, you'll help Cendron in the capacity of engineers. Let's get on. Champeaux?"

"Me, I'm from Saint-Claude. I was a lathe operator, specializing in egg-cups and napkin-rings."

"Ah! A lathe operator? In the munitions factory—you'll turn shells."

And so on. Everyone was attributed a branch of industry conforming more or less to his aptitudes and previous experience—and on that very day, buildings and materials were requisitioned, Moorish or Spanish workmen hired, and everyone set to work.

To tell the truth, the majority of these enterprises were unable to deliver immediate results, but what did that matter? The future was there! And almost everyone was a director; they saw themselves making millions, like "those in clover behind the lines."

The example of the manufacture of alcohol, at any rate, sufficed to justify all hopes. Thanks to Cendron's efforts, with the aid of local boilermakers, his still had been set up in an old convent near the palace, and four workers were toiling away there under the direction of Thomassin and Domec. Every day, ten liters were produced of an eau-de-vie of mediocre taste but considerable potency. That was a big deal for the *poilus*, and that general activity at least had the advantage of keeping them busy and putting a break on the perpetual blow-out in which they lived.

The monk, however, who was following their endeavors passionately, was astonished by checks that it was impossible to hide from him. Thanks to his reading, he was already able to form an idea of the industrial apparatus comprising 20th century civilization, and he imagined that a tiny French colony ought to be able to reconstitute it in its entirety, in a matter of weeks. He was astonished, most of all, that they had not yet instituted railways and telegraphic communications.

Monocard, who delighted him with the spectacle of his youthful enthusiasm and rivaled him in his determination to accomplish his "mission," never tired of enlightening his ignorance. He did his best to explain to him the principal reason that was limiting their civilizing effort: they lacked specialists.

"And they're rare, in each branch. Of a hundred thousand individuals transported by locomotives, not one of them is capable of designing one correctly, or even of constructing the smallest component of it!"

For Geronimo, however, the division of labor was a closed book. In his view, Monocard and Renard, not to mention the major, ought to be capable of realizing, or supervising the realization, of everything they knew theoretically.

Despairing of his cause, de Lanselles fell back on the shortage of natural products. There was, for example, no coal in Valencia; copper was scarce, and so was iron...

"Why don't you go find them?" the monk replied. "Andalusia is a land of mines. Send someone with the motorbike to the Caliph of Cordova, on behalf of the Emir..."

Seduced by this ingenious idea, de Lanselles persuaded Geronimo to accompany the motorcyclist Vidal, the latter holding a baccalaureate and being sufficient well-educated to help him in his research.

Such was the origin of the communications established, in the second month of the occupation, between Valencia and the kingdom of Grenada. First the truck, and then caravans of horses, mules and camels, brought coal, iron pyrites, copper, mercury, wines, Cordovan leather, dates...and they returned with gold and jars of alcohol.

Thanks to these imports from elsewhere and the ingenious perseverance of some of the troopers, some factories delivered more than hopes. With sulfur, carbon and saltpeter scraped from cellars and dungeons, the munitions factory was already producing sufficient powder to load grenades for the Moorish police. Rifle cartridges and shells would come later. A modest gas plant permitted the lighting of the palace, in anticipation of that of the city. Dupuy extracted an ammoniac salt from camel dung with which he equipped his piles, originally charged with sea-water. He had established a wireless telegraphy link with Port-sur-Seille and dreamed of linking Valencia to Grenada by means of a telephonic wire. The laying of temporary wooden rails was begun on the road to Andalusia.

The development of movable type, for official documents and newspapers, was not yet complete, but lithographic presses facilitated the work of impression. As paper was still awaited, they employed the pages of antiphonaries and the folio volumes of the monastic libraries, washed with oxalic acid. "The just revenge of the palimpsests!" proclaimed the major. It was on parchment that Lénac, in superb posters, boasted of the perfection of the Debray bicyclette, in guaranteed dogwood, or celebrated the benefits of the "Alcohol of the Eighth," "Nénesse Orangine" and "Duranton Anisette."

For alcohol no longer emerged from the distillery in the single coarse form of the early days. The distillation of wine had been combined with that of oranges and lemons, and even the confection of a redoubtable kind of Pernod, originally based on marine wormwood, *Artemisia maritima*.[22] Several factory directors, tempted by the

---

[22] The production of artemisia-based absinthe had been banned in France in 1915, primarily because of the damage inflicted on the war effort by its consumption. The consumption of Pernod rocketed in consequence, the color and taste of the anise-based liqueur being not dissimilar to that of absinthe, but the

169

benefits, had abandoned their manufacture in order to lend themselves to the industry of their peers. Fifty workers were employed there; alcohol flooded from the stills. Initially sold cheap, the price had risen rapidly as profit and speculation had entered into the picture.

In view of the increasing demand, Jews and Moors formed syndicates in order to buy up all the factory's produce and inaugurate the rein of mercantilism. Melchisedech, the licensed victualler of the occupying troops, bought up food commodities. The cost of living rose. Gold, monopolized by a few trusts, soon imitated by the *poilus*, became scarce. Seduced by the mechanism of fiduciary circulation, the monks suggested to Renard the idea of creating banknotes, and pretty vignettes bearing the stamp of the eighth were soon issued in place of quadruples and dinars, augmenting the economic difficulties...

Civilization extended its benefits throughout Valencia.

Thanks to the multiplied relationships between the troopers and the feminine fraction of the population, the initial prejudices concerning the Demons were gradually attenuated. The priests and Tortorado's secret agents found it harder to exploit the fear of Hell and patriotism. The hatred of the strangers no longer had the original strength and unanimity. If alcohol and banknotes had

---

replacement of Pernod by a kind of absinthe in the repertoire of the timeslipped soldiers—the *Artemisia maritima* cited here presumably has the same properties as *Artemisia absinthium*—would have been accompanied by a considerable increase in toxicity. Many of the other products of the amateur distillers would probably have been polluted by similarly toxic methyl alcohol.

transformed the factory workers into Blue-Helmet fanatics, directly interested in their preservation, the liberty that everyone enjoyed under their reign also won them a considerable number of partisans. The Jews, in particular, since the famous proclamation decreeing equality of rights and freedom of religion, had become partisans of the new regime *en masse*. As for those who, like Melchisedech, who were making enormous profits from the perturbations of the economic equilibrium, they knew that they would be doomed if Tortorado and the Inquisition ever returned to power.

The mass of the population bowed their heads and sighed over the hardness of the times.

Only the nobility and the temporal clergy held firm in their absolute faith in the Holy Office. The religious orders were divided. Without mentioning the nuns of Santa Cruz, plunged into the cycling lessons, the Franciscans had, for the most part, turned a blind eye to the singular circumstances of the return of their superior, Geronimo. Out of hatred for Toledo and the Dominicans, they affected publicly to see him as the glory of their Order, and to exonerate him as far as possible from the reproach of heresy. Secretly, however, they lamented the scandal, and were only awaiting the expulsion of the strangers to reject him and offer him up as a scapegoat.

For Geronimo, in the intoxication in which he lived, was not taking any precautions. Stuffed with all the half-digested knowledge of his new reading—he no longer slept, sustaining himself with the strength of alcohol, and was heartbroken by the rapid flight of the hours, continually consulting the chronometer given to him by the major—he devoted the rest of his time to reorganizing the University on a new footing and producing a seed-bed of propagandists. He had surpassed Voltaire, Rousseau and even Victor Hugo, and saw in integral social-ism the salvation of humankind. Karl Marx and Jean Jaurès became his idols.

His own pupils and another group of students fol-lowed him on this adventurous path. He even persuaded Monocard to help him select twenty of the most zealous as military students destined to form the superior ranks of the future Army of Progress, which would be set up once the armaments factory was producing better results. In the meantime—that surplus of combatants might be precious, in caste of revolt or external attack—Lebels were entrusted to these substitute *Saint-Cyriens*,[23] and Cipriani drilled them every morning in the palace cour-tyard. In addition, as they all spoke tolerable French, Monocard began his philosophy course, and excited the enthusiasm of his young listeners, accustomed to intri-cate scholastic dissertations, by talking to them about Henri Bergson, *"élan vital,"* "psychological duration" and "space-time."

In spite of his cynical indifference, the major took a real pleasure in inculcating healthier medical notions in his respectful and attentive pupils. Since the establish-ment of relations with the kingdom of Grenada, the re-nown of his science had spread, and a number of young Moors from the best families in Andalusia, who were destined for medical careers, had come to train at the University of Valencia. They were the most brilliant of his pupils. For them, especially, he stitched, dislocated, sawed and operated in every fashion on the invalids who flooded into his clinic in spite of the repeated excommu-

---

[23] Saint-Cyr-l'École near Versailles was the site of an elite military academy founded in 1802, an approximate analogue of Sandhurst or West Point.

nications. In the beginning, he used chloroform for major operations, but he soon renounced it, because the Emir had developed a taste for that anesthetic, whose use he alternated with that of ether to "give him dreams," in spite of Thévenard's charitable advice. And my word, Abdul Khan paid handsomely for his flasks...

"I've kept back enough for us," the major told the mess. "As for the patients in the clinics, they can howl. It only impresses my pupils more on seeing them cured. For I cure them, me, and they know full well that new patients are flocking in. I'm forced to entrust three-quarters of them to my young apprentices and swarthy assistants. In any case, it's better than the remedies of the local priests. Some of them are priceless. I've told you about a few, but what I saw and heard this morning beats the lot. A woman who couldn't walk as brought in; her anus was encircled by tumors as big as a fist, badly infected. I had her interrogated by the interpreter, and she finished up confessing that they'd started off as simple hemorrhoids. Instead of coming to see me right away, she'd gone to consult a holy bone-setter, the bell-ringer at the cathedral, and that bugger had sold her an ointment—you've guessed it, gentlemen—a greasy black ointment that he called bell-unguent: old axle-grease, which the good woman applied religiously; whence the tumors. I lanced them, and she was cured, but if she didn't get tetanus, that's not the bell-ringer's fault. Oh, the prejudices of these clerics! One could fill volumes with them!"

"These clerics," of course, hated the doctor cordially, and opposed him by every possible means. The dissections of cadavers that he undertook, in order to reveal the mysteries of the human body to his pupils, were an admirable pretext; preachers thundered in their pulpits against his sacrilege; he was called "the Ghoul." People even went as far as to accuse him, in certain right-thinking circles, of violating female cadavers. Several successful childbirths, which he deigned to supervise in person on behalf of the wives of hidalgos, and for which he was well paid, annoyed the midwives whose function he was usurping. A conspiracy was formed against him, which found an echo even in the University, among the students of theology and canon law. On several occasions the latter invaded the operating theater and manhandled the less numerous medical students. The major had to draw his revolver to drive the aggressors away.

Geronimo's lectures were also disrupted on several occasions by irruptions of the same sort, and brawls broke out around his presence in the city, between his partisans and the enemies of the strangers. It was necessary to provide him with a escort of two Moorish policemen for each of his comings and goings between the Palace and the University, whose clubs and grenades kept the boldest individuals at bay.

Irritated by these attempts, the monk no longer relented in his anger. Since the hand-press had started functioning, printing a kind of weekly newssheet in French and Spanish. The *Liberté-Libertad.* Geronimo had written several editorials therein of a rare vehemence, under the title "Clericalism is the enemy!" He recognized the hand of Tortorado in every new obstacle raised by the opposition to hinder the march of Progress, and warned his colleagues in the General Staff explicitly that they would never achieve serous results—and that all the ground they had gained might one day be lost—so long as the Grand Inquisitor was alive and fighting them in the shadows. His style was reflected in the fulminations that the priests of the various parishes launched from the height of their pulpits—not to mention the con-fessional—in reply to the articles in the *Liberté-Libertad*, in spite of fines and proclamations. Renard ended up issuing an order to search the Convent of the Incarnation, but the entrances to the crypt where the rebel Dominicans were hiding were too well-hidden; again, nothing was found.

Geronimo nearly had a fit of apoplexy on hearing of that failure. The others consoled him as best they could and reiterated their promise to name him as pope—which would permit him to issue an *urbi et orbi* bull against the Inquisition. But his faith in their success was eroded; he saw the future painted in dark colors, and on the day when he got his hands on the first fake bank-notes issued by the Holy Office, permitting Tortorado to fight his enemies henceforth with similar weapons, he warned his colleagues that the days of their reign were numbered.

All that was attributed to fits of bad temper. The General Staff, along with the *poilus*, did not believe that there was any danger. Fake banknotes or not, they felt that their domination was firmly established by the terror of their weapons and their personal prestige. The distill-ery now had two hundred workers, and its example showed that other manufactures could be carried out eventually; alcohol was flowing in rivers; gold was pil-ing up in the cellars; two banknote-presses, one a new model, were functioning incessantly; the caravans from Andalusia were bringing treasures of art and Arab lux-ury, and giving the palaces an atmosphere of the Thou-sand-and-One Nights.

Enfevered by an unprecedented agitation, Valencia lavished the fruits of autumn and its voluptuous daugh-ters upon the conquerors. In addition to one-night stands, everyone had an official mistress or mistresses. Even Renard, who only attached a minor importance to such trivia, allowed himself to enjoy the charms of a young Jewess, Myriam, the daughter of Melchisedech, the licensed victualler—and the Genera Staff, following their leader's example, immersed themselves in Hebraism. A dozen of Myriam's young friends frequented the Palace, and the gentlemen's bedrooms, every day.

II. Geronimo, Antipope

"Put a tablecloth on the sideboard too, for the aperitifs…but no napkins, idiot! Yousouf, set another place at the General Staff's table! I told you there were seven! And sixty-six at the Troopers' table. Mohammed! The champagne corks! Have you brought the snow? Yes? Set them out at the last moment. And the wine? White for the entrées…the Chief Cupbearer will organize the rest. Flowers, Haydé! Little shrew—I'll put my boot up your backside!"

In the Lion Hall, harassing a dozen Moorish domestics and slaves, Duranton, in an immaculate white uniform with insignia identifying him as the Palace Majordomo embroidered on his sleeves with arabesque curlicues, was supervising the final preparations for the feast that was about to reunite the General Staff and men of the eighth, for the occasion of the sanctification of Geronimo. The sight of the two tables, the noise of the saucepans and the perfumes rising from the kitchens, promised marvels.

Duranton stopped in his pacing to call out to a *poilu* who had just come in—a new-style *poilu* clad in gold-embroidered white and a white helmet.

"Ah, Père Jasmin, you've returned to the mess. What about the others? Are they coming?

"Close behind me. I came out a little in advance to supervise the aperitifs. My colleague the Chief Bread-Supplier has gone directly to the kitchens.

"To see to my vol-au-vents. His bakers haven't yet brought them. Hey, Margarita—run and see what Monsieur Saucisson is doing. And tell the chef to get the

177

minced langouste ready. Well, Jasmin, did everything go well at the ceremony?"

"It was magnificent," said the Chief Cupbearer, heading toward the credenza where the bottles were lined up in several neat rows. "You missed out by not coming."

"I don't doubt it," Duranton replied, following him and fanning himself with a menu. "I never see anything, me—I'm always busy with my ovens. I'm well-paid, but there's too much to do. At the end of the day, it's worse than in the trenches. Come on, pour me a picon-curaçao. Hey, Yacoub, a fresh jug, at the trot. So tell me about it. He's been crowned pope, Père Geronimo?"

"He's crowned—but first there was a high mass. A splendid ceremony, my dear. The cathedral full to bursting—all the people, all of high society, including the governor and his noble spouse, seemingly quite content, but there by order, like the rest; the choir dressed in velvet, tapestries from top to bottom, candles by the thousand, floods of incense, al the clergy in golden chasubles...and the orchestra! Violins of a sort, and our accordionist played so that he could accompany Lénac, who sang Gounod's *Ave Maria*..."

At that moment several *poilus* in white with gold braid—the factory directors—came in, went straight to the sideboard to quaff an aperitif, and joined in the conversation.

"Oh, yes, that fellow Lénac," said one of them. "Talk about a tenor—he'd make a fortune at the Eldo. And Monsieur Thévenard sang bass..." He trumpeted: "*I believe in God, master of nature...*"

"Shut your gob!" they protested. "You're not Thévenard."

"Lénac retaliated," Jasmin continued, while filling the glasses. "He got his revenge with the *Angelus de la Mer*. It was a triumph. Women wept. Madame Casanova was in a spin. The mass continued. At the moment of the elevation, Père Geronimo came forward to the middle of the choir, in his all-white cope, and received the papal tiara from the hands of the new bishop..."

"And what a tiara! Barbarin put a month into making it, with six workers from Grenada. All in aluminum, encrusted with gems pinched from the churches. It was at least a meter fifty high..."

"A meter fifty! You're joking! Why not the Eiffel Tower?"

"Hey, Jasmin," Nénesse cut in. "Why aren't you pouring us that liter of genuine Pernod? The new Progressinette's strong, I don't deny, but it tastes lousy. You could mistake it for bleach."

"That liter? It's the last one. Reserve stock—for the gentlemen at the high table."

"Oh, it's always the same...anyway, to yours, lads!"

"The bishop," Jasmin continued, "wanted to crown him, but Père Geronimo, lifting up the tiara, put it on his head himself, while we applauded fit to bust and the trumpets sounded boots and saddles. Only, there were a few murmurs in the audience..."

"They didn't grumble for long. The guy beside me was muttering between his teeth. *Sacrilegium!* I gave him a kick in the shins."

"All things considered, they have some reason to protest," Paincarat insinuated, his eyes lowered. "I'm just a humble medical orderly, a poor numbskull—I don't have factories like all of you, but if I might be permitted a word of criticism, papal dignity..."

179

"Oh, you can talk, seminary boy. Here, drink a glass of *gnôle* instead."

"Is it true, Paincarat, that you're going play aeronaut tonight?"

"It's still on the program of public rejoicing. Look, here's the official poster that Lénac gave me. Read it: 'At seventeen hundred hours, great aerostatic ascension over the Palace square. The spherical balloon Geronimo I, four hundred cubic meters, manned by Monsieur Galfart, pilot and Monsieur Paincarat, passenger…'"

"You won't dare go up, Jelly-Legs!"

"Bet you choke at the last minute."

Tumultuously, however, a crowd of troopers and the General Staff made their entrance, acclaiming the new Pontiff, his tiara on his head.

"Long live the Pope!"

"Long live Geronimo I!"

"Long live the Holy Father!"

"Long live our worthy chaplain!"

In the middle of a cordial bustle, Geronimo received the Pernod of honor from Jasmin's hands. Expansive and truculent, he turned round, glass in hand, and calmed the ovation.

"My dear friends," he pronounced, "I won't matagrabolize[24] your brains with a long speech. The supreme rank to which you've elevated me will enable me never to forget how much I owe to you—particularly to you, de Lanselles, who have initiated me into true Progress, and you, Renard, who were my liberator and have never

---

[24] The French verb *matagraboliser* [approximately, to confuse], rarely used except in literary texts, has no English equivalent, but that is surely an omission in need of repair. If not me, who? If not now, when?

ceased since to guide and support us in our efforts under-
taken against infamous Obscurantism. I shall prove to
you better than by words that I'm worthy of you by con-
secrating all my energy and all my thought to the triumph of the worthy cause, but struggling for it, if necessary, until the last drop of my blood...until the pyre! *In-
telligenti pauca.*[25] I drink to our valiant Director; I drink
to you all, noble workers for Civilization; a drink to a
better future for Humankind...to the Company!"

Renard attempted to reply, but cheers burst forth irresistibly. In any case, Duranton, anxious for his dishes,
scarcely waited until the toast had been drunk before
announcing in a stentorian voice: "His Holiness is
served!"

"To table!" bellowed the doctor, by way of an echo.

And in a hubbub of conversations already animated
by the distillery's violent aperitifs, the *poilus* spread out
around the large table, the General Staff around the
small one, which was raised on a platform, and the feast
commenced.

The Moorish lackeys, clad in felt, passed the plates;
the pretty scantily-clad slaves ran around pouring the
wine, all under the direction of Duranton and Jasmin.
Various wines, indigenous or Andalusian, washed down
a magisterial menu, from black and green olives, save-
loys, anchovies and tomato salads to cheeses and pyramids of fruits, via bouillabaisse, fried octopus, red mul-
lets, suckling pigs, poultry and lamb chops.

The Emir, prevented by religious observance from
taking part in the ceremony, arrived for the coffee, just
as the sorbets were being brought in, along with the

---

[25] Although often translated as "a word to the wise," a more
pedestrian translation would be "the wise need few words."

showpiece: an aircraft made of honey sugar, a delicacy suggested by the Protestant Bennsbury but which was not to be sniffed at. Diplomatically, Abdul Khan addressed discreet congratulations to Geronimo, and installed himself beside the doctor with the intention of obtaining a phial of sulfuric ether from him.

At the *poilus'* table, everyone was talking at once. The General Staff, scarcely less inhibited, swilled the last bottle of champagne originating from the Englishman's cellar, while lighting pipes and cigarettes. Liqueurs were poured. Renard, seeing the major preparing to get the new pope drunk—the latter having set down his tiara, his face as red as his hair, was taking enormous mouthfuls of his Jacob, and explaining his plans for social and ecclesiastical reform to de Lanselles—remembered that Geronimo still had to preach a sermon at vespers, shortly after the balloon ascent.

"Bah! He'll still be able to talk to those philistines, and anyone who doesn't like it..."

But an unknown voice interrupted: "*Ausculta novellas, Sanctissime Pater, quas ego, nuntius indignus, habeo tibi dicendas...*"

A Franciscan friar had come into the hall, darting scandalized glances at the "demonic" orgy, and had just knelt down beside Geronimo's chair. He spoke for a few minutes in Latin, in a low voice, and then retired as discreetly as he had come.

The new pope sat there frowning, his mouth twisted bitterly, the red of his face tending to violet.

"But you're exploding like a 420, old chap!" said the major. "What's up? What did the priest say to you?"

"He told me," Geronimo stammered, "that Tortorado...is going to have me killed...while I'm in the pulpit, shortly, at vespers."

"A bizarre coincidence!" remarked de Lanselles. "One might think that he has some suspicion of what you're going to say."

"He knows, the filthy swine!" exclaimed Geronimo, with a gesture so abrupt that his pipe fell on to the mosaic floor and broke. "He knows—he knows that I'm going to decree the suppression of the Inquisition. Founded by a pope, it requires a pope to abolish it. I only agreed to be pope in order to do that, anyway. Yes, Tortorado knows—he knows everything. He knows what we're saying at this very moment."

"You're exaggerating," Renard said, in his turn. "We've only talked about your plans among ourselves. Who could have reported it to him? And as for danger—we can answer for the Holy Father, can't we, Etcheverry?"

"I'll have the pulpit guarded by a cordon of troopers, Lieutenant. And I'll disperse police throughout the cathedral.

Geronimo shrugged his shoulders, brandishing the debris of his pipe. "You don't know them, Citizens, the dogs of the Inquisition. If I go up to the pulpit, they'll have me; it's as definite as the lines of a musical score."

"Then don't go up," the major cut in. "No one's forcing you, Jerome!"

"Except my duty! And Progress! And Liberty!"

The General Staff looked at him, embarrassed.

"Gentlemen," hazarded Dupuy, "if you'll permit, I think I have an answer. His Holiness can make his speech without going up to the pulpit personally."

"From the choir, then?" said the new pope, dubiously. "People won't be able to hear me."

"From the pulpit. Very Holy Father! But without moving from the choir, while remaining in our midst. We'll be able to protect you."

"How do you expect him to speak from the pulpit without moving from the choir?" asked Renard. "Have you a telephonic loud-speaker you can lend him?"

"No, Monsieur Renard—but there's a phonograph in the infirmary."

"Good idea!"

"Bravo!"

"He's found it!"

"Eureka!" exclaimed the monk.

Within five minutes, the apparatus was there, with a virgin disk and the recording stylus in place, in front of the orator, who collected himself. All the *poilus*, interested by the experiment, had turned toward the high table.

"A little hush, if you please!" shouted de Lanselles. "Over to you, Holy Father—speak into the microphone." He switched on the machine, and Geronimo commenced, in a vehement voice: "*Hermanos mios! Desde muy años. El tribunal de la abhorada Inquisicion ha hecho mas victimas...*"

"Pass me the Benedictine!" Thévenard cut in, addressing himself to Lénac.

"*...que las guerras, pestas, y uraganos. En cuanto a este animal feroz, Tortorado...*"

A loud belch, from an unknown source, inscribed itself like a punctuation mark on the disk, but Geronimo did not pause. He continued to address his vengeful tirade to an imaginary audience, punctuated by various noises and drink-induced remarks in spite of Monocard's order. Even the major, during the final excommunication, amused himself by launching a few solid Spanish oaths learned from his pupils into the microphone.

Renard was not pleased, and wanted to re-record the speech, but the monk refused, and Dupuy affirmed that the superfluous ornaments were scarcely audible. He changed the phonograph stylus and closed the box again, and then went to place it in the pulpit, ready for the appropriate moment.

Reassured, Geronimo resumed drinking, and lit another pipe—a briar that Jasmin had given to hm.

At five o'clock, following the program, they went out for the aerostatic ascent. Made of oiled silk by the local couturiers, inflated with the aid of the gasometer serving for the palace lighting, the yellow rotundity of the *Geronimo I* was swaying gently above the amazed crowd.

The medical orderly and ex-seminarian Paincarat, scorned by all because of his venomous slyness and cowardice, and forgotten—perhaps deliberately—in the distribution of expertise, had finally got the job, a month before, of supervising the construction of the balloon, provided that he took his place in the gondola during the ascent. Livid, but not daring to retreat under the jeers of his comrades, he followed the pilot, climbed over the wickerwork rim and, with a shout of "All away!" and to the rhythm of trumpets playing "Is there're anything to drink up there?" the balloon lifted off in the midst of crazed shouts, triumphant among the partisans—Moors, University students and factory workers—reproving among the supporters of the Inquisition.

A light north-westerly breeze pushed the aerostat toward Port-sur-Seille.

"Even if they fly over the village, there's no risk," Renard replied to an objection by the major. "Our friends the Moors have been alerted."

But the balloon was gaining altitude. It must have penetrated a violent counter-current, for after five minutes, it passed over the square again, at great speed, at a great height, heading westwards. It disappeared behind the domes of the cathedral.

"The idiots! Why haven't they opened the valve? They'll kill themselves if they come down in Spain!"

The incident caused a chill, but no one could do anything to save the two unfortunates. It was even necessary not to let the population know that anything abnormal had occurred.

On Renard's orders, the troopers went back into the palace, and took off their fantasy uniforms in order to don battle dress; then, surrounded by an armed guard, preceded and followed by Moorish police, Geronimo and his retinue went into the church and arranged themselves in the choir stalls to the left, next to the door of a hidden passage that communicated with the palace. To the right, facing them, were the Franciscans, the bishop and the clergy. In front of the choir, a dozen Moorish policemen on horseback—in order to be able to fire from higher up—took up their positions, clubs in hand and a bag of grenades slung over the shoulder. Twenty more were hidden in the nave, among the dense crowd. At the foot of the pulpit—a white marble platform supported by giant gilded cherubim, on which the loudspeaker of the phonograph was glittering—four *poilus* were on guard, with fitted bayonets.

No manifestation troubled the beginning of the service celebrated by the bishop. Orders had been given, and in the nave, partisans and adversaries were measuring one another with their gazes, awaiting the new pope's speech. But when a Franciscan announced that His Holiness, afflicted by a sudden paralysis of the vocal cords, would harangue the faithful from the pulpit through the intermediary of angels, and not in person, the assembly became restless.

When the loudspeaker of the phonograph began to speak, with the distorted but recognizable voice of Geronimo, there was amazement to begin with. Everyone looked at one another, terrified. When the bacchic utterances, the belches and the doctor's interjections and the footsteps of the barefoot slave-girls—all the noises of the feast, pitilessly recorded—were mingled, like an entire demonic choir, with the fulminations against Tortorado and his allies; and when the *poilus* in the choir, unable to contain themselves at these reminders of merriment, started laughing out loud; panic took hold of the people, who ran for the doors.

The doors, however, were guarded by Moorish police. In the milling crowd, trampled women howled. One even began to give birth in terror, and her crazed neighbors angrily stamped the child of Hell to death. The phonograph was still declaiming over the indescribable tumult.

Suddenly, a Dominican appeared on the choirmaster's podium: the notary Alvarez himself—who boldly launched an anathema against the sacrilegious pope. Then, in a surge of madness, a riot broke out.

The Geronimist students grouped around the pulpit took the offensive, and fell with shortened arms upon the Tortoradists. Nothing could be seen but raised fists, and the sonorous vessel of stone filled with vociferations and frantic howling. Under the impulsion of unknown hands, the bells started ringing and the tocsin burst forth. From the choir, trumpets sounded the charge.

The Moorish policemen, in order to get clear, lashed out randomly with their clubs; several used their grenades, and the detonations and the acrid smoke completed the pandemonium. The troopers at the pulpit drove back the assailants with rifle-butts and bayonets, and carried away the phonograph, bent low over the choir.

The French, with Geronimo, beat a retreat by means of the hidden door and went back to the palace, while the people, forcing the barricades, spread out into the square, reinforcing the townspeople who had come running in response to the tocsin. A few rounds of machine-gun fire, however, followed by a cavalry charge, soon quieted the revolt and dispersed the rioters.

By eight o'clock in the evening, order was reestablished. The Tortoradists, vanquished, had gone home. There was no longer anyone in the streets but Geronimists, who were demanding that the remainder of the program be carried out. It was decided to satisfy them. A few fountains established in front of the palace, each one provided with two nozzles, began pouring out free alcohol, in the midst of a joyful turmoil, and acclamations celebrating the new pope and the French.

The inventors of the new liqueurs had used this distribution as a means of commercial propaganda, and artistic posters, stuck above each jet of alcohol, enjoined drinkers to: "Ask for the incomparable Progressinette in all the bars," informed them that: "The only possible aperitif is Duranton Anisette," or exhorted them to "Demand the genuine Nénestine."

As an accompaniment to the dances that were immediately organized, a few films were projected on s screen erected on the façade of the cathedral. From behind the main altar Lénac had filmed a part of the scene at vespers, and had the unfortunate idea of concluding the session with that overly recent memory.

Overexcited by the new libations of the fountains, groups ran through the city streets howling the *Marseillaise*, the *Internationale* and the *Ça ira*. Doors were broken down, houses invaded and looted. It was necessary to send out the police again. All night, the bawling of drunkards, the screams of violated women and the explosions of grenades rose up toward the stars, and the cadenced tread of patrols resonated on the cobblestones.

In his room, the new pope, exhausted by the glorious day, fell asleep, his pipe in his mouth and a mug of Benedictine within arm's reach, over *Paroles d'un croyant*.[26]

---

[26] *Paroles d'un croyant* (1834; tr. as *Words of a Believer*) by the rebellious priest Robert de Lamennais is an aphoristic denunciation of the present world order, especially of monarchy and the Church's role in supporting it. Although the author was not excommunicated he was expelled from the clergy in consequence.

III. The Messengers from Toledo

Six days after the events that we have just reported, toward sunset, three individuals stopped at the door of the inn kept by Master Alfonso Escobardo on the outskirts of Valencia on the road to Toledo. It had rained during the day—for it was the end of November—and their mules, mud-stained to the withers, attested that the travelers had scarcely rested all day. Having confided their mounts to the stable-lad, they went into the main hall, after a second of hesitation at the sight of two customers—Moorish policemen—who were sat at a table drinking in the company of agreeable serving-girls, Carmencita and Rosina. Policemen though they were, attached to section three of bureau B, who had come to interrogate the innkeeper, suspected of harboring agents of Tortorado, the Moors, having completed their search without result, had allowed themselves to be offered a glass of Alicante, and then another, and were now larking about with the girls, having completely forgotten their mission. They were even chatting with scant restraint, and Master Alfonso Escobardo, while attending to his bottles and jars, was listening with interest as they talked about the actions and intentions of the "devils."

"You're well in with them, are you, you big rogue?" said Rosina tenderly. "I'll give you a kiss and you can tell me more."

They only darted a vague glance at the newcomers, whose features were hidden beneath wide-brimmed felt hats that were pulled down, and capes pulled up to their eyes.

"What would you like, my lord pilgrims?" enquired the innkeeper.

"We've come for the cheeses," replied the shortest of the three, who seemed to be the leader.

"They're ready," said Alfonso.

"That's good," the stranger concluded.

Without another word, the innkeeper went through a door with them, which he closed again carefully and bolted. After which, lighting a lantern, he took them along a corridor, then down a stairway, into a cellar cluttered with bottles and enormous jars. Moving aside an old round millstone lying on the ground, he uncovered a trapdoor, beneath which a wooden ladder plunged into darkness. He pointed to it with one hand and held out the lantern to them with the other.

"Have a good trip, my lords. My humble respect to His Paternity."

"Silence!" the leader ordered.

And the three travelers disappeared, one after another, into the tunnel. But Escobardo remarked, silently, that he only knew two of them, and that those two seemed to be keeping a close eye on the third.

"Bah!" he concluded, closing the trapdoor. "A new recruit."

In his monastic cell, with a smoking torch in his hand, Tortorado was examining with meditative attention the contents of a vast cupboard hollowed out in the thickness of the wall. There were eight Lebel rifles there, two light machine-guns, two revolvers, and a heap of grenades and cartridges—in brief, all the booty taken five months previously from Venette's unfortunate *poilus*.

Grim attention contracted the Inquisitor's hate-filled face, and his bulbous nose quivered, while he contemplated the diabolical weapons.

"He who has killed with the sword shall perish by the sword," he murmured. "The fake banknotes have begun their work of liberation. These will complete it...if someone will reveal their manipulation to us!"

In the narrow tunnel, Master Escobardo's two acquaintances marched one in front and the other behind their companion. Whenever he slowed down, the first pulled him brutally, and the second pricked him with the point of his dagger. The light of the lantern illuminated muddy pools, slime, fleeing rats, and even bones on the floor. Spiders' webs hung down from the vaults; bats took fright, brushing the travelers with their silent flight. The heavy atmosphere, saturated with a sepulchral odor, was only refreshed at long intervals, when they passed under shafts at the top of which daylight could be glimpsed, in a tangle of brambles.

The three walked for an interminable half-hour.

Three light raps on the door of the cell interrupted Tortorado's sinister reverie. Closing the cupboard, he went to open the door.

A Dominican bowed in front of him.

"The messengers from Toledo for Your Paternity," he announced—and, on a sign of assent, he introduced the mysterious travelers who had gone into Master Escobardo's cellar half an hour earlier. As soon as they were in the cell they uncovered their heads respectfully.

"It's you, Pedro...and Sanchez...good," said Tortorado. "But who's this?" And he pointed to the unknown man whom the other two had treated roughly, and who was looking at him, pale and trembling.

"I'm a faithful servant of the Church," the wretch stammered, in bad Latin. "My name is Paincarat."

Pedro interrupted. "He's one of them, Reverend Father. A demon from Valencia—one of those who fell in Toledo and whom we captured. He affects to hate his own kind. He claims to be the author of anonymous notes that Your Paternity has been received for some time."

The Inquisitor's nose quivered as he listened to the story of the balloon's catastrophic crash, which had delivered this traitor to him.

In Toledo, a procession had been organized in order to enthuse the minds of the faithful and prepare for the general crusade demanded by Tortorado against the demons of Valencia. It was the day after Geronimo's consecration. The balloon, whose pilot had been trying all night to free it from the current that was drawing it over Castille, had arrived over Toledo out of ballast and had landed just at the moment of the elevation on the temporary altar, whose candles had set fire to the envelope. The gas exploded. Of the two aeronauts, one was killed on the spot; the other—Paincarat—had fallen on an awning and had been retrieved unharmed. Because of the frightful panic accompanying the fall of the diabolical machine, the Inquisitions hirelings were able to protect the survivor from the holy fury of the crowd and lock him in the dungeons of the Holy Office, which fully intended to torture and burn the demon from Valencia.

It is certain that any other of the *poilus* of the eighth, fallen into the hands of the Inquisition, would have conducted himself properly, and would have died on the pyre mocking his executioners—but Paincarat, alone among them, was a coward, and had long been holding a grudge against his leaders and comrades. The major, the anticlerical Thévenard, had taken a dislike to him and showered him with rebukes. Renard was almost openly scornful of him. Moreover—a supreme grievance—he had been overlooked in the distribution of new grades; he alone did not have his manufacture, and it was with great difficulty that he had obtained the job of supervising the construction of the aerostat. Stupid and sectarian, incapable of any understanding of the work of civilization that Monocard and the monk were attempting, he had seen nothing but a frightful sacrilege in the battle conducted against the Inquisition, the methods of which he had always admired since his days in the seminary. The remorse of collaborating, even indirectly, in that impious work had driven him to redeem his sin in the possible measure and to send Tortorado notes in Latin in which he denounced the plans of the Blue-Helmets.

Thus, as soon as he was in the presence of the judges of Toledo, the traitor had thrown himself on his knees, had implored their clemency and recalled his secret services. In brief, he had shown himself to be so vile, so abject and so resolute in all ignominy that he had been sent to Tortorado, who would be able to make the best use of him.

The good news that Pedro and Sanchez had brought—among other items, that a royal army was being prepared to come to deliver Valencia—and the heavy bag of gold that they gave him were not as gentle a balm for the Inquisitor as the sight of Paincarat. Finally, Divine Providence had sent him the instructor necessary for the sacred battalion of resolute Dominicans that he intended to form!

He fixed the wretch with a profound and penetrating gaze, then took him to the cupboard, which he opened.

"You regret having made a pact with demons; you repent your crimes; you have decided to redeem your soul by absolute obedience to my orders? That's good. But in order for me to give you absolution and for me to snatch you from the hellfire that is ready to devour you, it is first necessary for you to show me, in the greatest detail, how these weapons are used..."

For an entire week, the medical orderly, closely watched by Pedro and Sanchez, who had orders to stab him at the first suspect gesture, trained Tortorado and eight other inquisitor in the employment of Lebels, revolvers and grenades. As for the machine guns, as one of them jammed at the first shot and the other was damaged, they were kept in reserve.

The sessions had taken place in the inferior crypt, with all openings blocked, in order that the detonations would not be heard outside, by the light of smoky torches—and once or twice, Moors of Bureau B, captured by stealth in taverns, served as targets.

At the end of the week, Tortorado judged that his men were sufficiently instructed. It was necessary, in any case, to economize with the ammunition. He told Pedro and Sanchez to thank the Inquisitor in Toledo and to take Paincarat back to him. The latter received a sealed letter, which he was told to deliver himself.

"Go, and sin no more, my son. This is your reward. It is the finest you can receive."

The wretch threw himself on the ground and kissed Tortorado's feet. The latter raised him up gently, gave him the accolade, and confided him to the care of Pedro and Sanchez.

The secret letter addressed to R. F. Esteban Segura said:

I have obtained from the bearer information pre-cious to the good of the Holy Church. Pedro and San-chez will explain how I hope soon to put an end to the demons with their own weapons. Spare him torture, therefore—but the leaven of evil persists in him; he can-not be returned to the demons without danger, and he would risk contaminating our brothers if he lived among them. For the good of his soul, therefore, and for the greater glory of the Church, have him put on to the pyre after he has been given absolution.

Clutching the precious note to his heart, dreaming of the magnificent reward that awaited him in Toledo, Paincarat meekly followed his guides into the tunnel.

IV. Attrition

The rain fell interminably for days on end, from a leaden sky: a December rain, penetrating the entirety of the old Moorish palace—so cheerful and pleasant in summer but direly uncomfortable in winter—with an icy damp. For want of chimneys, they were reduced to braziers, which were toxic and asphyxiating. Furthermore, the gas-plant broke down and they no longer had anything but candles by way of illumination, and they had run out of coal; the bunker was empty and the weekly convoy from Andalusia was already more than a week late, probably because of the waterlogged roads. The poor lighting was not the most painful restriction, however; tobacco and coffee had been totally lacking for a fortnight and their substitutes—dried lettuce leaves and roasted acorns—made no contribution to reviving the good humor of the Frenchmen.

The rain was falling, therefore, that morning. Having no desire to go to the factories—which were mostly stagnating—the melancholy troopers strolled around under the arcades of the Court of Myrtles, pausing on each circuit at the braziers smoking at the four corners. No more summer uniforms, cork helmets, espadrilles and naval costumes! The ten men of the daily guard in Port-sur-Seille or at the palace machine guns were not alone in dressing in regulation uniforms; they had all readopted blue caps, the heavy boots and steel helmets. Balaclavas and mittens made their reappearance, and sheepskins hid the insignia and decorations stitches on sleeves during the initial intoxication of the conquest.

Those triumphant illusions were far away now...the conversations reflected the mournfulness of the sky.

"Bloody hell, is it going to rain like this all the time?" complained Pilon, between two bouts of coughing. "It's worse than in the trenches. Hurrah for the war in which one can get killed!"

"There's no need for war; we'll all end up kicking the bucket here. Count up the chaps we've lost—not to mention the Moors—since we've been in the Golden Age, as the doc calls it. Twelve the time Nénesse came back all alone; Titi-la-Vache, Haricot; and then there's been Chabert, Delesalle, and I don't know who else...the five or six who weren't seen again after boat races and blow-outs with the girls..."

"That's true; there's only sixty-one of us in the company now..."

"Bah!" said Totor, in another group. "Don't go on about it. Winter only lasts a couple of weeks here. It's like in the colonies. My brother was in Tonkin; it was wet like this there, but it won't last."

"I bet it wasn't freezing there. When we were at Verdun, remember, before coming to Port-sur-Seille, what did we get? It was so cold they were handing out our wine in pieces."

"I wonder what's become of the lads in the trenches—the ones who stayed in Lorraine?"

"Doesn't matter—we're better off here. Do you want to go back there?"

"I don't know. There's real tobacco there, and real juice, not salad leaves and bits of wood...but what's lacking here most of all is furloughs. Just for twenty-four hours, to take a little trip to Montparno...to see the Rue de la Joie—I'd like that."

"You can't complain—you've got full pockets, you're rolling in gold. We've never had so much moolah."

"Yes, but with all these fake bills…another four got passed off on me yesterday…"

That same day, Major Thévenard showed Adjutant Cipriani out of his office. The latter was abashed and crestfallen.

"There's no doubt about it, my friend—you've got it. You need treatment. Do what I told you, and come back tomorrow.

Cipriani drew away, but Lénac was waiting on the landing.

"You've come for the photos," said the major. Can you imagine, that bugger Cipriani has the pox!"

"Oh! Him too?"

"You know about others, then?"

"Yes. At least one other."

"The Emir, I'll wager?"

"No, I know him better than the Emir. I believe it's me."

"Shit! Where the devil did you catch it?"

"Must be a gift from the Italian."

"Madame Casanova? Him too! Good God! What about Christopher Columbus, then? Who could have…not a Spaniard, or a Moor…no, you must have had it before."

"I swear to you that I've never had anything."

"They all say that. I want to believe you, mind—but it'll be necessary to do some research. Fortunately, there are mercury mines here! Come on, show me…"

The reader may consult *Candide* if he wants to imagine the ulterior propagation of the scourge in Valencia, where relationships between the sexes had the ingenuous facility to which the American importation put an end. As for the discovery of its origin, that took place a few days later, dramatically.

Like many others, and in spite of Renard's exhortations to prudence, Jasmin and Saucisson frequently left their beds and spent the night with the cyclist nuns, but their duties recalled them to the palace at dawn—in the brief days of December—and the hirelings of the Inquisition, informed of this particularity, took advantage of it. Lénac, returning from a party himself, found them one morning lying on the flagstones at the crossroads of the fountain. Saucisson was already cold. Jasmin was dying with his throat cut.

"I'm dying, don't go," he stammered to the photographer, who was leaning over him. "Let me confess, like the first Christians. You can pass my words on to our Holy Father..."

He confessed his sins—but suddenly, Lénac straightened up. "You...you...with the governor's wife? Oh, you thought you were cured, did you? So it's you who has contaminated...me and Cipriani, and the governor, and who knows how many more!"

But poor Jasmin was dying; nobly, Lénac forgave him."

The victims of this double murder were given funerals appropriate to their rank. The *croix de guerre* was conferred on them posthumously. Geronimo officiated, but as a state of reinforced siege had just been pronounced, as the *poilus* had taken immediate reprisals against the Valencian masses, demonstrations were held at the exit from the mass. A riot broke out, more serious than all the preceding ones. The police charged, and there were dead and wounded on both sides.

Before Jasmin and Saucisson, five or six men of the eighth had disappeared inexplicably—in the course of excursions at sea, mostly. Afterwards, as if a wind of desperate fanaticism had over the city, seven other troopers of minor rank had their throats cut in less than a week, in taverns and whorehouses. It was necessary to renounce going out alone or without an escort.

By virtue of a circumstance that was more than inconvenient, the aura of fear that surrounded the Moorish police had diminished considerably; their grenades, charged with poor quality black powder, only went off half the time, and sometimes in the hands of the grenadiers. That black powder was the sole result obtained by the munitions factory; all other efforts had failed pitifully, or had not even been attempted, and one of Renard's gravest anxieties was the shortage of ammunition. All that remained in the palace were a few machine-gun strips and three thousand cartridges—and as many more in Port-sur-Seille, where the guard redoubled its vigilance.

The rumor soon went around that the convoy from Andalusia, awaited in vain for a fortnight, had been attacked by considerable Spanish forces, the merchandise stolen, the truck and motor-cycle burned, and the Moors of the escort massacred, along with three troopers, including the motorcyclist Vidal.

The news was all too true; a cavalry reconnaissance confirmed it, and also reported that the Spaniards remained camped in large numbers on the sides of the road. To dislodge them would require a serious operation, which the execrable winter weather required to be postponed. Communications therefore remained cut off, and the isolation in which the Frenchmen and Abdul Khan's Moors found themselves henceforth augmented the discouragement in the palace and redoubled the audacity of the Tortoradists in the city.

Deprived of raw materials, the half a dozen factories that were still functioning were closed down; only the alcohol factory remained. In the course of recent weeks it had attracted the majority of the directors, disappointed in their hopes of unlimited profits. The financial success of the liquor-manufacturers excited competition, and everyone strove to invent a new product endowed with a prestigious name. Lénac's poster business boomed, and he could not keep up with demand.

In the city, riots and skirmishes multiplied. The people rendered unemployed by the factories, who had been conclusively laid off, were organized into gangs subsidized by the Inquisition, and became the most determined adversaries of the Blue-Helmets. High food prices, and the looting in which the Mors and *poilus* were indulging again, completed the indisposition of the rest of the population. The *Liberté-Libertad*'s propaganda was increasingly impotent to combat Tortotado's occult opposition. The false banknotes multiplied with fantastic rapidity. The newly rich, half the students and the distillery workers, numbering four hundred and fifty, were soon virtually the only defenders of the new regime.

To complete the misfortune, the pro-Stranger party, whose strength had previously frightened even Tortorado, broke up into political sects—humanitarians, socialists and anarchists—at odds with one another. Geronimo, the apostle of Progress, was bitterly disappointed, and his partial responsibility for the disarray completed his demoralization. He was as angry as a hen that has hatched ducks' eggs to find his pupils becoming enemy brothers, proselytes held up in various phases of the progressivist evolution that he had traversed like a meteor and surpassed successively. Poor great man! The increasingly clear mistrust, the half-confessed hostility that he encountered in the bosom of his Order—the Order that he had raised so high by virtue of the abasement of the Dominicans!—ended up making him doubt everything, even religion. He abandoned socialism for the anarchism of Elisée Reclus and Sébastien Faure. He had just discovered Nietzsche, and regretted only having in his library a single volume of his *Selected Works*.

The major's disappointments were no less. Seduced by the ease of assimilation of his Moorish pupils, he had galloped ahead and led them with drums beating. Amazed by the revelations of anatomy, the young students had taken to carving and stitching with increasing boldness. Several times, the doctor was obliged to intervene and repair the mistakes of the apprentice surgeons. In spite of that, he had the temerity to give them a lecture on animal grafting and the work of Alexis Carrel.

He had been back in the palace for two hours and was playing cards with Dupuy and Lénac, waiting for the Emir, when his laboratory assistant irrupted into the room in panic. The experiment, although carried out according to his indications, had not succeeded; the hemorrhage had not stopped...

Thévenard was alarmed by his inference, and ran to the University at the double, in spite of his paunch—which had increased significantly. Horror! He had guessed only too well. The students, jealous of Carrel's laurels, had embarked upon a super-graft. Enthusiastically, hoping for marvelous results of such a hybridization, which would realize Geronimo's long-term educational utopias immediately, they had taken two Moors who were being treated in the clinic for minor wounds, and two Spaniards, one of whom had had a recent operation for appendicitis, and, slicing through their necks—*secundem artem*,[27] and with the requisite antiseptic precautions—had attempted to suture the Spanish heads on the Moorish bodies, and *vice versa.*

"Oh, the little rascals!" the major repeated, nonplussed, and foreseeing the capital that the Tortoradists would extract from that scientific sabotage.

Henceforth, he renounced instructing his students, went to the University less and less and spent the greater part of his time with the Emir. The latter caused him a great deal of anxiety, for his narcotic use had brought him to death's door. The ether, cocaine and laudanum having run out, he had confined himself to chloroform, and there was no means of stopping him. In response to a refusal by the major, he had nearly run him through with his scimitar; then he had begged, offering him the free disposition of his harem.

And he's big enough to take care of himself, damn it, Thévenard thought.

He made use of the harem and ceased remonstrating.

As for Renard, he was eaten away by cares and anxieties. Two new developments that further aggravated the situation, already severely compromised, ended up depriving him of sleep.

For some time, the aviator had been giving unequivocal signs of mental derangement. Since Renard had put the brake on his excursions of platonic conquest by means of little Union Jacks, he had remained perpetually angry, and it was difficult to persuade him to undertake authentic reconnaissance flights—a service all the more

---

[27] In the accepted manner.

necessary because of the major troop movements taking place in the vicinity of Toledo. He lost his temper and hurled the contents of his glass of progressinette in the lieutenant's face when he was held responsible for the loss of the Andalusian convoy, which effectively resulted from his neglecting to fly over the route in advance. He was put in irons for two days.

One morning, having given the slip to Etcheverry, who had been commissioned to accompany him in the air and to furnish him with the alcohol required by the aircraft, he took off without warning, with two choirboys to whom he was supposed to be teaching English. He was never see again, and the Emir reported that he had offered to take him "to heaven" with his little passengers.

The Emir's death, caused by an excessive inhalation of chloroform, had consequences that were just as grave and more immediate. The question of succession gave rise to battles and massacres in the Moorish palace, between the partisans of his multiple offspring, legitimate and natural, and those of the collateral branch. The rupture of communications with Cordova, prevented them from obtaining the advice of the Caliph, who would have cut the dispute short, and Renard could not intervene in a problem of internal politics. The regent finally elected by the army was a young Islamic fanatic. Conflicts were immediately produced between him and the General Staff, and it became impossible to count on the Moors in case of need. Even the police relaxed their control considerably.

That was tested when an operation was decided against the Convent of the Incarnation, that hotbed of revolt and false money, which Geronimo never ceased to denounce. Three *poilus* who had ventured in had not returned. The Moors refused to venture into the lair. The secret exits having remained undiscoverable, as well as the subterranean floor whose existence was certain, it was decided to blow up the entire building. Two tons of black powder were taken inside, and policemen charged with digging a hole for the mine. Avoiding the surveillance of Cipriani—considerably weakened by his disease and the intensive mercury treatment—the faint-hearted Moors thought they could see a ready-dug mine-hole in the gaping orifice of a conduit that slanted beneath the walls of the convent, and placed the explosive there. The conduit ended in a cistern. It rained. The mine fizzled out.

Renard sensed that this ridiculous error was heaven's final warning—something akin to the "prodigies" in which the Ancients recognized the precursory signs of the fall of Empires. An atmosphere of menace and imminent catastrophe enveloped the land. The men of the eighth were murmuring, having observed that thirty-one out of the original eighty had perished since the timeslip. The General Staff themselves, except for Monocard and the monk, no longer believed even in the partial success of their fine humanitarian projects. Far from having been able to extend beyond Valencia a domination that they had thought at first was destined to subjugate Spain and the world, they sensed that their last partisans were tightly grouped around them.

Several of the newly rich had left the city with their hoards, in solid gold, attempting to reach Andalusia in order to shelter themselves from the reprisals that the Inquisition would not fail to exact, when it returned to power. There were smiles among the hidalgos as they passed on news in whispers; the priests were announcing openly that all the Blue-Helmets would perish within a week. One morning, the governor, having been summoned to the palace, did not come; he had left the city during the night.

Renard saw that departure as an exceedingly ominous sign. He resolved to speak out.

It was an evening at the end of December. Jasmin's successor, the new Chief Cupbearer, sorry to have been taken away from the alcohol factory and its profits, fulfilled his duties reluctantly. He had let the provisions of wine run out, and they would have had none, but for Myriam. That daily visitor to the palace, informed of the difficulty—as of everything else that happened; she was a member of the family—remembered that her father Melchisedech possessed, in a suburb of Valencia, a highly-reputed winery—famed for the 1338 vintage, in particular. Specimens were sampled, and the deal was concluded. The barrels had just arrived at the palace for bottling. The new wine—the Melchisedech plonk, as the major had baptized it—was to be drunk for the first time that evening.

Toward the end of the diner, when the decoction of roasted acorns that was such a poor replacement for coffee was served and the most hardened smokers had stuffed their pipes with the infamous leaves of the lettuce known as "Valencia tobacco," and lit up disgustedly, Renard took the floor.

"Gentlemen," he began, addressing de Lanselles, Thévenard, Geronimo, Etcheverry, Dupuy and Lénac, "I don't think, if you agree with me that we'll be drinking Melchisedech plonk for long...at least in this palace. I think the time has come to submit to the inevitable. There's no need to tell you that things can't go on any longer. We're short of ammunition, our factories have stopped, the reverend fathers are inundating us with

forged currency, the Moorish police are no longer reliable, our troopers are discontented, and alcohol is insufficient to maintain our dominant prestige. Progress is an
admirable thing, but it can only be realized in a propi-
tious atmosphere, in its own time. And the civilization of
the 20th century, which we have the honor of
representing, certainly seems to be incompatible with
that of the fourteenth, into which we have intruded. In
other words, it's time to go back to the Lorraine front."

"My God," said the major, "we haven't been bored
here, but I agree with you, Renard: these harem ladies
and Myriam's little friends become monotonous in the
end, and I wouldn't be displeased to get back to my
chick in Landremont."

"You're not going to abandon me!" cried Geronimo, raising his arms to the heavens.

According to Monocard, the situation, without being brilliant, was not desperate. Should they allow themselves to be put off by a few temporary snags? Ought
they not, on the contrary, to stick to the task, to devote
all their energy to it?

"Whatever you decide," he concluded, "my resolution was made a long time ago. I've interrogated my
conscience, and it has dictated my highest duty. My battalion of *Saint-Cyriens* has more than confidence in me.
I dare to say that it's hero-worship. A part of the population is ready to march with us. Go on, go—and take your
poilus with you. The manufacture of alcohol will
cease—so much the better. And the debauchery, and the
mercantile traffic. All of that has held back our
progress...

"Yes, go! Me, I'll stay with the Holy Father, that
noble apostle of Freethought! We'll do our duty until the
end—all of our duty! And if, some day, having returned

to the century which has enough enlightened men without you, you change your minds and think about the marvelous task that you might have accomplished here with a little perseverance—well, come back! Come back with specialists, munitions, books above all, good books! I'll welcome you as brothers, without rancor."

The monk spoke in the same vein, and asked for the complete works of Nietzsche. It was impossible to make any impression on the two of them; they were committed.

Renard put the motion to the vote. The departure was decided, by five votes to two—within the week, in principle. The exact date would be fixed according to circumstances.

De Lanselles, offended by a slightly lively riposte from Renard, got up, threw down his napkin, and refused to sleep under the same roof as "the deserters of Progress." He went to join his students at the University.

The monk remained in the palace, but also went up to his bedroom, in spite of the major's amicable nudges.

When they had gone, Renard admitted that, in anticipation of the departure, He had already ordered preparations to be made for the relocation.

"In addition," he said, as enemy galleons are gathering off the coast, and seem to be threatening a disembarkation, I've doubled the guard in Port-sur-Seille. We now have five hundred Moors and fifteen *poilus* there. Here, in that matter, a sign of the times: Nénesse, whom I ordered over there this evening, replied insolently, and I had to threaten him with a week in the slammer..."

It was eight o'clock. Myriam arrived with her companions. They were welcomed, all the more so because, beneath their capes, they were dressed as bayaderes. The major, who was pouring a round of the new wine, offered them a glass. Myriam refused, on behalf of them all; it would have slowed down their dance.

"Give some to the poor *poilus* instead," she suggested.

They could hear the men singing and the strains of the accordion downstairs. By way of condescension to Myriam's desire, twenty bottles were sent down to them.

The tambourines and castanets struck up a prelude. The dancers, dressed in gauze sashes, launched themselves forth, whirling...

"And to think," Dupuy sighed in Etcheverry's ear, "that perhaps we'll be in Lorraine tomorrow, at Port-sur-Seille!"

"To Myriam's health!" the major proposed, filling the glasses. "A true nectar, this little Melchisedech!"

V. The Return of the Holy Office

Renard awoke. But open his eyes or make a movement…no, not yet! The slumber that had just cradled him in its unfathomable depths left him with a strange physical numbness, sweet to savor before the return of lucidity. He was initially conscious of piercing headache, an abominable dryness in the throat and a vague but all too familiar sick feeling.

"What a hangover!"

And, in an instant, it all came back to him: the deliberation of the General Staff, the decision to return to the front made in principle, in spite of the defection of Monocard and the monk; the evening of libations with Myriam and her little friends…

What an abominable hangover, indeed! He had drunk too much. Drunk too much? But no…somewhat less than the others…

The torpor that was making his thoughts sticky was dissipating. What were those noises, those cries, those clamors? Was the party still going on? And this ultrahard bed? The floor of the Lion Hall?

Overcoming the crushing listlessness, he made his first gesture, to stretch himself. Resistance, pain in his wrists, metallic cold…what the…?

He opened his eyes, and uttered a hoarse cry.

In chains! On the bare stone floor of a cell, with Dupuy, Lénac, Etcheverry and the major, lying inert—perhaps dead!

And the shouting—there was a crowd outside, glimpsed through the barred skylight, around a pile of wood…a pyre surmounted by a huge green cross…the pyre of the Inquisition!

With all his might, he called out to his companions.

One after another, they opened vague eyes.

"What?" said Thévenard, stupidly. "Good God! This is it! We've been caught!"

"What about the mates?" moaned Dupuy.

"In another cell, evidently," said Renard. "Who can save us, then?"

"Myriam, damn it!" roared Thévenard. "The little cow! It wasn't for nothing that she bragged to us about her father's wine, that vile Melchisedech plonk!"

The major was not mistaken. It was, indeed, Myriam's treason that had facilitated the success of the plan worked out by Tortorado, in collaboration with his friend Segura. The Blue-Helmets no longer having an airborne spy, since the loss of the aircraft, the Castilian army had been able to arrive from Toledo, by means of a forced march, in three days. The day before, it had camped in the woods four kilometers from Valencia. At eleven o'clock in the evening, Myriam had come to tell the Inquisitor that the drugged wine had taken effect, and that the entire General Staff, as well as all the *poilus* except those on guard, had been plunged into sleep.

Poison would have been more radical, but the politics of the Holy Office demanded that the greatest possible number of "demons" be taken alive.

The dozen *poilus* who had sent the night at the convent of Santa Cruz had already been massacred, along with the Moorish sentinels at the gates of the ramparts. The Castilian troops entered the city, cheered by the population. In five minutes, in spite of a salvo from the machine-guns, whose servants had escaped the drugged wine, the palace was invaded and all the Frenchmen captured in their sleep. The Moorish police, crushed by the weight of numbers, had only put up token resistance. All the cavalrymen were killed on the spot, along with the new Emir and his concubines. In the city, an enormous sweep delivered into the hands of the Holy Office the distillery workers, the profiteers of the occupation, the Jews and all those who had allied themselves with the strangers. Monocard, assisted by his sacred battalion, had taken refuge in the attics of the University, where they had held out until daylight.

A detachment of five hundred men, sent to attack Port-sur-Seille, was repelled with heavy losses, but as they retreated southwards, the Moorish cavalry had abandoned their French allies in order to reoccupy their former camp. Only the fifteen *poilus* remained to watch from the advance posts, listening from afar to the tocsin and the crazy tumult that was rising up in Valencia, horribly anxious about the fate of their comrades, who were not responding to radio calls.

All night long the populace had pillaged the homes of the profiteers, set fire to the factories, plundered the alcohol plant and smashed the stills. The army was obliged to put out the fires, which had spread.

Tortorado's first concern, as soon as he was master of the city, was to retake possession of the palace and the treasures that the demons had accumulated with so much foresight in the Inquisition's own coffers, which would make it richer than ever. Dominicans, notaries, clerks and hirelings—the entire personnel of the Holy Office—was triumphantly reinstalled, and after a rapid provisory exorcism and purification, all of the rooms and courtyards sullied for six months by the presence of the Blue-Helmets and their infamous orgies recovered their pious purposes, from the Grand Inquisitor's cell to the torture-chamber and the dungeons.

In spite of their number and capacity, the latter were overflowing, and it was necessary literally to pile up some of the multitude of captives. The newly rich and the students and the factory-workers occupied the four upper floors of the prison tower next to the torture chamber. Down below, in the crypt, the thirty-four *poilus*—still plunged into the comatose sleep induced by the drugged wine, which they had drunk in much greater abundance than the members of the General Staff—had been thrown pell-mell. The latter, carefully separated according to Myriam's indications, were on the ground floor of the Palace, in a cell situated directly beneath the Tribunal Hall.

Through the barred window they were able to witness the first burnings of the monstrous auto-da-fé that would take all day, as the sentences were pronounced. For Geronimo the Antipope, the sacrilegious and apostate monk, no simulation of a trial was necessary. He had been outside the law for a long time. He was executed at eight o'clock in the morning, to the roaring cheers of a delirious crowd swarming in the square, on the terraces and in windows, all the way to the highest galleries and domes of the cathedral.

Placed on a vast pyre of pine-wood, sprinkled with alcohol and constructed, with delicate attention, within view of the prisoners on the ground floor, were, firstly, the cadavers of the machine-gunners killed at their weapons and the *poilus* slaughtered in the nunnery—fourteen in all. One by one they were secured upright, dressed in their uniforms, against stakes bearing the label: DEMON. Then, in the middle of this macabre display, at a higher level, was Geronimo, in a sulfur-dusted chemise and tiara. His label read: ANTIPOPE AND ACCOMPLICE OF DEMONS.

He was still somnolent, and paraded his stupefied gaze over the multitude stamping their feet on the ground and on the balconies of the palace, where the entire personnel of the Holy Office was enjoying its vengeance. The lugubrious psalmody of the ritual maledictions rose up, followed by the anathema launched by Tortorado.

At the voice of his enemy, the unfortunate antipope woke up. Comprehension of the unexpected disaster in which his magnificent hopes were sinking shot through him. And in the formidable clamor that rose from the crowd at the moment when the executioner set fire— ironically, with the aid of a kerosene lighter—to the faggots of the pyre, he recognized the eternal hue and cry with which the vulgar and stupid herd condemn geniuses and the masters of thought. He gazed bitterly, and with infinite sadness, at the society that he had attempted to save, and his head fell back on to his breast.

The roaring flames of the immense alcohol-soaked pyre shot up; they enveloped him. Suddenly, dominating their roar, in the restless silence of the crowd, breathless with joy, a supreme cry of revolt sprang from the hectic flames, directed by the victim at the better future, at his naïve and radiant utopia:

"Down with the Clergy! Long live Anarchism!"

In their cell, the prisoners had watched the auto-da-fé, chilled with horror. Not one thought of smiling at the grotesquerie of Geronimo's appeal. They perceived its sublimity, and remained mute and trembling while the crowd roared and the flames rose into the sky.

"Poor old Jerome! He was a bit crazy, but he toughed it out to the end," remarked Thévenard, with a tear in his eye.

"Did you recognize de Lanselles among the cadavers?" Renard asked.

No one had seen him. Nothing but the cadavers of simple troopers.

"So much the better. He might have escaped with his battalion of students. Who knows whether he might try to rescue us?"

"Let's hope so—but he hasn't much chance of success. We'll be roasted like the old man, that's obvious."

With that first execution under way, Tortorado and his assessors went back to the Tribunal Hall to prepare for the next burnings. The merchants and other accomplices of the Demons, taken from prison one by one, were subjected to a summary interrogation before being thrown on the pyre that was consuming Geronimo and the fourteen corpses, which was fed in the meantime by pine logs and alcohol. The thirty-four *poilus* piled up in the subterranean dungeon were still asleep; they were being saved for a *bonne bouche*. As for the leaders of the General Staff, there would be time to confront them with certain profiteers—Melchisedech, for example.

They were only waiting, before summoning him to appear, for the arrival at the palace of certain items found during the night in the home of the Licensed Victualler in the course of the domiciliary visit. One of the items, probably of capital importance for the trial of the Demons, was also of considerable material weight, and a crew of twenty robust hirelings took nearly two hours to effect its transportation into the vestibule of the palace. According to the express denunciation of Myriam, an unnatural daughter, the object in question was nothing less than the secret treasure of the Blue-Helmets.

Some six weeks earlier, the Allies' Licensed Victualler, on gong to Port-sur-Seille with two carts of foodstuffs and straw intended for the garrison, had noticed the singular object in an unmanned shed. A cylinder as tall as a ten-year-old child and as broad as his head, the lower two-thirds made of copper, it was terminated by a tapered top of polished steel that seemed to form a lid. The considerable weight of the implement—which was evidently hollow—was judged by Melchisedech to be evidence that it was an important treasure, perhaps the strong-box of the monopolists of gold and silver.

The fact of its being thus abandoned to public view was, according to the cunning miser, a trick on the part of the Blue-Helmets. They imagined that no one would take it, he thought. And as the *poilus* of the guard, used to the old Jew's foraging, let him come and go freely, he was able to take possession of the mysterious object with the aid of his acolytes, hoist it on to a cart and take it away, hidden under straw, to his house in Valencia.

Once there, he made no attempt to open it. His possessive mania was satisfied. He limited himself to going to visit the treasure every evening in the hiding-place to which he had relegated it. Myriam discovered it there in her turn, and recognized it as a Blue-Helmet object. Insidiously, she interrogated her father—who, sure of his hiding-place, swore by the horns of Moses that he had never possessed anything of the sort. Piqued to the quick, she had not hesitated to denounce the stolen goods in one of her reports to Tortorado. As soon as the Blue-Helmets were defeated and Melchisedech was under lock and key, Tortorado had given the order to fetch the object.

The treasure hidden by the Licensed Victualler had finally arrived, on the stroke of ten o'clock, in the ante-chamber of the palace. Tortorado came to cast a glance over it, and attempted to open it. He had to give up, but his conviction was confirmed that there was a secret involved of some importance to the trial of the demons. He resolved to interrogate Melchisedech.

The Spanish army, with the entire population of the city, continued to applaud the successive burnings of the merchants thrown on to the fire one by one as they were sentenced. At first the alcohol had produced a superb and vigorous flame, but, one jar having exploded in the hand of a maladroit aide, they ceased to spread it; the fire became redder and the last few victims did not burn as well. The people of Valencia became impatient. The auto-da-fé of Geronimo and the French cadavers had given them an appetite; at the sight of each new victim cries of disappointment went up. It was the Demons they wanted to see perish, without further delay. In certain groups, people were beginning to talk once again about their omnipotence.

"You'll see," said one old fisherman in a red bonnet, squeezed between the peasant at the entrance to the street running alongside the palace. "You'll see that, at the last moment, they'll escape. The Vampire will come back in the air, and launch thunder to save them."

"But they're in chains, I tell you. I saw them being carried into the dungeon; they were asleep."

"They were pretending. It's a ruse in order to find out who their friends are. Their vengeance will be terrible. Remember..."

That anxiety, fuelled by sharp memories, found echoes almost everywhere...

In the torture chamber, the Grand Inquisitor, assisted by Alvarez, the torturer and some hirelings, proceeded with the interrogation of Melchisedech.

The Licensed Victualler was stripped of his clothing and attached by his wrists to a pulley in the vault. A clever system of bondage prevented him from bending his legs. A brazier full of burning coals was placed under his feet.

"You have stolen the Demons' strong-box?"

The unfortunate confessed.

"What does it contain?"

"I don't know."

A lie, evidently! The rope grated on its pulley and Melchisedech, lowed by a notch, touched the coals with his feet. A frightful odor of grilled flesh, which Tortorado breathed in with a quivering nose, spread through the room.

"Confess," the inquisitor resumed. "There are secret documents?"

"I confess!" Melchisedech replied, very rapidly, howling in pain. "Yes, yes—secret documents!"

"Would you care to open the coffer?"

"Yes, yes, I'll open it—but let me go, for pity's sake!"

"That's good," said Tortorado. "Suspend the questioning. Take the accused into the vestibule, so that he can open the coffer. Give him a hammer and a chisel. The Demon leaders have been unchained, have they not? Bring them here as soon as the Jew has opened the coffer, for the confrontation."

The orders were carried out. Two minutes later, the sound of hammer-blows on metal began to be heard. Melchisedech, the Licensed Victualler, was doing battle with the detonator of the 220mm shell...

VI. At Top Speed

In their dungeon, the prisoners of the General Staff were indulging in pessimistic comments. Four guards, armed to the teeth, had just unchained them, and were watching them while waiting for orders.

"This is to put us to the torture. What are they going to use?" groaned Dupuy, rubbing his aching wrists and ankles.

Etcheverry addressed the question to the guards, but they contented themselves with sniggering and spitting scornfully.

"Me, I think I might prefer to be burned right away, like the old man," Lénac opined.

"They might at least give us something to drink!" the major exclaimed. "I've never had such a thirst. And a stomach-ache to boot. It's an infection, this! Oh, the swine, the swine! What did they use as a narcotic to knock us out? Henbane? Belladonna? Opium?"

Lénac began to speculate as to the probable varieties of torture that awaited them; the rack, water, the pincers, splinters under the fingernails, molten lead...

"I've also heard mention of a little bath in boiling oil. Do you think one can survive that, Doctor?"

"It's driving me mad. I've got a belly-ache, that's all I know. Too bad—I have to relieve myself!" And he retired to a corner to pull his trousers down.

"Tell me, Doctor," said Lénac, following his train of thought, "what about twisting the testicles—is that very dangerous?"

Renard intervened: "Enough, Lénac—you're boring us with your stories. Let it go. We'll soon see..."

But he did not finish. The thunderclap of a mighty explosion close at hand threw all five of them into the air, opening a flaming crater in the wall. Stones tumbled from the vault; the entire palace seemed to be collapsing...

In the acrid yellow asphyxia, a gaping breach appeared—and behind it, daylight, and liberty! Still stunned by the blast, but alive and almost intact, the five prisoners pulled themselves together. Of the jailers, only one was lying under a section of masonry, crushed. The other three staggered to their feet—but Etcheverry, Renard and Dupuy launched themselves upon them, hitting them with bricks. Then their arms were distributed: daggers and halberds.

Outside, heavy smoke was stagnating over the rubble, from which groans and cries for help in Spanish rose.

Renard hesitated momentarily. "What about Monocard? It's him who's come to our rescue! Perhaps he's still under that, a victim of his devotion!"

"We can't hear him, at any rate," the doctor retorted, pulling his trousers up again as best he could. "This isn't the moment for pity. There's the street—it's a matter of getting through. Let's go!"

"At top speed." Dupuy put in, stumbling over the debris of the corner tower. "To the Machine!"

"We'll never get to Port-sur-Seille!" moaned Lénac.

"God, I'm thirsty!" croaked Etcheverry.

"Go, go!" Renard repeated, taking the lead.

In the frightful disarray that followed the explosion of the shell—whether provoked by a Jew's hammer or not, the explosion of a 220mm makes a lot of noise and packs quite a punch—no one dreamed of trying to stop them. The entire Castilian army was in the cathedral square watching the execution of the newly rich with the people. In the street into which the escapees emerged there were only peasants who had arrived too late to get a good position, and who had been occupied at the moment of the explosion in discussing the chances that the Demons had of getting out of it.

"There they are! I told you they were all-powerful!" cried the old fisherman in the red bonnet, on seeing the five Frenchmen appear, daggers and halberds in hand. "Their spells have brought down the walls. Every man for himself! They'll blast us with thunderbolts!"

The women were already running away, screaming; the rest, gripped by terror, piled into the side-streets. The way was clear, and the Blue-Helmets passed by. At the crossroads of the fountain they stopped for ten seconds to drink, then ran into the street of the Puerta del Sol. It was swept clear by the same panic. At the gate, two sentinels opposed them with their pikes. They were knocked down—but poor Etcheverry fell too, his heart transpierced.

"Dead!" the major diagnosed, at a glance.

The fugitives, now only four in number, left the city. The plain lay before them, deserted—and a league away, on the tower of Port-sur-Seille, the tricolor flag was flying.

"They're holding firm over there!" said Renard. "Courage! They can see us—they'll help us."

"Oh, my asthma," wheezed the major, still feeling the effects of the wine. "I'm going to throw up."

"Get a move on, doctor—hurry up!"

Dupuy and Renard each took one of his arms and dragged him at a run. Lénac followed, groaning.

In the distance—the far distance—was the Machine, their salvation. An enormous tumult went up in the town behind them, but no one was pursuing them—yet.

They gained ground...

In the Tribunal Hall, Tortorado, thrown to the ground by the blast, was the first to get to his feet, covered in plaster. He was grinding his teeth, epileptically, foaming at the mouth at that supreme revolt of Hell. In the midst of the smoke, he called out to his colleagues in a thunderous voice.

"To arms, the sacred battalion! Rally at the Arsenal!"

Grabbing his own Browning and his bag of grenades, he strode out of the room. Outside, however, there as a void: the staircase had disappeared. The prison tower, adjacent to the vestibule, had collapsed *en bloc*, and from the mass of rubble emerged groans, croaks and cries of distress—but not one of them in French. Death had been merciful to the thirty-four *poilus* in the subterranean dungeon, all crushed in their narcotic slumber, perhaps in the middle of blissful dreams!

Tortorado leaned over the gaping gap, and his vile nose quivered. "Finish them!" he ordered the hirelings who were arriving behind him. "Pour boiling oil into the fissures." But there were none below but the ordinary Blue-Helmets. The leaders, lodged elsewhere, perhaps having more powerful spells at their disposal...what had become of them?

The Inquisitor went back through the Tribunal Hall, found the other stairway intact, and joined the six Dominicans assembled in the Arsenal, rifles shouldered and cartridge-belts buckle over their habits.

"Where are the other two?"

"Dead, Reverendissimo."

"The idiots! Follow me!"

He took them to the General Staff's dungeon. The sight of the breach and the halberdiers' cadavers drew a frightful blasphemy from him. He grabbed a stupefied hireling who was contemplating the effects of the explosion and shook him ferociously.

"The Demon leaders—where are they? Speak!"

"They've gone, Reverendissimo."

"And you didn't stop them, wretch? Die, then!"

Foaming at the mouth, Tortorado aimed his pistol at the man and fired; then, stepping over the cadaver, he launched his militiamen through the breach into the street.

There, it took several minutes to disentangle the truth from the exclamations and fantastic tales of the peasants. According to some, the five demons had vanished into thin air; according to others, they had projected flames from their eyes and mouths. Two Castilian soldiers, who had arrived from the square, had seen nothing...thus, the fugitives had gone in the direction of the fountain.

Drunk with fury, Tortorado lost another ten minutes; he went down the street as far as the Puerta del Sol. On discovering the corpses of the two sentinels and that of the adjutant, he finally understood...

There was a further delay, in order to return to the cathedral square and choose fifty horsemen from among the people and soldiers filling it. Six of them took the armed Reverend Fathers up on to the rumps of their mounts. Tortorado leapt on to a horse, and the pursuit began.

On the plain, beneath the lukewarm winter sun, there was no one to be seen, but the fugitives could only find refuge in Port-sur-Seille. The Inquisitor, at the head of the troop, galloped straight for the tower.

"There they are! There they are!"

Between the bushes of Barbary figs in the distance, they perceived the four men. They only had five hundred meters to cover, and at the entrance to the village, a dozen *poilus* were running over the bridge, coming to met them...

"Fire! Fire!" howled Tortorado.

Awkwardly, the inexperienced Dominican fusiliers, on the rumps of their horses, shouldered arms and fired—but the discharge had no effect. They were too far away—six hundred meters. Furthermore, the horses, frightened by the detonations, scattered, and it was necessary to bring them back.

The gallop continued...

Out of breath and exhausted, Renard, the major, Dupuy and Lénac ran toward the footbridge, while announcing the catastrophe, in the scraps of halting sentences, to the men of the guard that Nénesse was bringing to them *en masse*, by virtue of an uncomprehending solicitude.

"They have firearms!" Renard gasped. "You'd have done better to pick them off without moving from cover."

"I saw that you were all in, Lieutenant. It was to put steel in your legs..."

"Thanks anyway. You still have ammunition?"

"Ten cartridges apiece, Lieutenant. We've been shooting all night to defend ourselves."

The major, who was supporting himself on two halberds in the guise of crutches, staggered and fell, dragging Dupuy down with him. At that sight, the pursuers howled with joy and increased their speed—but a volley from the *poilus* felled three horses, one of which was carrying a Dominican rifleman. Dupuy and the major got up, but their fall had rendered the dire situation critical. Could they get there?

Protecting the retreat, the *poilus* turned around every ten paces, methodically, in order to fire and shoot down the horsemen.

Tortorado, leading his troop, was only thirty meters away when Renard, Lénac, the major and Dupuy reached the bridge. The Reverend Fathers fired again, killing two *poilus*. Both sides were firing relentlessly, and the grenades came into play. The last six *poilus* succeeded in getting back over the Seille, but four fell reaching the left bank. The Inquisitors' fire, well-nourished, was becoming more accurate; the grenades were raining down...

The French had to recover the dead men's cartridges...

"Quickly, Dupuy, to the Machine," Renard croaked. "Get it going!"

"I can't do any more," Dupuy moaned. With a supreme effort, however, he reached the tower and crossed the threshold, followed by the three others. He let himself fall into the seat of the Machine, and with his trembling, exhausted hands he pressed the switches, one after another...

At the bridgehead, only Nénesse remaining standing. All his comrades had fallen, slain by the Inquisitors' grenades and bullets. The latter, howling, had got down from their mounts and were preparing to descend into the bed of the Seille. The village's last defender used his bayonet to drive back Tortorado's first advance on to the bridge, but with a pistol shot, the Inquisitor smashed his right arm. He dropped his rifle, but threw himself upon his adversary furiously, gripping his cape with his left hand.

A grenade exploded. Nénese fell dead, in the middle of a supreme cry of "Death to the..." But he did not let go. Tortorado, blinded by the discharge, took two steps and fell into the Seille with a despairing roar, amid the frantic cries of the Spaniards...

At that exact moment, Dupuy tripped the last switch. The machine went into operation, and in a clap of thunder, the tower and its perimeter escaped, to surge forth once again in their original time and place, on the rainy night of January 17, on the Lorraine front.

VII. The Pact of Silence

After the fulguration and the formidable jolt of the transfer, the four escapees remained vertiginous, dazed and bewildered for several minutes, Dupuy in the bucket-seat of the Machine, Renard, the major and Lénac where they had thrown themselves down, panting hard, after their long flight from the Inquisition's dungeon. The rectangle of the doorway, through which the soft Mediterranean winter sunlight had been flooding a short while before, was open on darkness now. The glacial cold of the night invaded the tower, A cannonade was rumbling to the north.

Suddenly, there was a sound of footsteps approaching across the square. The four men started, and the frightened Lénac threw himself toward the door in order to close and bolt it. Renard pulled him back brutally.

"Stay calm, idiot!"

"Hey, Dupuy!" someone shouted from outside. "Are you up there?"

"No," Dupuy replied. "I'm down here, at the bottom. Is that you, Chabert?"

"Yes, of course! With Vuillemin. We've brought the accumulators."

The accumulators! It was the two assistant radio-operators, with the accumulators, still stranded in undisplaced Port-sur-Seille. With a huge sigh of relief, Dupuy whispered the news to his three accomplices. Aloud, he added: "Come in!"

"And above all," Renard whispered, "complete silence about our absence."

The two radio-operators came in, groping in the dark. "But there isn't any light here, Dupuy! What are you doing, then?"

"It was the earthquake that put out the lamp," pronounced the hoarse but familiar voice of Thévenard.

"Oh, beg pardon, Major, sir...we didn't see you. We thought that a mine had gone off...two, in fact, a few minutes apart. Here's your accumulators, Dupuy. Shall we take them up?"

"Yes, yes, go up, lads—go on up, and I'll join you."

Fortunately more preoccupied with their burden than with trying to make out the watchful faces around them, the two radio operators, without noticing their sergeant's anxiety, climbed up the rigid ladder, lighting their way with a pocket torch, and disappeared.

"Light something, then," whispered Renard, when the noise of a closing trapdoor resounded from above. "We need a serious talk."

Dupuy unhooked an oil lamp and generated some light. All four of them looked at one another.

"Oof!" gasped the major. "We're back at Port-sur-Seille, at any rate, for sure. They didn't get us, the swine!"

"Saved! Saved!" exclaimed Lénac ecstatically, with a wide grin—and, hiding his face in his hands, he burst into tears.

Dupuy and the lieutenant breathed in the icy night air voluptuously.

"It's not over yet," Renard said, suddenly. "We don't have any time to lose. I don't need to tell you that if we utter a single word about what we've done during these last six months—or the last six minutes, which comes to the same thing—we'll all be court-martialed."

"There's more chance that we'll be locked up as lunatics," the major sniggered.

"One's as bad as the other. So, silence all down the line. You hear, Lénac? And now, we have to restore a little order here. But first, what's that shining on your sleeve, Thévenard?"

"My insignia, of course! My insignia as Minister of Hygiene…and yours as Director of Operations."

Feverishly, using pen-knives all four of them returned their uniforms to the regulation appearance.

"What about the others?" Dupuy exclaimed. "The lads who are lying on the ground outside, decked out from the shoulders down?"

"No one must find them like that. Take care of it, with Lénac. Your two radio operators aren't going to come back down, are they?"

"Them? Come back down? No, they were on duty, the night of the departure. It was…it still is…me. They'll take a nap up there.

"Go, then—take care of the cadavers. Search their pockets too. Get rid of everything recalling Valencia. There are twelve, aren't there?"

"No," said Lénac, "two fell on the other bank, in Spain. I saw them when I turned round. There can't be more than ten here…and Nénesse; that makes eleven." He went out with Dupuy, armed with a lantern, to accomplish the macabre task.

Renard and the major set about restoring the plausible appearance of an office to the ground floor of the tower. Before the Machine was moved there, it had first served as a guard-room for the Moors, then as an arsenal. Finally, after the death of the Emir, Lénac had stored all his photographic and cinematographic apparatus there, of which he was no longer making use. In preparation for the departure, however, all the original furniture and the typewriter had been brought back. As best they could, the two officers finished restoring order; they made a bundle of everything left over from the occupation.

"What about that?" said Thévenard, pointing to the Arabic *graffiti* inscribed on the walls.

"Too bad!" Renard replied. "That won't bother anyone. What bothers me is this Machine. Inventions are all very well, but we've seen enough of them, haven't we?"

"Couldn't agree more. Get rid of it. Hold on—an idea. Dupuy can dismantle it, and we'll take the pieces into the crater when the four shells from Metz fall every morning on the dot of eight o'clock. This evening, they'll be gone forever."

The office was presentable again when Dupuy and Lénac returned from their expedition with pockets full of insignia, Spanish and Arab gold, eighth banknotes, photographs of Valencians chicks and other compromising souvenirs. The gold was shared out, the rest taken to the cellar and locked away with the bundle of film canisters, posters and so on.

The dismantling of the Machine took Dupuy and Lénac the rest of the night. Renard and the major busied themselves concocting the report to the colonel. A difficult task! After long discussion, they arrived at the following text:

Report of Lieutenant Renard to Colonel Sausse

Last night at twenty-three thirty, the enemy launched an abrupt attack on our sector. Our advance posts, rapidly overrun because of the deplorable func-

231

tioning of the light machine-guns, engaged in combat, but a numerous party of assailants succeeded in crossing the Seille and penetrating into our trenches, where they carried out grave depredations. Supported in admirable fashion by all the men, I took measures to hold back the movement. I must signal in this regard the heroic conduct of Adjutant Etcheverry, Sergeant Cipriani and even those whose employments dispensed them from participating in the attack: orderlies, cooks, the medical orderly. All of them were killed, victims of their devotion. My colleague, Sublieutenant de Lanselles, launched a counter-attack from his side—in the course of which he disappeared—and our combined efforts finally drove the enemy back to the other side of the Seille and beyond the barbed wire, at about one o'clock in the morning.

We have, unfortunately, to deplore an extremely high percentage of losses: eighty-one men killed, wounded, taken prisoner or unaccounted for, out of a hundred and twenty-two presently in the Company.

Notification was given during the combat of the landing in our lines of a British aircraft gone astray. Its pilot took off again a few minutes later, after having received the care of Major Thévenard in the infirmary.

In addition, at two-fifteen in the morning, the considerable shock of an earthquake—or perhaps the explosion of a mine—followed at a six-minute interval by another of similar violence, disturbed the vicinity of the sector and caused some damage. The death of several men might plausibly be attributed to that seismic phenomenon.

"That's fine—good job!" exclaimed Thévenard, when his companion read it back to him.

"What can you do? What's necessary is necessary," Renard pronounced, stoically.

Dawn broke. Dupuy and Lénac, for their part, had just finished with the Machine. It was too late to carry the parts to the shell-crater. Noises could be heard I the other half of the village; the men were waking up. The unrecognizable heap of metal was therefore covered with a tarpaulin until nightfall—which would soon arrive, give that it was January. The four men, utterly exhausted, would gladly have gone to bed, but they were far from having finished yet.

"Hey, Duranton!" shouted several jovial voices outside. "Where's the juice?"

Renard came out of the tower.

"Duranton's dead. Don't you know? He was killed...or taken prisoner, like many other poor chaps, last night."

"What, Duranton?" one man groaned. "No juice, then?"

"And there's nothing at all in the kitchens," said a second, who had gone in through the open door.

"Hang on, lads," the major intervened. "I've got something here for you." And he offered them a demi-john of Nénestine, from which he had just scraped off the superb label.

"Funny *gnôle*. No matter—it's warming. We can have it?"

"As much as you like."

"Let's fill our bottles, then, lads!"

It was necessary to appoint new cooks, re-man the deserted advance posts, send a detachment for new supplies. There were still two donkeys in the battery shed. The remaining men of the company—some forty of them—were hardly sufficient for all the tours of duty. The enormous proportion of the killed and missing plunged them into amazement.

"What! Jasmin too! And Saucisson! Everybody, then!"

The attack, however, had seemed relatively benign to them.

"You're forgetting that it wasn't just the attack," the major replied, making every effort to come to Renard's aid. "You're forgetting the earthquake that followed it. Two very violent shocks, which you mistook for the explosion of mines."

They listened to him deferentially, but there were whispers. His very appearance provoked comment. The major had put on a lot of weight since the previous day, and the lieutenant, Dupuy and Lénac were tanned, as if bronzed by the sun!

The discovery of the bodies—very few in number! how many prisoners!—passed without too many comments, save for Nénesse's. In the dark, the two scavengers had not noticed that in his extended left arm he was still holding the inquisitor's hooded cape, and that the latter's rosary was lying, along with an aspergillum, a few meters away in the barbed wire.

"He had a funny overcoat, the Boche! Are their chaplains taking part in their attacks now?" they joked, around these bizarre trophies.

"It's probably the trench-cleaners new costume. One of them seems to have done for Nénesse."

"Poor Nénesse—he was such a laugh!"

The radio was receiving, but the telephone wire had been cut. While awaiting its repair by Dupuy's aides, Renard had sent a cyclist as soon as it was light to take his report to Colonel Sausse. The supply crew had just come back with abundant provisions of every sort when the reconnection of the wire was announced. Immediately, a telephone call informed Renard that the colonel intended to come in person, at about two o'clock, to assess the situation of the eighth.

While awaiting his arrival, the four escapees from Valencia had lunch in the cellar. They were famished, and the cuisine of Duranton's successor seemed delicious to them. The presence of the man who had replaced Jasmin initially restricted their speech to discreet allusions and winks, but he was dismissed during dessert. The apples, the taste of which they had forgotten months ago, the coffee, genuine juice and no longer the ignoble substitute of roasted acorns; and the regulation *gnôle* all delighted them with ease. During the morning, they had already been able to smoke a pipe or two of old shag, but now—oh joy!—there were cigars.

The four accomplices considered one another in silence at first; then they all began laughing at once—laughing immoderately, in irresistible bursts, which set them writhing on their chairs for several minutes.

"Damn it!" the major finally exclaimed, wiping his eyes. "Why are you laughing, Renard?"

"I don't know. I'm happy, free, glad to be here. What about you?"

"Me, I was thinking about the Emir."

"Me too," said Lénac.

"Me," said Dupuy, "I've got leave coming up in a fortnight…and party time!"

Lénac had to wait a month for his turn, Renard six weeks, the major eight.

"Bah!" the last-named philosophized. "I've got my little chick in Landremont. I'll go see her tomorrow. And after all, we've spent six months away from the war. That was overtime!"

"And how!" added Lénac.

They remembered the mates left behind, buried under the ruins of the tower. They discussed the explosion that had freed them. Had it really been Monocard's work? And what had become of him? Dead, no doubt, with his *Saint-Cyriens*...

"At any rate, he'll have difficulty rejoining us, poor fellow," said the major. "With a handicap of several centuries..."

Colonel Sausse—a short man with a gray beard—arrived sooner than expected. He came into the cellar like a blast of wind, and Lénac did not have time to put away the collection of photographs that he had just taken out of the bookcase in order to examine them. After a "Well, it seems that it was ugly last night" by way of a *bonjour*, however, the colonel came to an abrupt halt, his eyes wide, in front of the major, and cut off the reply commenced by Renard.

"But you're enormous, Major! What's happened to you, my friend? Have you copped a dose of mustard-gas?"

The three accomplices were covertly amused by the lamentable: "Yes, Colonel, I have indeed," that Thévenard stammered.

"You'll have to be evacuated," Sausse went on. Then, noticing the bronzed faces of the others, he exclaimed: "And you! Your faces are burned, all three of you. The Boche must have attacked with flame-throwers!"

"Er...yes, Colonel," Renard replied.

"You're not suffering too much?"

"No, not too much, Colonel. It's rather mild."

The sight of the artistic poses destined for the Emir, distracted the officer's attention. He cast a semi-indulgent, semi-severe eye over them.

"Always with your naked ladies? Look, she's not bad, that little one. One might think she was a Algerian. She has a Moorish look about her..."

Beneath the snapshots he noticed half a dozen gold coins—quadruples and dinars.

"Tee hee—you have gold here. That'll have to be sent to the Banque de France...but these are old coins. Where did you find them?"

Père Sausse was keen on numismatics.

"It was last night's earthquake that unearthed them, Colonel," the major replied. And, seeing the colonel's questing gaze settle on a halberd forgotten in a corner, he added: "Along with other objects—that weapon, for example. It must be a Medieval burial-site..."

"Oh yes—your report, Lieutenant, mentioned an earthquake. You were here, then, last night, Thévenard."

"Yes, Colonel. I stayed here."

"Very good, very good. I noticed your zeal a long time ago...and you were gassed as well..."

They passed on to serious matters. Renard gave another detailed—and imaginary—account of the attack. He spoke again about the courage of de Lanselles, Etcheverry and Cipriani, the orderlies, and so on. But their disappearance irritated the colonel. He wanted to see the corpses arranged on a canvas sheet behind the infirmary.

"Eleven. No more than that? What about the others. How many prisoners and missing did you say?"

"Sixty-six, Colonel."

"That makes no sense. How did it happen, then?"

"Sublieutenant de Lanselles carried them all away. I shouted at him to stop, but he pressed forward...and no one came back."

"It's annoying that we don't know whether they're alive or not...at any rate, we'll put them down as missing."

"Oh, in my opinion, they're alive," said the major, with a wink at Renard.

Having inspected the advance posts, and commented on the disappearance of the machine guns, the exhaustion of the ammunition and other damage, the colonel concluded: "I've rarely seen a sector so sorely tried. You can't stay like this. I'll send you half a company today, and then I'll get busy having you relieved. In three or four hours, you can get some rest."

When he went back to the office, where he had parked his bicycle, he came to a halt in front of the graffiti.

"What! That's very odd. I've never noticed those inscriptions before. Have you, Renard?"

"No, Colonel—but they've always been there."

"And astonishingly well-preserved, considering their antiquity. That's ancient Arabic, there's no doubt about it; they're as old as the tower. I've always thought that the Arabs got as far as Port-sur-Seille...those coins are abundant proof of it too. I must take photographs one day, when I have time, and put together a note for the Académie des Inscriptions..."

Ready to get astride his bicycle, he considered Thévenard's monstrous paunch one last time. "You don't want me to have you evacuated, then?"

"I have my wounded to care for, Colonel."

"Those are the words of a hero. I won't insist—but I'm going to recommend you for the Légion d'honneur."

That evening, the pieces of the Machine having been placed in the crater, the four accomplices, locked away in the cellar, proceeded with the destruction of the souvenirs of Spain. The gold, the halberds, the daggers and the photographs of women could be kept, but the banknotes were incinerated and long with the printed matter. As they went along, they reread some of the posters.

"Program for the celebrations of the coronation of His Holiness Geronimo I..."

"Proclamation of the state of reinforced siege..."

"To the people of Valencia: the cowardly assassination of two high-ranking French officials, the Chief Cupbearer Jasmin and the Chief Bread-Supplier Saucission..."

"Rise in the price of raw alcohol..."

"Workers required for the distillery..."

"Debray bicycles in guaranteed dogwood..."

"The Andalusian convoy will bring..."

"Nénestine and Progressinette, available in all good bars..."

A nearby detonation, closely followed by three others, made the accomplices jump, having become unaccustomed to them. Then they remembered: eight o'clock! The four shells from Metz! With half-smiles, they looked at one another, and the major, with a hand gesture, waved a definitive farewell to the Machine.

"Bye bye...*au revoir*..."

Lénac broke the silence while throwing a wad of banknotes on to the fire: "There goes another million."

"More!" said Dupuy.

"Well, those are fake..."

The auto-da-fé came to an end. There remained the films. On a sheet, standing in for a screen, Lénac proposed to show them one last time. Once again they watched the explosion of the gate of Valencia, the triumphant entry of the Emir and the monk on the truck with the green palms, the riot at the cathedral...

"We're there—we're still there! Oh, they were good times, all the same."

"Yes, but with those bastard Inquisitors, it wasn't really tenable."

"And we have to destroy all this? What a pity! It would be so amusing to look at them again from time to time, when we four meet again..."

"In fact," said Dupuy, "we could keep the portions of film in which we don't appear, or the *poilus*, and connect up the pieces. It would be a historical reconstruction film!"

Lénac declared the plan quite feasible. He projected all of it a second time, for the purposes of censorship, and carefully made a note of the cuts to be made.

By half past nine—twenty-four hours having gone by since they awoke in the Inquisition's dungeon—all four of them were falling down with fatigue. Renard gave a signal to Dupuy, who went to fetch an earthenware bottle from the Henri II bookcase.

"Gentlemen," said the lieutenant, while filling their glasses, "I found this bottle of Alicante. It was a gift from the Caliph of Cordova to the Director of Operations. I shall assume that title one last time in order to drink a probably-posthumous toast to the noble and chivalrous Monocard, to his colleague in generous madness the monk and late pope Geronimo, to Etcheverry, Cipriani, Jasmin, Saucisson, Duranton, Nénesse, and all our brave friends, the troopers who remained out there, victims of the Inquisition!"

"You're forgetting the Emir, old chap," the doctor replied. "He liked us a lot, although he had his faults...I shall add to those toasts, for my part, the health of the Director of Operations, who always showed himself to be on top of things...and that of the three of us who are lucky enough to be here this evening. Drink!"

The glasses clinked; they drank.

"And now," Renard continued, "with the few drops that remain, we're all going to swear a solemn oath never to mention again, except between ourselves, the adventure that united us all in good and bad fortune, without distinction of rank. This will be the Pact of Silence, a worthy pendant to the Pernod Alliance!"

Epilogue

It was four days after Colonel Sausse's visit. The Eighth Company, so terribly tried, was sent to rest at Liverdun. A parade was held in the morning. Renard and the major, wearing the decoration of the Légion d'honneur, Dupuy the military medal and Lénac the croix de guerre, dined with a few other guests at the colonel's residence. He congratulated them publicly, and requested a cinematic presentation from Lénac. On the way to the barracks where the *poilus*, notified of the windfall, had assembled in haste, Captain Loubet of the tenth came to clap Renard amicably on the shoulder.

"Well, have you still got any of it left?"

"Any what?"

"The Pernod, damn it! You haven't emptied the cellar already, I suppose?"

"My God! Yes, I'd better confess—it's completely empty."

"Damn! You lot go at it hard. In ten days! There was enough of it to keep a regiment going for a month."

The Pathé News, the grotesque misadventures of Charlie Chaplin and the exploits of the detective launched in pursuit of the odious kidnappers of the billionaire's daughter obtained their customary success, of crazed laughter and respectful attention respectively, on the part of the *poilus* packing the wooden benches. On their chairs, Colonel Sausse and his guests occupied their eyes while digesting dinner. To close the session, Lénac announced one last film—a new one, he said, which he had just received: *Spain under the Inquisition in the 14th Century*.

And they saw minarets appear, sharply outlined against the sky, terraces and palm trees, crenellated walls garnished with archers and arbalesters. On a tower, the bishop and his clergy were brandishing aspergillums. The breach was opened in a cloud of dust. Cavalrymen in burnooses launched forward at a gallop, returning waving severed heads with a striking realism...

"There's a *poilu*!" an overexcited voice in the crowd suddenly exclaimed, during a confused episode of a brawl in the nave of a church.

A *poilu* in the Middle Ages! The interrupter was jeered. Such an anachronism on the part of the scenarists would be too stupid...but the film, with all its great spectacle and luxury of depiction, merited criticism nevertheless.

"It's well-made, I admit," the colonel concluded, leaning toward Renard's ear. But even so, one can see that they aren't people of the 14th century. Those fellows have obviously just taken off their false collars to put on coats of mail. They're all very well, these historical reconstruction films, but they always reek of fakery!"

Afterword
Loose ends and Inconvenient Knots

La Belle Valence was written in a era when it was considered compulsory that a work of fiction must leave the world of the present unaffected—i.e., that its plot must be "normalized," all *ad hoc* innovations being somehow tidied away in order that the *status quo* could remain unaffected. It is therefore not surprising that the narrative voice of the text, like the principal characters, does not even consider the issue of whether their trip into the past might have altered history—any such alteration being, of course, literally out of the question.

It was not until 1939 that L. Sprague de Camp, in the magisterial *Lest Darkness Fall*—perhaps the finest science fiction novel of its era—bit that particular bullet and allowed a timeslipped hero bent on introducing the civilization to the past to obtain a measure of success—without, in so doing, canceling out the history that had produced the hero, enabled the novel to be written and given it meaning, in a seeming flourish of textual suicide. Our modern familiarity with such texts allows us to take in our stride the assertion of de Camp's narrative voice that his hero has simply started an "alternative branch" of history that will grow "sideways" into some kind of "parallel world." Blandin and Varlet were not equipped to make that imaginative leap—or, if Blandin was, Edgar Malfère, acting on behalf of their potential readers was not, and instructed Varlet to put that particular plot twist in irons.

Because of prevailing *a priori* assumptions, therefore, there was no way that *La Belle Valence* could end except with the massive tidying-up of the final chapter, in which the Great War is allowed to resume its course and the returned soldiers their roles therein, without any disturbance of any conspicuous kind. Modern readers will probably feel as disappointed and frustrated by this imaginative pusillanimity as contemporary readers might have been had things not worked out according to their conservative expectations. There is, however, clear evidence in the text that, even though the characters and the narrative voice observe a strict pact of silence with regard to the possibility of time paradoxes, the authors were well aware of the potential logical problems, and might perhaps have been prepared to undertake a bolder solution to them, had they been allowed—or had circumstances prompted them to write a sequel.

The most interesting feature of the narrative as recorded, in fact, is not the way it tidies up its plot into a slightly untidy but nevertheless conclusively-sealed knot, but the way in which it carefully leaves certain loose ends awkwardly dangling. The dangling in question is undoubtedly deliberate, and might even qualify as calculatedly provocative, so it makes perfect sense, having finished the novel, to return to some of the questions that the plot conspicuously refuses to answer, and speculate as to what possibilities are thus opened up.

The first such question, which is raised explicitly but not answered, is: "What happened to Monocard?" We are told that he and the "*Saint-Cyriens*" took refuge in the attics of the University when the Castilian army attacked, and that they held out there until morning, but we are not told what became of them when they could no longer hold out. Obviously, Monocard was not captured or killed, or he would certainly have been put on the pyre with Geronimo and the cadavers of the murdered troopers—which was not the case—so what did become of him?

Even if he managed to escape from Valencia to remain stranded in the past, of course, de Lanselles might still have remained impotent to carry forward his civilizing mission, especially if most of his *Saint-Cyrien* acolytes had perished in the battle—but it is not impossible that one man, adopting cunning methods, might have succeeded at least in introducing some small changes into the pattern of history, as L. Sprague de Camp attempted to demonstrate.

Corollary to this question is, of course, the issue of why none of the innovations introduced by the time-slipped soldiers survived. Having been introduced to the secrets of distillation, gunpowder, lithographic printing and the bicycle, would the Valencians really have forgotten them entirely, even if the Inquisition condemned them as unholy? And what about the Cordovans, with whom Renard was in communication? Perhaps they did not have the technological sophistication, as yet, to build printing-presses with movable type, but why could they not have simulated a typewriter? Then again, there is one innovation introduced by the time-travelers that could not possibly be contained or canceled out, as the text explicitly informs us: syphilis. Whether or not one accepts the common thesis that syphilis was imported to Europe from the Americas after 1492, there is no doubt that the appearance and spread of the disease a century and a half ahead of its time would have made a significant difference to the subsequent pattern of history.

Perhaps, though, if a disease was the most significant factor capable of changing 14th century history, it was another disease that prevented it doing so. The text never makes any comment on the significance of the choice of the year 1341, mainly because it has no particular significance in the chronicles of European history—but it is not so far removed from one that has: 1348 saw the emergence of the single factor that probably had a greater and deadlier influence on the progressive course of European history than any other: the advent of the Black Death. Perhaps it was the slaughter of a third of Europe's population by that uniquely destructive plague that wiped out all trace of the innovations deliberately or accidentally introduced by Renard's timeslippers, including any modifications subsequently made by Monocard, thus preserving the history we know (and cannot entirely hate) from fatal disruption.

As to that, we can only speculate, because the authors never produced the sequel that would have tracked Monocard's continuing adventures and endeavors in the dangerous world of the 1340s. Given that he could remember that the papacy was in Avignon at the time, though, it is unlikely that he did not remember the imminence of the Black Death, and his first priority, once he was certain that he was stranded in the past, would surely have been to take up arms against it. Alas, he knows nothing about sulfa drugs, let alone penicillin, but he does know something about modern hygiene and he knows that rat fleas probably played some part in spreading the plague before it became directly transmissible from human to human. Surely he could have used that knowledge to help himself, and others...and any help he rendered might have lessened the disaster sufficiently to change history.

As well as these corollaries, however, the question of what happened to Monocard also has an inverse counterpart, which is equally intriguing. What happened to Tortorado? We know that he fell into the depleted Seille while temporarily unsighted, but we have no reason to believe that the fall killed or injured him. We know, too, that both banks of the Seille were within the perimeter of the Machine's operation. We have every reason to believe, therefore, that he could have been transported, alive and well, to the Western Front in 1917.

That was, of course, a very dangerous place to be, especially for a man as confused—matagrabolized, even—as Tortorado would have been, on finding himself dragged into what he would surely see as a kind of Hell, but we know that he is a man capable of great determination, tenacity and ingenuity, and not everything is against him. He is, after all, in a world where the Dominican Order still exists, if not the Inquisition, and in which Latin is still the language of a Catholic Church that is not without power and influence.

If he can only make it to a monastery...

Like the sequel following Monocard's exploits in the 14th century, the sequel detailing Tortorado's trials and tribulations in the 20th century remained unwritten, but perhaps not unimagined—and even if it was unimagined by Blandin and Varlet, it need not stay that way. We, at least, are free to wonder, and are by no means shackled by the same narrative assumptions and prejudices that prevailed in 1923. We are not in the least afraid of alternative histories; indeed, we love them. For us, therefore, there is no intimidation, editorial or otherwise, requiring us to tone down our flights of fancy.

We know, too, that what has been learned cannot really be unlearned, shells and the Black Death notwithstanding. We know that if the mysterious Englishman who filled that enchanted cellar in Port-sur-Seille with lovely booze could design and build a hyper-Wellsian time machine, then so could someone else—and another thing the text refuses to tell us is what happened to the black notebook. In the fullness of time—in the fullest possible meaning of that phrase—Renard and Dupuy might well be able to go time-traveling again, and might even be able to meet up with Tortorado in a more complex narrative context than simply trying to settle old scores in the most vulgar fashion imaginable. In time—somewhen and somewhere—any and all of them might yet make contact with Monocard again; and after that, the possibilities become endless...which is, of course, exactly what Pope Geronimo the Alcoholic Anarchist Antichrist wanted them to be.

And who among us cannot sympathize with that glorious dream?

SF & FANTASY

Henri Allorge. *The Great Cataclysm*
Guy d'Armen. *Doc Ardan: The City of Gold and Lepers*
G.-J. Arnaud. *The Ice Company*
Cyprien Bérard. *The Vampire Lord Ruthwen*
Aloysius Bertrand. *Gaspard de la Nuit*
Richard Bessière. *The Gardens of the Apocalypse*
Albert Bleunard. *Ever Smaller*
Félix Bodin. *The Novel of the Future*
Alphonse Brown. *City of Glass*
André Caroff. *The Terror of Madame Atomos; Miss Atomos; The Return of Madame Atomos; The Mistake of Madame Atomos*
Félicien Champsaur. *The Human Arrow*
Didier de Chousy. *Ignis*
Captain Danrit. *Undersea Odyssey*
C. I. Defontenay. *Star (Psi Cassiopeia)*
Charles Derennes. *The People of the Pole*
Georges Dodds (anthologist). *The Missing Link*
Harry Dickson. *The Heir of Dracula*
Jules Dornay. *Lord Ruthven Begins*
Alfred Driou. *The Adventures of a Parisian Aeronaut*
Sâr Dubnotal *vs. Jack the Ripper*
Alexandre Dumas. *The Return of Lord Ruthven*
Renée Dunan. *Baal*
J.-C. Dunyach. *The Night Orchid; The Thieves of Silence*
Henri Duvernois. *The Man Who Found Himself*
Achille Eyraud. *Voyage to Venus*
Henri Falk. *The Age of Lead*
Paul Féval. *Anne of the Isles; Knightshade; Revenants; Vampire City; The Vampire Countess; The Wandering Jew's Daughter*
Paul Féval, *fils. Felifax, the Tiger-Man*
Charles de Fieux. *Lamékis*
Arnould Galopin. *Doctor Omega; Doctor Omega & The Shadowmen*
G.L. Gick. *Harry Dickson and the Werewolf of Rutherford Grange*
Edmond Haraucourt. *Illusions of Immortality*
Nathalie Henneberg. *The Green Gods*
V. Hugo, P. Foucher & P. Meurice. *The Hunchback of Notre-Dame*
Michel Jeury. *Chronolysis*
Gustave Kahn. *The Tale of Gold and Silence*

Gérard Klein. *The Mote in Time's Eye*
Jean de La Hire. *Enter the Nyctalope; The Nyctalope on Mars; The Nyctalope vs. Lucifer; The Nyctalope Steps In*
Etienne-Léon de Lamothe-Langon. *The Virgin Vampire*
André Laurie. *Spiridon*
Gabriel de Lautrec. *The Vengeance of the Oval Portrait*
Georges Le Faure & Henri de Graffigny. *The Extraordinary Adventures of a Russian Scientist Across the Solar System* (2 vols.)
Gustave Le Rouge. *The Vampires of Mars*
Jules Lermina. *Mysteryville; Panic in Paris; To-Ho and the Gold Destroyers; The Secret of Zippelius*
Jean-Marc & Randy Lofficier. *Edgar Allan Poe on Mars; The Katrina Protocol; Pacifica; Robonocchio; Tales of the Shadowmen 1-8*
Xavier Mauméjean. *The League of Heroes*
José Moselli. *Illa's End*
John-Antoine Nau. *Enemy Force*
Marie Nizet. *Captain Vampire*
C. Nodier, A. Beraud & Toussaint-Merle. *Frankenstein*
Henri de Parville. *An Inhabitant of the Planet Mars*
Gaston de Pawlowski. *Journey to the Land of the 4th Dimension*
Georges Pellerin. *The World in 2000 Years*
J. Polidori, C. Nodier, E. Scribe. *Lord Ruthven the Vampire*
P.-A. Ponson du Terrail. *The Vampire and the Devil's Son*
Henri de Régnier. *A Surfeit of Mirrors*
Maurice Renard. *The Blue Peril; Doctor Lerne; The Doctored Man; A Man Among the Microbes; The Master of Light*
Jean Richepin. *The Wing*
Albert Robida. *The Adventures of Saturnin Farandoul; The Clock of the Centuries; Chalet in the Sky*
J.-H. Rosny Aîné. *Helgvor of the Blue River; The Givreuse Enigma; The Mysterious Force; The Navigators of Space; Vamireh; The World of the Variants; The Young Vampire*
Marcel Rouff. *Journey to the Inverted World*
Han Ryner. *The Superhumans*
Brian Stableford. *The New Faust at the Tragicomique;The Empire of the Necromancers (The Shadow of Frankenstein; Frankenstein and the Vampire Countess; Frankenstein in London); Sherlock Holmes & The Vampires of Eternity; The Stones of Camelot; The Wayward Muse.* (anthologist) *The Germans on Venus; News from the Moon; The Supreme Progress; The World Above the World; Nemoville*
Jacques Spitz. *The Eye of Purgatory*

Kurt Steiner. *Ortog*
Eugène Thébault. *Radio-Terror*
C.-F. Tiphaigne de La Roche. *Amilec*
Théo Varlet. *The Xenobiotic Invasion; Timeslip Troopers* (w/André Blandin); *The Martian Epic* (w/Octave Joncquel)
Paul Vibert. *The Mysterious Fluid*
Villiers de l'Isle-Adam. *The Scaffold; The Vampire Soul*
Philippe Ward. *Artahe*
Philippe Ward & Sylvie Miller. *The Song of Montségur*

MYSTERIES & THRILLERS

M. Allain & P. Souvestre. *The Daughter of Fantômas*
A. Anicet-Bourgeois, Lucien Dabril. *Rocambole*
A. Bernède & L. Feuillade. *Judex*
A. Bisson & G. Livet. *Nick Carter vs. Fantômas*
V. Darlay & H. de Gorsse. *Lupin vs. Holmes: The Stage Play*
Paul Féval. *Gentlemen of the Night; John Devil; The Black Coats ('Salem Street; The Invisible Weapon; The Parisian Jungle; The Companions of the Treasure; Heart of Steel; The Cadet Gang; The Sword-Swallower)*
Emile Gaboriau. *Monsieur Lecoq*
Steve Leadley. *Sherlock Holmes: The Circle of Blood*
Maurice Leblanc. *Arsène Lupin vs. Countess Cagliostro; Lupin vs. Holmes (The Blonde Phantom; The Hollow Needle)*
Gaston Leroux. *Chéri-Bibi; The Phantom of the Opera; Rouletabille & the Mystery of the Yellow Room*
Richard Marsh. *The Complete Adventures of Judith Lee*
William Patrick Maynard. *The Terror of Fu Manchu*
Frank J. Morlock. *Sherlock Holmes: The Grand Horizontals; Sherlock Holmes vs Jack the Ripper*
P. de Wattyne & Y. Walter. *Sherlock Holmes vs. Fantômas*
David White. *Fantômas in America*

SCREENPLAYS

Mike Baron. *The Iron Triangle*
Emma Bull & Will Shetterly. *Nightspeeder; War for the Oaks*
Gerry Conway & Roy Thomas. *Doc Dynamo*
Steve Englehart. *Majorca*
James Hudnall. *The Devastator*

Jean-Marc & Randy Lofficier. *Royal Flush*
J.-M. & R. Lofficier & Marc Agapit. *Despair*
J.-M. & R. Lofficier & Joël Houssin. *City*
Andrew Paquette. *Peripheral Vision*
R. Thomas, J. Hendler & L. Sprague de Camp. *Rivers of Time*

NON-FICTION
Stephen R. Bissette. *Blur 1-5. Green Mountain Cinema 1*
Win Scott Eckert. *Crossovers* (2 vols.)
Jean-Marc & Randy Lofficier. *Shadowmen* (2 vols.)
Randy Lofficier. *Over Here*

HEXAGON COMICS
Franco Frescura & Luciano Bernasconi. *Wampus*
Franco Frescura & Giorgio Trevisan. *CLASH*
L. Bernasconi, J.-M. Lofficier & Juan Roncagliolo Berger. *Phenix*
Claude Legrand, J.-M. Lofficier & L. Bernasconi. *Kabur*
Franco Oneta. *Zembla*
L. Buffolente, Lofficier & J.-J. Dzialowski. *Strangers: Homicron*
Danilo Grossi. *Strangers: Jaydee*
Claude Legrand & Luciano Bernasconi. *Strangers: Starlock*

ART BOOKS
Jean-Pierre Normand. *Science Fiction Illustrations*
Raven Okeefe. *Raven's L'il Critters*
Randy Lofficier & Raven OKeefe. *If Your Possum Go Daylight...*
Daniele Serra. *Illusions*